Mad About YULE

GENNY CARRICK

ISBN (print): 978-1-957745-13-8

ISBN (ebook): 978-1-957745-12-1

❀ Created with Vellum

For anyone who needs the reminder: Don't settle for less than what you want just to please someone else.

And for everyone who secretly thinks nutcrackers are creepy. You're not wrong.

WHAT TO EXPECT

This book includes a main character dealing with grief over the loss of a parent, living in a sibling's shadow, creepy nutcrackers, stray two-by-fours, heated kisses, and mild innuendo.

ONE
HOPE

AN EIGHT A.M. phone call from my mother is a bad omen, right?

I want to let it go to voicemail, but her motherly freak-outs have quadrupled since I volunteered to revitalize our town's Christmas festival. She already operates at Defcon Two, I really don't want to find out what happens when she reaches Maximum Hover Mother.

"Good morning." I flash a mega-watt smile—she can't see it, but I put on my armor anyway.

"How's my little event planner?"

"Everything's going great." A blatant lie. My Winter Wonderland is turning into a Merry Mess, but Mom will swoop in like a coddling vulture at the smallest sign of weakness. I need this win. So I lie like my pants are on fire. "We're right on schedule."

"Really? I heard about Silas."

All the air whooshes out of my lying sails. *Well done, Sunshine gossips.* It's only been two days, but she probably heard his whole medical report in the frozen food aisle at Ray's Grocery. My sole volunteer handyman no sooner opted into my project than he *noped* right out again. He strained his back lifting a sheet of plywood.

So no, my project isn't *quite* on schedule.

"It's totally fine," I say, hoping to soothe her with my calm confidence. That's also a big old lie, so I'm on a roll. "I've got a replacement."

"Already? Who did you find?"

I straighten yellow tubs of Bee's Knees body butter in their honeycomb-styled shelf. *Calm and confident.* "I don't know his name yet."

Impossible for me to spin that into a positive, but at least it's true. She hesitates a fraction of a second on the other end, like a shark smelling blood in the water. A too-sweet, motherly shark who will swim right over to bandage up the poor injured fish.

"I'll phone my contractor in Bend. I'm sure he'll be willing to rearrange a few things in his schedule as a favor to me. It's just the Christmas village, right? That can't be too hard."

I'd drawn out plans for five whimsical little houses reminiscent of vintage Christmas displays, each with a different style and theme to make a pretty little Winter Wonderland in town square. But sure. Just a Christmas village.

"I have it covered, Mom. Kat McBride said she knows a guy."

"Kat? That's a relief I guess, but why did you go to her?"

Kat runs the town's largest landscaping company with her grown sons and is on the town council, but Mom makes it sound like I asked an outsider for help.

"She was in the store when Silas called yesterday." I'd also told my best friend Wren that I'd rather eat a whole loaf of fruitcake every day from now until Christmas than ask for my mother's help with the festival, but who's keeping track? "She said she had someone in mind and texted me last night to let me know he'd agreed."

"And you don't know who it is?"

With only three weeks to go until tree lighting, I can't be too picky. The closer it gets, the more the festival hemorrhages volunteers. At least Silas's back strain is a more believable excuse than *my dog has pneumonia*. I didn't research it, but that one sounds like a scam.

"One of her employees, I assume. I'm sure it will be fine."

I need it to be fine. I have too much riding on this for it to be anything but fine.

"This is a big undertaking, honey, and you've been working so hard to make it happen."

She sounds more like she's consoling me than praising me, but I'll take it. I *have* been working like crazy to pull this together.

"Just remember, Lila and I are always here to help if you need us," she adds.

It's too early in the morning for this. The last thing I need is for my mom and sister to parachute in to save the day for me.

"I have to go, Mom. I'm meeting Kat and her guy in a few minutes."

"Let me know if I need to call Andre to help you out."

"I will."

To be clear, I absolutely will not. Mom bringing in her contractor—no doubt at her own expense—would be the opposite of what I've been going for on this endeavor.

I hang up and do a quick walk-through of the three aisles of handmade goods in my sliver of a gift shop, making sure everything looks just right. Full of handmade jewelry, purses, pottery, and screen-printed T-shirts with quirky sayings on them, The Painted Daisy is my happy place. It's a spot to connect with and support local artists of all kinds, even if I don't have the guts to put my own artwork on display. Just standing in the store clears my head.

Lately, I haven't spent nearly enough time in here.

Volunteering to organize Sunshine, Oregon's Christmas festival seemed like such a great idea back in September when I made the offer at a town hall meeting. Downtown's holiday event needs a refresh, and small businesses like mine could use the sales boost.

I'd camped out in City Hall, cornering council members to make my case every time they walked by until I'd secured their approval. I can't let them down now. If I think being known as *Hope Parrish, Well-Intentioned Screw-Up* is bad, being known as *That Girl Who Ruined Christmas* would be so much worse.

Wren pops her head in the open doorway between The Painted Daisy and Blackbird's next door. Up until a year ago, The Daisy's tiny space used to be an overflow seating area for the Krause family bakery, but I convinced Wren's mom to let me sublet it. I painted the walls a soft butter yellow and hung floating shelves—well, Mom's contractor installed all the shelves. I hadn't minded accepting help with that. But I haven't bothered to close off the Daisy from the bakery. Customers can wander from one shop to the other, ideally increasing business to both. Mostly, Wren and I use the pass-through to keep an eye on each other.

"What's with the pacing?" she asks. She smooths her blond hair along the ponytail she typically wears in the bakery, trying to tame the loose strands. "I can hear you sighing all the way over here."

I pause my third loop of the store. "I'm thinking about running away to that commune up in Bigleaf Canyon until Christmas is over."

I could use a little Zen. Isn't that what they find at retreats like that?

"You'll never last that long. It's clothing-optional. What's wrong?"

I stop myself mid-sigh. "Mom heard about my handyman's injury. She offered to help find someone to replace him."

"We all know how much you hate help."

"Not true. I just dislike help from my mother, especially since her advice is mostly to ask Lila for help." Nothing says *I have confidence in you* like *Go ask your sister what to do*.

"Yeah, Lila would probably turn your Winter Wonderland into a holiday-themed fashion show or something."

"And it would be amazing, but not remotely what I'm going for."

"Aw, come on, she's got some great tips for accessorizing for fall."

I stare hard at my wonderful, beautiful, traitorous friend. "You follow her on Instagram now?"

"What can I say? She's an unstoppable juggernaut whose sphere of influence can't be contained."

I snort-laugh at Wren's over-the-top description, but she's not far from the truth. My sister has amassed a small army of followers eager for her lifestyle posts and chic selfies. Meanwhile, I've mostly made fans of bots and trolls. Not that any of that matters. I don't care about the online popularity contest. Even if it makes me unaccountably sad when my bot friends unfollow me.

I grab my purse from behind the counter. "I have to go meet Kat and get my new handyman up to speed, but I'll be back in time to open the store."

"I'll just be snooping around and adding to my Christmas list," she calls after me.

Keeping watch for patches of ice on the sidewalk, I scurry down Maple Street to Perk Me Up, the coffee shop where I agreed to meet Kat. I need to make a good impression here—her contact is my last hope to save face with my Winter Wonderland. I should have had my volunteer handyman start on the buildings as soon as the town council gave the okay, but instead, I've spent most of the last few months arranging everything else: decorations, the choir, refreshments, the Christmas market.

But for me, the Winter Wonderland means everything. Those buildings will be my artistic stamp on the festivities, proof I'm capable of more than just being Lila Parrish's little sister. My plans for the renewed festival will still be a huge step up without the Wonderland, but those little buildings will be the icing on the Christmas cookie.

Thank goodness for Kat. When I see her, I'll probably pull her into a bear hug and raise her up into a *Dirty Dancing*-style lift to show my gratitude.

I walk through Perk Me Up's doors and spot my handyman-producing angel bundled in a slick brown parka. Kat's at the counter chatting with a tall man who has his back to me. As I get closer, he turns around, and his eyes hit mine.

Holy jawline, Batman.

My heartbeat goes into red alert, one heel skidding awkwardly on the floor, and I almost fall over my own feet.

Wait.

Oh, heck no.

TWO
HOPE

HIM? This is who Kat convinced to help me?

I should have asked for his name last night, but I'd been too busy doing a happy dance in the middle of my apartment to question anything. Not that I'm in any position to turn him away, but it might have prepared me for the shock. Give a girl some warning when you're going to spring a blast from the past on her.

And not the fun kind of blast—more like an explosion that leaves my pride in ribbons.

I fix on a smile and close the last few feet to Kat and *her guy.*

"Hope." She welcomes me over like I couldn't possibly have reservations about her pick. "You know my son Griffin."

"Kind of."

That's about as accurate as I want to be. Most of my high school stress had *kind of* been caused by Griffin McBride. He had *kind of* spewed criticism I'd felt compelled to combat with positivity at every turn. I had *kind of* drawn devil horns on every picture of his smug face in my senior yearbook.

Sure. I kind of remember Griffin.

His hazel-green eyes drift down my body in a brief once-over and snap back up to meet mine. Can I see the green parts in his eyes from here? Nope. But not even ten years could make me forget those eyes critiquing me on everything I said or did.

I love Kat McBride, but her son? Hard pass.

"We haven't kept in touch," I say, as though we might have been secret pen pals all this time. "But I know of you."

Who in town doesn't? He had a reputation as a bit of a bad boy, with his attitude and all the parties and the one *oops* fire in the canyon that had never been officially pinned on him but everyone knew he'd started during one of his bonfires gone awry.

"I know of you too, Hope," he returns.

Okay, fine, it sounds stupid when he says it. We went to school together from kindergarten through graduation, often shared the same classroom, and were once lab partners in chemistry. We'd had about nine thousand arguments during those years, and he'd made me lose my cool for about eighty-seven hundred of them. The point is, we aren't close.

A small smirk touches his mouth, and déjà vu gets my stomach squirming. That smirk used to haunt my teenage nightmares. I have fewer stories about me in circulation than he does, but I can guess the one on his mind. Every year, our debate class instructor gave out little statuettes to her Number One Debater, and he'd won ours right out from under me.

Not that I truly loved debating, and obviously Griffin comes by arguing naturally, but whatever. I'd wanted that award.

But wait...does he know about last summer's humiliation? People in town have gotten a lot of mileage out of my rumored engagement exploding to bits so publicly. The fact that I was never actually engaged just makes the story even juicier. I want to believe he has no idea, but that curl along his mouth doesn't settle my stomach.

"Come on up, coffee's on me this morning." Kat waves me to the counter and the young barista who waits to take my order.

I ask for a caramel macchiato and stand between the two McBrides, my stomach clunking around like a washing machine with an unbalanced load. I want to see my Winter Wonderland come to life, but I'm not sure I want it *this* much.

"I adjusted Griffin's schedule around so he can make those buildings for you," Kat tells me. "He jumped at the chance to get involved in the Christmas festival. He's very civic-minded."

She shoots him a huge smile, clearly giving him a hard time. Safe bet she didn't offer him any other choice. Roughly the same age as my mom, Kat has a tough-as-nails attitude mixed with warmth and understanding. My mom's affection usually comes with a thick blanket for smothering.

I scramble for something helpful to say to my new volunteer.

"We're going to have a lot of fun together."

I probably shouldn't have said that like I'm talking to a two-year-old, but my brain hasn't fully adjusted to the situation yet. His eyes land on me, and I really wish I owned higher heels so he couldn't look down his nose at me so easily.

"Can't wait."

His smile makes my churning stomach swoop like I've time-traveled back to debate class, and how he'd smirk through every one of my speeches. I hated that smirk. Now I have to see it every day for three weeks?

What did I do to tick Santa off?

Kat laughs. "He's awfully good with a hammer. I'm sure he'll get that Winter Wonderland built for you in no time."

She lifts her eyebrows at him in a silent command, all but saying out loud he doesn't really want to help me with this. Usually, I like my volunteers to be willing and eager. I don't know how I feel about the silent arm-twisting.

Griffin gives her a brief nod. "It won't be a problem."

I should appreciate his confidence and leave it at that, but his brush-off hits me wrong. People in town have been shrugging off my project ever since I stepped up to run it—I don't need my volunteer looking down on it, too. "You don't know what I have planned yet."

He ticks his head to the side, facing me more fully. "Do you *want* it to be a problem?"

"Obviously not, but what if I ask you to build thirty houses? What if I want a replica Bavarian village in town square? What if I want a life-sized Christmas Town complete with Jack Skellington and Sally? None of that would be a problem?"

"Are you asking for any of that?"

"No."

"Then it won't be a problem."

Amazing how quickly he can crawl right under my skin.

The arrogance that had rubbed me wrong in high school now makes me want to start a fight right here in the café—which probably wouldn't be very smart, considering everything I'm about to ask him to do. His blunt criticisms always drove me crazy. I couldn't understand his need to be so negative, and it looks like that hasn't changed.

I take a deep breath, imagining how magical my Winter Wonderland buildings will look when they're done. *That's* the main thing, not Griffin's excess of self-confidence. And definitely not that whenever I used to play the Kiss, Marry, Kill game, I always axed Griffin without a trace of guilt.

In another minute, the barista passes around our coffees. Kat takes hers and hitches her purse farther up her shoulder. "Well, I'll leave you to it. Check in with me later, son. Bye, Hope."

My mouth falls open to say something to get her to stay, but she hustles out the door before I can come up with a plea.

I risk another glance at Griffin.

Big mistake. He's watching me a little too avidly, and I get the feeling he's already tallying up faults and failures to point out later. I've had enough hazel-eyed condescension from him to last a lifetime. We'll just have to build the Wonderland with a minimum of eye contact.

"Do you want to sit down?" I ask. "I can tell you more about the festival, and then we can go to the warehouse around the corner to look over the plans."

"I'd rather see what you've got in store for me now."

I will just chalk that up to unbridled enthusiasm and not the low-key dread it sounds like. "Okay then."

We leave the coffee shop and set off for the warehouse a few blocks away. Now that I don't have his eyes boring directly into me, I can think for a minute. Mostly, I think about my regrets.

When Kat said she knew someone, I never guessed she meant Griffin. One of her *other* employees, maybe. A friendly neighborhood handyman I've never heard about. *Not* her cocky younger son I've been doing my best to avoid since he came back to town.

He was some kind of construction guru up in Portland since high school, but he moved back after his dad suddenly passed away nearly a year ago. I've heard a few colorful stories about his poor customer service skills over at his family's landscaping business, but he wasn't on my list of people to reconnect with.

From the way he eyes me, I'm not on his, either.

"Did your mom tell you anything about the Winter Wonderland?" I ask to fill up the silence.

"Just that you need something built."

"I really do. You know those light-up miniature Christmas villages people put on their mantels?"

He arches an eyebrow at me. Right. This is Griffin McBride.

He doesn't seem like much of a Christmas decorator. He probably staples his stocking to the wall and calls it good.

"Anyway, I got the idea to make one of those, but person-sized, to be the backdrop for Santa visits in town square."

"So you're putting a replica little town in the middle of an actual little town."

He doesn't *say* anything critical, but it's implied.

"It's going to be cute. Kids will love it." *I* will love it, but that's implied, too.

His mouth tugs into a dismissive frown. I guess Griffin isn't in the *love it* column.

I should have been more specific when I told Kat I needed a new handyman. I need someone interested. Invested. Definitely not someone who's going to make me doubt this whole project with one twitchy eyebrow.

I let him into the warehouse and pull my coat a little closer around myself. The uninsulated walls and bare cement floor leave the warehouse an icebox this time of year. With the flip of a switch, the fluorescent lights come on high overhead, flickering to life one by one, revealing my dreams laid out piecemeal in the cavernous room.

"All the decorations for the festival are stored in here." I step farther inside, waving my arms vaguely. "We planned to do all the work on the Winter Wonderland here, too. It's big enough to hold the buildings when they're done, kind of a staging area before we take them to town square on the day of the tree lighting."

Griffin follows me into the warehouse, one hand jammed into his jeans pocket against the cold, the other lazily holding his coffee. I try to see the warehouse through his eyes. It isn't much to look at. A sheet of plywood laid over a pair of sawhorses form the workbench. Next to it sits a pile of two-by-fours and a stack of uncut plywood, the main components of the buildings I have planned. All just plain wood now, but in my mind, they'll come together to create Christmas magic.

With any luck, Griffin will see it, too.

"It's freezing in here," he says.

Or not.

"We can turn on the industrial space heaters if we need to." I flash him a smile. I want to look reassuring and calming, but I probably look more like Buddy the Elf grinning his head off.

"Space heater's a fire hazard with all this lumber," he says.

You would know about fire hazards. Not that I dare say that out loud.

He scowls around at the supplies. I need to win over my volunteer, or I don't have much hope of him making the buildings I dreamed up. If he thinks the project is too much—or worse, too little—he might decide not to get involved. I might have to turn to my mother for help after all.

Ha, no way. If it comes down to it, I'll build the Wonderland myself.

I shudder, imagining the bloodbath. So many power tools. So many severed fingers.

"We'll just use the space heaters as a last resort, then." I follow him on his circuit of the warehouse, watching his face for any sign of—well, it's already too late to hope he might be impressed. I would settle for less disdain, but the scowl stays on his face.

"Pretty basic supplies," he says, walking by the boxes of metal fasteners, shingles, and buckets of paint.

Again with the brush-off. Most of my volunteers at least *want* to be part of the festival. Somehow, I got stuck with the least-invested person to do the most important part.

"Then it should be an easy job for you."

His mouth curls at that—Smile? Sneer? I can't tell—but he goes on looking through the warehouse like a drill sergeant inspecting pathetic recruits. In addition to all the wood for the buildings, I rounded up the town's old holiday decorations from storage units far and wide. Six-foot-tall candy canes lean against one wall next to a haphazard assortment of lighted wire snowmen, wreaths, and bells. A few items turned up broken and too expensive to replace, like the plastic reindeer team that each have a crushed leg, but I found enough to make a merry, vintage scene.

"How many buildings?"

"Five. Sort of a mini elf village."

He cuts his eyes to me. "Elf village?"

"It is the North Pole." I smile again, but he doesn't return it. Mine crumbles away. "I've got blueprints, so you don't have to worry about any of the designs."

He looks over the collection of power tools, most of them borrowed from my original handyman. "Where'd you get the designs?"

"For the buildings? I designed them."

He stops to toss a skeptical look over his shoulder. "You designed all the buildings for this?"

"Yes."

"Do you have a degree in architecture or something?"

"No. I just like art." I'd minored in studio art in college, paint nearly every day, and run a store devoted to all things crafty, but I don't feel like telling him any of that. "I referenced old Christmas movies when I came up with the building ideas. You know, for the nostalgia."

He doesn't seem moved by the image. "Right. Let's see the plans."

I go over to the workbench and pull out a sheaf of papers. He takes the stack and flips through them, stopping now and then to examine a drawing or note. I hold my breath for about fifteen seconds—long enough to realize my hopes for a smile or an appreciative nod over my designs aren't going to materialize —and I huff it out again.

Silas had just accepted my plans for the whimsical buildings, he hadn't critiqued them. Of course, he doesn't have years of experience building actual houses behind him—he just happens to have a garage full of tools.

He doesn't cut the same figure that Griffin does, either. Over six feet tall, with an athletic build and a stern expression, Griffin probably doesn't mess around with things like paints or heartwarming Christmas movies. Combine that with our sketchy history together, and I feel even more awkward than I ordinarily would.

And ordinarily, I can be pretty dang awkward.

"These aren't blueprints."

"Sure they are." I point out some of the more detailed pages. "They've got all the dimensions here."

"That doesn't make them blueprints." He spreads the pages out on the workbench. "These are sketches and estimates. They're guesswork, that's all. I'm going to have to figure out how to make them."

First, I don't appreciate his accusatory tone, as if I intentionally tricked him. Second, I don't appreciate him looking directly at me. With all the arrogance in his gaze, his eyeballs must weigh a hundred pounds each.

"I thought you said it wouldn't be a problem."

He shakes his head and shuffles through the papers again. "Five houses, each with different decorations, none of them the same size or shape. You're really going all out."

Between his deep voice and obvious lack of interest in the project, I can't tell if he's complimenting me or mocking me. Always a tough call, in my experience. Normally, I assume positive intent, but that doesn't come easily with Griffin. Even the way he drinks his coffee feels like a judgment call.

I'm so much better than you, with my plain black coffee and smoldering good looks.

"That's the point. We're going to create a little bit of Christmas magic right here on Maple Street."

He lifts one eyebrow like a die-hard skeptic.

"Come on, don't you remember the way the festival used to be? All the events, the lights, the music? The way we would run through town square to see Santa?"

He goes on staring at me, unmoved. I feel like a cheerleader accidentally doing her routine in front of the opposing team's fans, and my Christmas *rah-rah* fizzles out.

"That's what you're trying to capture with this?" He tosses a hand at the pile of boards.

"Well, yeah. We're bringing back some of the old stuff, like the decorations and the choir, but hopefully, we can make it even better than it used to be."

"We're talking about sheets of plywood."

This man has no vision at all.

"Plywood that you're very helpfully going to turn into my Winter Wonderland. Aside from the tree, it's going to be the centerpiece of the whole display. It will be the highlight of the Christmas season."

No pressure or anything.

"How many people are you thinking are going to come to this?"

He might as well have asked me "How many people do you think live on the moon?" I take a step back, giving myself space. Talking to him is like trying to impress a manager who's hell-bent on firing me, and I need a second to shore up my morale.

"We should see several thousand people."

He makes a sound that might be a snort. "That's not going to happen."

A tsunami of irritation washes over me, along with a renewed extreme dislike for hazel-green eyes. "Excuse me?"

"I saw the Christmas festival last year. How many came to that? A thousand people, tops? You can't just throw some plywood buildings together and expect that five times as many people will show up to this thing."

His cynicism was one of his most prominent traits in high school. Clearly, Griffin hasn't stumbled on a latent optimistic streak.

"How many Christmas festivals have you put together?" I ask.

He lifts his eyebrows rather than answer.

"I've done the research." I work on staying calm and collected even though I'm tempted to get shouty. Yet another déjà vu about being around Griffin. "It's a reasonable number to expect from all of the ads and promotions I'm doing."

One of his eyebrows ticks even higher, and I seriously want to flick it back down. Get back where you belong, you thick, skeptical caterpillar.

"You did the research and advertising, too? Shouldn't the town have hired a firm for that?"

I stand straighter. "My degree is in marketing. It's not a stretch for me to do the research."

He tilts his mouth into a brief frown. "If you say so. But I think you should aim lower."

"Always a garbage piece of advice, in my opinion."

"I'm not saying to cancel the thing. I just wouldn't count on that kind of a turnout."

Would punching my volunteer in the nose make a bad first impression?

"I'll note your concerns in my log."

His smile is relaxed and easy, like my chilly retort hasn't fazed him a bit. Meanwhile, my blood burns through my veins with every angry heartbeat. This is part of what had driven me so crazy back in high school—he could criticize and nitpick until I totally lost my cool, but he never got worked up no matter how much we argued. He remained totally unbothered, which only made me furious back then.

Just like it's starting to do now.

"What are you doing here with a degree in marketing?" he asks. "Last I checked, there aren't many jobs like that in Sunshine."

"I worked in marketing for a few years in Portland after college."

"But...?"

"But now I'm back." Those years had been a failed experiment in living the Big City Life: sharing a tiny apartment, working at a high-end firm downtown, and ultimately realizing none of it suited me. The strange loneliness in the middle of a constant rush of people, the corporate craze of nonstop deadlines, knowing I was just a worker bee in my company hive—it had all been an epic disaster.

Not that he'll get any of the gory details. He would just use them as ammo one way or another.

"Huh."

He looks me up and down again like maybe he has more questions. Whatever he wants to know about my time in Portland, he can keep it to himself. Reliving the low points of my life with him isn't part of our deal.

I clear my throat and nod at the papers on the workbench. "Are you going to be able to make these or not?"

"Sure."

"That's not very reassuring."

"It's more reassuring than if I'd said no."

I groan over his perverse need to win the simplest conversations. "Will figuring out the designs cause a delay?"

"Shouldn't. You've got plenty of notes."

See? Even that sounds like an insult.

"It's called being thorough."

That smirk touches his mouth again. "Who's going to paint and decorate all this?"

I raise my hand like a kid in school.

"You're a regular one-woman band around here. Is there anything you're not doing?"

"I'm not building them. Like I said, I'm not handy."

"Right. I guess I'd better get started."

Finally.

"Sounds great."

He might be an arrogant, condescending volunteer who'd possibly been coerced into this by his mom, but at least I have someone to build my Christmas dreams.

If I don't kick him out of the warehouse first.

THREE
GRIFFIN

I SHOULD HAVE LEARNED by now to be suspicious whenever my mom asks me to do something with a big smile on her face. She'd fed me this sob story about how the Christmas festival organizer needed a replacement handyman ASAP or hundreds of little kids would have their hearts crushed. Wouldn't I like to put my carpentry skills to use again? Don't I want to save Christmas? Yada yada.

But I've been doing anything she asks for a solid year—of course I agreed.

Just hadn't expected Hope Parrish to be the mystery organizer. I'd figured it would be some gray-haired old lady ready to reward me with butterscotch candies whenever I made sufficient progress. Not the former Homecoming Queen with the long dark hair and big brown eyes.

Standing here in her lime green sweater, she doesn't seem so different from the girl I remember. Sky-high ambitions make her a little too eager to be taken seriously. Snarking at me comes as naturally as it had then, too. And her wide smile never leaves her face, like everything makes her crazy happy.

Not that she's all that happy with *me*. I didn't miss how her smile disappeared when she recognized me at the coffee shop. She'd smiled again even brighter right after, but too late. I'd be lying if I said her disappointment hadn't dented my pride a little. Crazy smiles or not, the woman is gorgeous.

Always has been, in a *Do Not Touch, No Admittance* sort of way.

Hope had been voted Best Smile by our senior class. I'd been voted Most Likely to Burn the Woods. That never stopped me from admiring her, though. Even when frustrated with me, she was the prettiest girl I'd ever seen.

She's the prettiest girl I've ever seen even now.

I tuck all of those thoughts into a mental lockbox, wrap it with a couple of chains for good measure, and toss it into the abyss of Things I Do Not Think About. Because this particular Hope Parrish also happens to be engaged.

"These are pretty simple designs." I ran through the papers for the two bigger buildings already, marking down proper measurements and tallying up exactly what supplies I'll need for each one. Basically oversized dollhouses, they'll be easy enough for me to put together, given a little time.

I still maintain they can't possibly deliver on her overblown expectations. That part isn't my problem, though. I only need to worry about building them. She can deal with the results.

"So you said." She hovers close by, trying to watch what I'm doing without looking like she's watching.

"I could improve them if I—"

"What's wrong with my designs?"

Her eyes shine with annoyance and probably a touch of hurt feelings. Great. First morning in, and I've already got off on the wrong foot with her. I do that with people sometimes. Well —most of the time. Not everybody responds well when I see a better way of doing things.

Case in point: my brother Caleb.

But she asked me here to build these for her—it only makes sense she'd want my advice on how to improve her project.

"Nothing's wrong, but if I make a few changes—"

"If you don't want to build them, I can find somebody else." Her annoyance flares even brighter with the challenge.

We both know she's bluffing. I already heard about the festival's plight from my mom. She doesn't have a line of people knocking down the door dying to make this stuff for her—she only has me. Lucky for her, I'm her best option anyway.

I set my pencil down and face her fully. "Are you going to let me finish?"

She twists her mouth like she has another defensive remark at the ready but manages to hold it back. She still glares a silent *You're not the boss of me*, but waves a hand my direction. "Go on."

I wait a second for her glare to die down. When it becomes clear that isn't going to happen, I explain. "I could improve them if I make them 3D."

"They are 3D. They're real houses, not just front façades." She pokes a finger at the pile of papers as though I didn't just look through her three-dimensional designs.

I take a deep breath, glowering at her a touch so she'll chill out. Which of course, she doesn't.

"The *fronts* can have more depth," I explain. "Bump out the section beneath the awning here, or make the painted dormer real on this one. It will add dimension to the designs and give you a little more realism."

Her angry veneer melts away. "Oh."

"It looks like you were just planning to paint on all the designs, but I can make frames around the windows and doors to give them depth, too."

She looks from the sketches to me. "I didn't want it to be so elaborate my volunteer couldn't do it."

"Maybe it would have been too much for your previous volunteer, but you've got me now."

Her little frown says that's not as reassuring as I'd intended.

"Well. It's a really good idea." That faint praise sounds like it was offered at gunpoint.

"I know."

Her mouth thins. "You're so humble."

"I'm not familiar with that word."

"You haven't changed much, have you?"

I toss her my most charming grin. "I haven't had any complaints."

She rolls her eyes. "I feel like you throw your suggestion box straight into the trash. If you need more supplies, Luke at Bridger Hardware is donating all that stuff. Don't go overboard or anything, but he'll help you out."

"I won't abuse his generosity by stocking up on plywood for the year."

I get back to my notes for the buildings, trying not to think too hard about what my old construction crew would say about me building *elf houses*. A year ago, I did custom carpentry for multi-million dollar houses. Now, I'm the guy people call when they want a life-sized gingerbread house.

Not exactly moving up in the world.

"I'm going to get my tools out of my truck."

"You brought your own tools?" Hope looks like I just told her Grandma got run over by a reindeer.

"You should thank me." I hook my thumb at the ratty selection of tools by the so-called workbench. "Using any of those comes with a serious risk of electric shock. You don't want me to wind up in the hospital next to your original handyman, do you?"

She tries to look stern. "I'm still debating."

I walk out the warehouse door smiling to myself. Working

with her might be more fun than I'd thought. Too bad about the whole *engaged* thing.

I let the cold mountain air fill my lungs, pushing any regrets about her out of my mind. Coming back here wasn't my plan—the grief of losing my dad still rattles through me, knocking me flat on my back and putting a lump in my throat—but I can't deny Sunshine has a certain draw.

Not enough for Hope's grand scheme of pulling in thousands of tourists, though. Between mountain bikers on McKenzie Peak, boaters on Jasper lake, and fly fisherman on the Olallie River, we get a good amount of outdoor tourism, but events like she's planning? They haven't made it happen yet.

Sure, Portlanders like vintage these days, but not enough to drive four hours to the middle of the state for it. Maybe she'd get a few hundred from Bend, but when the day comes to light up the tree and sing all the songs, safe bet she'll wind up disappointed by the low turnout.

Everything inside me bristles at attaching myself to a project destined to fail, but like I said, my mom asked. She believes in this thing, and wants me to see it through. I can't let my family down again.

And hey, at least I'll get a reprieve from working with my brother for a few weeks.

I park closer to the warehouse now that I know where I'll be spending my days and cart my things inside. Getting down to business, I pull off my coat and start measuring and cutting two-by-fours to form the first wall.

While I throw together the basic frame, Hope inspects plastic bins full of light strings, untangling someone else's shoddy work. At least, I assume perfect Hope Parrish isn't the one who threw dozens of strings of lights into a pile. She plugs each one in to test before neatly winding them into a loop and noting something on a sheet of paper. Probably how long they are and what they're destined to festoon.

She looks slightly ridiculous in her knee-length wool skirt and heels in the middle of a warehouse, but she has plans, I have to give her that. I like these hints of her Type A traits, since they match mine. Just one flaw in her plan.

"You should sort them by light type," I tell her. "If you string incandescents with LEDs, you'll ruin the LEDs."

She looks down at the open bin in front of her and then at me. "I didn't know you majored in Christmas Lights in college."

The hint of challenge in her voice warms me up. So does the curl along those berry-colored lips.

Remember why you're here, McBride.

"I majored in Efficiency," I return. "With a minor in Doing Things Right the First Time."

She exhales a soft groan at me. I like that, too, but everything will be easier if I pretend I didn't hear it.

"Am I doing anything else that needs improvement?"

"I'll let you know what else I find."

"I was being sarcastic. You joined *my* project, you know." She waves a finger between the two of us. "We're supposed to be a team here."

"We are. I just don't want my teammate to blow out light strings because she mixed the two types."

Frowning hard at me, she sits delicately on one of the bins and starts examining the bulbs. "It's high school all over again," she mutters under her breath.

I laugh softly—I don't need to *completely* tick her off. I'll do the work for her, but I'm sure not about to be her underling taking orders in silence, especially not when I see ways to improve business.

Hmm. Maybe I'm thinking of the wrong teammate.

I remind myself Hope isn't my brother and go back to work.

It isn't Caleb's fault I quit my carpentry job in Portland and came here to work with him and Mom. That was my choice.

The fact that we butt heads about as often as two rams eager to prove themselves the strongest of the herd? Might have a little more to do with him. Fifty-fifty.

Doing my best to focus on the simple tasks of drilling boards and tightening screws, I try to empty my head. Not think about family obligations or regrets and definitely not my pretty *teammate* wandering around fifteen feet away.

I zone out for a good while before Hope interrupts again.

"Look at how much you've done already!"

She's at the edge of my work, snuggled up in her bright red parka again, her dark hair spilling out beneath a red knit cap pulled low over her ears. The red makes her brown eyes even richer—another fact I need to throw onto the pile of Things I Don't Notice.

She acts out my own personal standing ovation for being less than five percent through a project. Gotta say, her applause gives me a nice flush of pride, but her excitement seems premature. Maybe this is how she normally cheers on her teammates, but I don't need empty praise.

I stand and dust off my jeans. "It's just a wall."

Not even that, just the frame for one. I haven't attached the plywood yet.

"I'm relieved, though. After Silas got injured, I was afraid all of this was dead in the water."

"I never heard what happened to him."

"He hurt his back helping me unload the lumber. I guess the project was a little too much for him. But look at all this!"

She grins, waving her hand over the not-quite-wall, and I have to wonder how badly she gets walked on if she treats everyone this way. Keeping her expectations low won't help her make those thousands of tourists roll in.

"I've got to go open my store." She twists her fingers, and a glint of something silver shines as she fidgets. "I have a part-time employee, but I usually come in even when she's there. I'd probably sleep in there if I could."

She gets this dreamy look on her face but shakes it off again. "Anyway, I've got a lot to do, and I won't be able to be in the warehouse with you all the time."

That brings a surge of relief. A smaller wave of disappointment follows right after, but I need to focus on the relief.

"I wanted to leave you this." She holds her palm out to me, revealing a silver key. I stare at it but don't take it.

"It's for the lock on the warehouse door." She flashes another smile. She probably honed those smiles in her run as Homecoming Queen. They're a little too perfect, a little too tight at the edges to be totally sincere. Kind of the way I think of her as a whole. "So you can work when it's convenient for you."

As though any part of this arrangement is convenient for me. I don't argue, though, and take the key. The stupid thought it's the first time a woman has ever given me a key to anything runs through my brain, and I have the urge to shoot myself in the hand with a nail gun.

"I don't expect you to work around the clock," she goes on. "Give yourself breaks, take the weekends off."

"I thought you wanted me to get this done as fast as possible."

"Well..." She looks past me to the solitary wall on the floor and back. "I wouldn't want to aim too high for you."

I laugh at her attempt to roast me. "You'd be surprised what I can do when I'm properly motivated."

A flush of pink spreads over her cheeks, and my stomach tightens in response. I'm not flirting with the engaged woman. Just stating fact. Probably shouldn't have dropped my voice like we're telling secrets, though.

She flashes that tight smile again. "We should exchange numbers. In case anything comes up."

Exchanging numbers with Hope shoots a stupid thrill through me, but I squash that out. My interest in her is instinct only, and wildly inappropriate.

We trade numbers, and she starts to leave but turns around again at the door.

"Thanks for agreeing to do this. I know your mom's behind it, but I really was up a creek. I appreciate it."

No Homecoming Queen smile peeks out now. I catch a glimpse of the real Hope—worried, a little bit out of her depth, and startlingly vulnerable. My heart kicks in my rib cage. I'm not sure I deserve her thanks, considering the doubts I have about the project, but I can't refuse her, either.

"I'm happy to help."

She gives a stout nod in return and disappears out the door.

Making these buildings for her will be easy. Watching Hope's face crumble when her dreams crash and burn in three weeks? That will be the real problem.

FOUR
HOPE

I ARRANGE gemstone necklaces on a rustic wooden display, turning them to catch the light, and try not to let the worries worming around in my stomach develop into big ugly worry moths.

Did I order enough stock to get through the major shopping days after Thanksgiving? If I ordered too much, how long will it take to sell the extras and recoup the investment? What if everyone is so busy online shopping, we don't get any sales boost at all?

And such and such. Ordinarily, I like to see the glass as half-full, and I believe in The Painted Daisy. But that isn't quite enough to keep the Business Failure Boogeyman away permanently.

My phone rings, and I pop it out of my pocket. Lila. Surprising, considering my sister is usually too busy Girl Bossing to call in the middle of the day.

"What's up?" I say.

"Just checking in. Is this a good time to talk?"

"It's fine. The store's not busy right now."

"That's not a good sign, is it?"

I can't help but roll my eyes at her concern. "Are you coming down for Thanksgiving, or are you going to stately Brandt Manor this time around?"

Last year, she'd sent pictures of her fiancé's family home. Pretty sure *our* family home has fewer square feet than their pool house. I've never bothered to look up what his parents do for work, but I'm betting her fiancé's wealth isn't solely from his successful tech start-up.

"Staying here this year. How are things in Christmas central?"

"Going great. Right on track." All virtually ninety-eight percent true. Mostly.

"That festival must be a pretty big undertaking." She sounds like she's at the top of a high dive looking down—a little bit excited, a little bit uneasy.

"It is, but I've got it all under control." Again...mostly.

"Is all the advertising taken care of? Do you need any help getting the word out? What does your social media plan look like?"

I sigh right into the phone so she can't miss it. "Mom put you up to this, didn't she?"

"What? No. I'm asking because I *care*."

Her Broadway play audition isn't going so hot.

"You're a terrible actress. You need to learn not to oversell it."

Now she sighs, managing to sound more put out than I am. "Fine. Mom hinted I should see if I can help you out. Don't you need a team working with you?"

Team gets me thinking about Griffin, and his apparent aversion to the word. Most of my volunteers want everything spelled out for them, but he waltzed in ready to take over. I resent his attitude...and that all his suggestions were spot-on. Which I will be taking with me to the grave.

"I'm not doing everything by myself. I've delegated a bunch of tasks—you know what, I'm not doing this. If Mom wants to know about the festival, she can come straight to me." She's already abused that privilege, but she doesn't need to send Lila to check in on me, too.

"She's just trying to look out for you. First you leave your job in Portland, then you start *and quit* doing real estate with her, then you open this pop-up store—"

"It's not a pop-up." True, The Painted Daisy is roughly the size of an average SUV, but I run it year-round. Not the same.

"And now the Christmas festival. I don't understand why you didn't ask me to help you in the first place. I put together big, successful events all the time, and you never have."

Harsh. True, but still harsh. Kind of a microcosm of our whole relationship right there.

"You don't want to put your job on hold and take vacation time for this." Also, it won't count as *my* win if I have to tag Lila in. "I'm sure you're busy with all the wedding planning too."

"Yeah." Her voice goes so soft I barely hear it. "There's plenty of that."

"Did you figure out a date yet?" My mother lost her mind with pride when Joshua Brandt III proposed over the summer— she would have shouted it from the rooftops if Lila and Josh had set a firm date. Engaged, working PR for her fiancé's uber-successful tech firm in Seattle, *and* a minor Instagram celebrity, Lila is basically the living embodiment of everything our mother has ever dreamed for us.

I flatten out my bitterness and fold it up into an origami box. Lila works hard for what she has, and I'm proud of her. I just don't love having her successes shoved in front of my face all the time in Mom's eternal hopes I'll achieve the same things.

"We haven't decided yet. You know how it is."

"I really don't." Lila found her Price Charming, but I

haven't found mine, despite Mom's aggressive attempts to help me with that.

"Have you heard anything from Mark?"

I shudder at the mention of his name. "No, and I don't expect to."

"It was a simple misunderstanding."

"Only from Mom's perspective." Lila has been happily paired up for years. She can't possibly understand the humiliation of having Mom mow down my dating life with her overzealousness. Lesson learned: I haven't told our mother a thing about my love life since.

Not that I've had anything to relate. The point remains—my dating life will never be up for public consumption again.

"If you really like him, you could reach out. Let him know you're still interested."

Lila just doesn't understand failure. She has about as much experience with that word as Griffin has with humility.

"No way. What would I say? 'Hey, sorry I came across like a psycho last summer. Want to give it another try?'"

"Maybe don't use those exact words."

"It doesn't matter anyway. His reaction to that whole thing was enough of a red flag, I'm glad it worked out that way." *Now,* anyway. Over the summer, I'd marinated in humiliation. And I've gone on soaking in it every time someone around town brings up my supposed fiancé.

Two women walk through The Daisy's door and start a slow browse up the aisles.

"I've got to go, Lila, I've got customers."

"Let me know if you need anything with the festival!" she chirps.

I greet the women with a warm smile, tucking away my frustration at the one-two punch of Lila fishing for information for our mother. As much as Mom wants me to succeed with this project, digging for information and offering to call in favors tells me she doesn't think I can.

Just once, it would be nice to hear her say "I know you can do it" without a *but* at the end of that sentence.

Wren steps over to lean against the pass-through. "So who did Kat find for you? Some hunky handyman ripped from the pages of a romance novel?"

My lips pull back into a sour face like I've had a sip of Sarah Gould's eggnog. Pretty sure bourbon makes up eighty percent of her recipe.

"Too close to the truth," Wren says, "or too far?"

Somehow both at once.

"She asked Griffin."

Her smile turns into a toothy cringe. "You're joking."

"Nope. He's in the warehouse right now. I assume." I've lost volunteers left and right, but quitting after a couple of hours would be a record.

"This is going to be an interesting Christmas."

"No kidding. Santa came early, and he brought me a big lump of arrogant coal."

She laughs, but we hush our gossip as one of the two women brings her purchase to me. I ring up the items while Wren loiters in the doorway, no doubt waiting to hear more about my surprise handyman.

"I love these little coin purses," the woman says. "It was hard to choose just one."

"The artist lives right here in town, and she gets all her fabric from estate sales and thrift stores." Also, my mother and sister are both getting one of these coin purses for Christmas.

"Oh, I like that. I like knowing I'm supporting local artists."

Pride glows through me like a Christmas candle. That's exactly why I opened my store.

"If you have time, you should stop in next door for a slice of pie."

The delicious smells of a dozen varieties of pies and cupcakes drift through The Painted Daisy, making it impossible to forget Blackbird's Bakery next door. Sometimes customers wander over for treats before they can buy anything from me. Heck, I nip over there for a goody most days, too.

As soon as the women cross the threshold into the bakery, Wren moves closer to me. "So how is this going to go? You working side by side with Griffin for the next three weeks?"

A jolt of excitement shimmers through me at the image of us close together, huddled over blueprints and designs, our arms brushing as we make plans.

Uh—no. The picture of us getting cozy is unexpected and totally unwelcome. I need to derail that train of thought ASAP. Push it off the tracks and into an abyss.

A handsome face doesn't make a guy *good*, as I learned with Mark.

"I don't even want to think about it. This was supposed to be my big moment, and now I have to deal with *him*."

"Yeah." Her slow nod goes on way too long. "He's looking good though, right?"

I try for my best angry romance hero growl, but I just sound like a frightened baby animal. "You're a traitor. You have no loyalty."

"I'm just saying. He's stopped in the bakery a few times, and...yowza."

I can't disagree...but I *really* can't admit it, either.

"Speaking of, you should probably get back in the bakery. Wouldn't want your customers to leave empty-handed." I sweep my hand to shoo her out, but she doesn't make a move.

"Nice try. Tess is on counter duty."

They keep Blackbird's Bakery in the family: Wren, her

older sister Tess, and their mom Maureen. Tess's five-year-old son acts as their unofficial cutie pie mascot and should probably be on the payroll for his adorableness.

I envy how well their family works together. I'd maxed out at eight months working for my mom's real estate firm, and I'd wanted to quit for a solid six of them.

Honestly, even the first two hadn't been so hot.

"Was he wearing a flannel shirt with the sleeves rolled up?" Wren asks. "I swear that's all that man owns."

I turn away before she can see the truth in my face. Sleeves rolled up, forearms at the ready—he'd shown me the works. Whatever else I want to pretend, I hadn't totally missed his looks. The flannel! The russet scruff on his jaw! His strong hands! Skill with power tools should not be a turn-on, but here we are.

"I'm too busy to think about Griffin."

It's like my new hobby consists solely of lying through my teeth at every opportunity.

"Come on," Wren says. "I tell you every time Shepherd comes into the bakery all broody and greasy and angry at the world to order his slice of pie for the week."

I spin back around. "You don't tell me what your next-door nemesis is wearing, though."

Nemesis feels like a strong word for a guy who's never done worse than goad her a little and buy a pie from her every week, but I can't dispute her inability to get along with the bike shop owner.

"Indulge me."

"Fine. Griffin was wearing flannel when he swooped in with a bunch of criticism and suggestions like he thinks he's king of the project. He's exactly like he was in high school—his confidence crosses the line into arrogance, and everything he says comes across as condescending. If anything, he's even *more* sure of himself now, which seems like it should be scientifically impossible. The ego on that man is blinding."

It wasn't all in the things he'd said—although that had been plenty. He'd walked around with this cocky swagger like he owned the whole warehouse. He hadn't asked questions so much as he'd demanded information and offered unsolicited suggestions. Maybe most obviously of all, he didn't care a bit about what I thought of him. That alone proves intimidating, since I care about what *everyone* thinks of me.

Wren looks like I just handed her a Christmas present. "You're *really* worked up about him."

She's right. I shouldn't let him rile me up this way. It's a bad sign for our working relationship for the next few weeks. Still, she doesn't have to bob her eyebrows as if that means something.

"You're a bad friend. Genuinely. The worst friend I've ever had for twenty years."

"Aw. You love me, though." Some of her giddiness fades out. "Do you think he'll do a good job with your Winter Wonderland?"

"He used to build houses for a living. I'm sure he can handle making a few fake ones." I chew my bottom lip, picturing the side of the house he'd had laid out on the floor when I left. "Actually...he's already done more in a couple of hours than Silas probably would have done all day."

There are some advantages to working with a guy under thirty. His massive ego being the most obvious disadvantage.

Wren keeps her eyes on me, applying pressure. "Are you two going to murder each other? Because there were some close calls in debate class."

And American History. And English Literature. We'd even found ways to argue in Chemistry, but that makes sense, considering we were lab partners. Two volatile substances forced to share the same desk for a year.

"It's fine. We're adults. We'll just...put all that behind us."

She looks like she's having flashbacks from all of our squabbles ten years ago. "That sounds real convincing."

"I can get along with him for the sake of my Winter Wonderland."

After that, he can go back to criticizing someone else.

FIVE
GRIFFIN

I WALK into McBride Landscaping's executive meeting before Mom and Caleb have a chance to sit down at the small conference table. They both hold paper coffee cups, ready to settle in for the weekly check-in session.

"I wasn't expecting you today." Caleb looks at me like my very existence baffles him.

"What? I still work here. Mom didn't trade me to the Christmas festival permanently."

"Wish she could," he mutters. He shoots me a grin right after, so I forgive him for the joke.

Even if I suspect part of him means it. We've been knocking each other's elbows ever since I took my place with the family business almost a year ago. Neither of us has enough room to spread our wings the way we want to, but we keep our scuffles to a minimum, for the CEO's sake.

"What do you think of Hope's plans?" the CEO asks. Mom's eager eyes tell me she won't accept criticism on the festival.

I dig deep, searching my brain for some tact. Putting things nicely isn't one of my stronger skills. I try sometimes, but to my way of thinking, truth is more important than sparing someone's feelings.

Unless that someone is my mom.

"It's ambitious."

Vaguely complimentary, that description might work. It used to be my usual response when someone presented me with a haphazard plan they didn't know how to execute. Make them feel like they'd had a good idea, even if I wound up shooting them down in the end.

Her frown proves my methods don't fly with her. "Can you make her buildings the way she wants?"

I splay my hands wide. "Look who you're talking to. Of course I can make them, that's not the problem. Doesn't mean they'll bring in the crowds she's hoping for."

She waves off my doubts. "What happened to my determined son with a vision and a plan to make it happen?"

"He's still here, but that only holds true if it's *my* vision. This is all Hope's rodeo. Me, I'm envisioning her Christmas village surrounded by a smaller crowd than she's thinking, that's all."

Much smaller, if I have to guess. The buildings will be cute, I'll make sure of that, but I just don't see the rest of it drawing in record-breaking numbers.

"You're such a Scrooge," Caleb says.

"It's not being a Scrooge to look at it logically. What does Sunshine have that's going to draw in that big of a crowd?"

"It's like you've never watched a Hallmark Christmas movie."

"Maybe you should think about how easily you just admitted that you *do*."

He shrugs. "They're Rowan's favorite."

"Sure. Blame it on your wife."

"Maybe you should help Hope revise her strategy," Mom cuts in.

Someone needs to, but that won't be me. "Christmas parties aren't my wheelhouse. I'll make her gingerbread village, but the rest is on Hope."

"Don't go giving her a hard time." Mom points her "I'm serious and I mean it" finger at me.

Seems a rude thing to lob at a guy. I look to Caleb for some backup. "Why would I give her a hard time?"

He chokes on laughter. "I don't know, maybe because you love giving people a hard time?"

I scoff, but arguments die before I can voice them. I do kind of like giving people a hard time. Only if they deserve it, though. A guy who wanted to pretend to be the foreman and bark out orders after being on a job crew for a week? Absolutely, I'll give that guy a hard time. But a woman who's simply overshot her goals of reigniting this town's Christmas spirit? I have no plans to butt heads with her over that.

"I can show you written feedback from our crew that says you have a tendency to be abrasive," he adds.

"Well, I don't tear down pretty women for the heck of it."

Except when I do. I shift uncomfortably in my seat. I'd razzed Hope enough in high school to prove myself a liar. It hadn't *all* been for the fun of it. I'd had genuine points to make most of the time. But some of it had been just because I could get under that veneer of perfection she wore so carefully.

I liked the glimpse of realness it showed me when she lost her cool, but my methods weren't exactly admirable. I don't really like the mirror they've held up.

"Don't forget, you're there to help her, not the other way around." Mom still waggles that accusatory finger in the air. "You need to be a good little soldier and do whatever she says."

"Ah, correction." Caleb stands from the table and ducks out of the conference room.

I turn to Mom, waiting for the rest of whatever's coming. The little smile that curves along her mouth makes my stomach cramp right up. Not a good sign if they're in on this together.

Caleb returns thirty seconds later with a paper bag. He pulls something red and green out of it, and that cramp hits even harder. Dread has my stomach in its snowy, Christmas-bedazzled grip.

"Not a soldier," he says, holding the hat in the air. "An elf."

The green hat has a red zig-zag crown and a freaking *bell* at the pointy end that jingles with every move he makes. He steps closer like he intends to put that monstrosity on me.

"No way. Get that thing away from me."

"Come on," he croons, trying to land it on my head. "You need to get into the spirit."

"If you put that on me, I'll stick a candy cane right up your—"

"Boys," Mom says into the fray.

"Nose," I finish.

Caleb smirks and tosses the hat at me. It hits my chest and *jingle-jingles* into my lap.

I flop it onto the table. "Mom just asked me to help out with the festival last night. You went and bought that today?"

He settles back into his chair. "I saw it in the pharmacy window and couldn't resist. It won't hurt to fit the part. You need to dress for the job you want."

"Believe me, this is not the job I want." I draw in a slow breath and cut my eyes to Mom. That sentence hits a little too close to the truth about more than just the Christmas festival. "But I'll see it through. I know it's important to you."

Her smile works between my ribs to expand inside my chest. I haven't been here nearly often enough in the last ten years—haven't stored up enough of her loving looks. I'd lost out on more of those moments with my dad, and I won't risk the same thing with her.

"Thank you, honey. I think this will be fun for you." Her smile grows wider. "With or without the elf hat."

Caleb's laughter roars through the conference room, but I do my best to frown at him. "Can we get on with this meeting, please? Or do you want to be late getting home to Rowan?"

I've hit his Achilles heel, and he settles right down. Married two years and with a baby on the way, his happiness can be a lot to take sometimes. Sure makes it easy to pull his strings, though.

He gets the meeting going with a recap of new business and expectations for the week. We have several yard and patio renovations to plan out for the spring, and while the actual designs fall under Caleb's expertise, I'll have plenty to do on the business end. Or I normally would.

Mom answers as though she plans to handle all that while I'm out at the warehouse working with Hope.

"You don't have to do that," I tell her. "I can make the calls for the permits and everything else. I can find time between building parts of the elf village or whatever."

Caleb snickers. "Elf village."

"That's all on Hope," I say again. "I didn't name the things."

But Mom shakes her head, already shooting down my plan. "Until tree lighting, I want you to dedicate all of your time to Hope. Whatever she needs, you take care of it."

I refuse to let myself take that the way I might like to. Hope is engaged to some mystery guy in Bend. Also, after this morning, she probably thinks I'm a jerk. Zero for two.

Actually, considering everything from high school, it might be closer to zero for two million. I've gone up against poor odds with a woman, but I don't like my chances here.

"Her project is your only job for the time being." Mom's

scolding look softens into a smile. "This will be good for you. I know it."

They carry on talking about projects, plans, and preparations, but they don't need my input. Honestly, they haven't needed my input much in the last several months. That never stops me from offering my opinions, but the business operated just fine without me until last year. I'm not all that convinced they need me now.

Maybe it's part of my *abrasive* personality, or maybe I leaned too hard into being a black sheep, but I never wanted to work here with my family, not even as a kid. I'd wanted something of my own and found it in custom woodwork. I'd built up a solid career—and then the world had dropped away beneath my feet.

Losing my dad changed everything. I stopped chasing my carpentry dreams and took my place at McBride's, right where Dad had always wanted me. I can never fill his shoes, but I can try to walk in his footsteps. I still feel like a square peg trying to squeeze down into a round hole, but I figure that pinching, poking feeling will improve with time. Has to.

Still. Being offered up to Hope for her festival plans confirms my "not needed" theory.

"I think we're good for today," Mom says. "See you boys tomorrow."

I stand to go, but she stops me before I get to the conference room door.

"I want you to try your best with Hope." She takes hold of my upper arm, a gentle but undeniable pressure. "I know you can be the man she needs."

Those words weave through me like a Magic Grow dinosaur, suddenly way too big for my chest. Doesn't make any sense, since I don't want to be the man Hope needs, and last I heard, that job is already taken.

"You mean all the handyman stuff." Feels like we both need the clarification.

She just smiles and squeezes my arm before letting go. "Mm hmm."

"Don't forget this." Caleb slaps the jingly hat into my hands. "Dress to impress."

I take it, but it will find its way into my trash can eventually. "I promise you, I am *never* wearing that elf hat."

SIX
HOPE

I COLLAPSE onto my sofa at nine-thirty on the nose—an early night for a change.

After I closed up The Painted Daisy, I met with the Christmas market volunteers for almost two hours, sorting out the arrangements for booths, tents, and awnings. Then I went to Fred Deckard's to take a look at his much-rumored model train collection. I want to put a few on display as a little something extra in the weeks leading up to Christmas, a throwback to the days of toy shop windows filled with elaborate mechanical wonder. I'd gently asked him about his trains for weeks, and he finally invited me to see them.

"I've got to be sure nothing will happen to them," he'd said as he led me down to his basement. "They're pretty special to me."

I'd been about to rattle off some reassurances, but the sight in the basement blew a fuse in my brain. I'd stumbled into a shrine for a cult that worshipped all things electric and scale-model. Shelves proudly displayed dozens of engines and freight cars carefully preserved beneath plastic cases, with possibly a hundred more stacked around the room in their original packaging.

One wall housed an intricate storage system of neatly labeled drawers filled with miniature figures, trees, and signs. Capping it off, an elaborate toy train set the size of my bedroom dominated the display. Track tunneled through a mountain as tall as me, crossed a tiny river on delicate bridges, and wove in and out through several detailed towns.

I think I know what Mr. Deckard has been doing since he retired.

"They'll just be on display in Henderson's department store window," I said when I could form words again.

"Hoodlums might break in and steal them."

I'd spent forty-five minutes trying to reassure Mr. Deckard that with all the increased foot traffic on Maple, the trains might be even safer in Henderson's window than in his basement. But after all that, he'd left me with a solid *maybe*. I think he'd just wanted to show off his mind-boggling collection.

I sprawl out on my couch and pull an afghan over my legs, trying not to think about how perfect that vintage Christmas toy display would be. I'll still do it without the trains if I can't convince him, but the trains would make the whole scene. Snuggling deeper into the couch, I try to shut off my festival worries, but my brain doesn't work that way.

I need self-care. A massage. Meditation. ASMR videos with all the tingles.

I crane my neck toward the kitchen in futile hope, as though maybe I fixed dinner for myself last night and forgot about it. But the only food-adjacent things on the counter are an empty cereal bowl and a soggy box from a microwave curry I ate last night.

Peanut butter and jelly it is.

My phone buzzes, and I roll over, hoping against hope Mr.

Deckard has had a miraculous change of heart, but no. Starting and ending the day with calls from my mother is the opposite of self-care. I remind myself she could be worse. I just can't really think how.

"Hi, Mom."

"I heard who Kat McBride found to help you with the festival."

I know my mother has an actual job, but sometimes I wonder just how much time she spends snooping around for local news. Has to rival her open house showings.

"Looks like Griffin's the man for the job," I confirm.

"Are you sure? I can still call Andre if you want."

No, not Andre, her favorite contractor who will apparently drop anything just for her.

But ugh, not Griffin and his condescending, handsome face.

"You don't need to call anyone. It's only been one day, but he got a lot done." I have to assume he completed more than what I'd seen when I left this morning. He might be patronizing, but he doesn't have the attitude of a slacker.

"As long as you think you've got it covered. I'm sure Andre wouldn't mind helping him out."

"Griffin's not really a team player." As he made abundantly clear today.

"Handsome though."

I squeeze my eyes shut, silencing all my internal organs shimmying around in agreement. My internal organs are dummies.

"He's okay."

"This could get interesting for you two, working together on a project like this for a few weeks."

She sounds like she's getting ready to roll up on the couch and watch her favorite reality show, *I Think You Should Date My Daughter*. I hate that show.

"I don't think it's going to be all that interesting." Borderline hostile, maybe.

"He hasn't dated anyone since he moved back home."

I like this news against my will, but I'm also appalled by it. "Why would you know that?"

"Everybody knows that. Working together might not be such a bad thing."

I want to laugh at how casual she's trying to be, but my Spidey Sense is tingling too hard for me to find it funny.

"It's for the festival, Mom."

"Mm hmm." She's not listening. She's probably already dreaming up flannel-themed weddings and big, grouchy babies. "But it doesn't have to be *all* work, does it?"

"Yes. There's too much to do to get the Winter Wonderland together for anything else." What does she think we're going to do, kiss in the warehouse?

I...should absolutely not be thinking about kissing Griffin in the warehouse.

"Well. It's nice for you to reconnect. You were always close in high school."

I toss the afghan off of my overly warm legs. "Where did you get that? We weren't *close*. We didn't get along at all. He was my nemesis."

Great. Now *I'm* using that stupid word.

"You're adults now. Maybe he's had a glow-up."

I press my knuckles against my forehead, desperately trying not to think about Griffin's undeniable glow-up, or that my mother said those words together.

"He still needs a personality transplant."

She just laughs. "Maybe he'll grow on you."

Like mold. Or gangrene. Handsome, handsome gangrene.

"Maybe he can get that door up between your store and the bakery."

"I like having it open."

"You don't want customers thinking you're some kind of off-shoot from the bakery. I can't tell you how many people have asked me if your gift shop belongs to Maureen Krause. I understand why you chose to sublease from her."

She pauses, her judgment silent this time around. She's a realtor—cutting out the middleman and going straight to Maureen showed a little bit of bad faith on my part. A tiny thread of guilt cuts through me, but it was the only way I could afford to open my own shop to begin with.

"But I still think you should have waited until you had enough saved up to open a legitimate business."

"It *is* a legitimate business." I sound like a mafia member running a front. *Legitimate Gift Shop.*

"You know what I mean. Your own storefront. If you had accepted Josh's offer to work for his company, you wouldn't have to worry about any of this."

It's been a year and a half, and she still gets wistful over that misguided job offer. "I don't think Josh really wants Lila and me working side by side."

The offer was flattering, but the thought of moving to Seattle makes me want to curl up into a ball and hyperventilate. Big city, crowded streets, a famous tech firm where everything I do would constantly be on display, *and* I would report directly to my older sister? Heck no.

"I'm so happy Lila found Josh." Her voice turns all syrupy the way it usually does when she talks about my future brother-in-law. "He's the perfect man for her, don't you think?"

She'll go on either way, so I just listen. I like him fine, but I don't need to write him fan letters or anything.

"They met working together on a project, too."

I groan. She's like a little kid with a favorite new toy, and her only option is to love it to death.

"I feel like working PR for Josh's tech firm isn't quite the same as working on a small-town Christmas festival."

"No," she says, still dreamy. "One of them's a lot more romantic. If I had to choose, I'd take the one with opportunities for walks in the snow and mugs of hot cocoa, wouldn't you?"

"Mom, please. We're not going on walks in the snow. I have a lot of volunteers working with me, it's no big deal."

Not that I've thought much about any volunteer aside from the one with the sharp jawline and judgmental eyes. Apparently, I have a teensy weensy thing for arrogant bad boys. But admitting as much would set off an avalanche of pushing and prodding, and I can't deal with that on top of everything else.

"I've seen your volunteers, honey. None of them are as good looking as Griffin."

"Oh my gosh, I have to go."

We hang up, and I drag myself off the couch for a quick dinner of a PB&J and an apple. It's a pretty pathetic dinner, but I don't have the energy for anything more ambitious.

I eye the canvas set up in the corner of my living room while I eat. My small apartment doesn't offer much room for my art, but I use what I have. I've been working on a piece for Wren's sister Tess—her son's favorite lovey perched in her mom's favorite chair. Something for her birthday in January.

Working on paintings I intend to give away means there's zero pressure to display them in my store. Finagling my way into small business ownership was easier than mustering up the courage to share my art with the world.

I'd participated in a few showings in college, but nobody had known me there. Whispers about whether my art is any good or even worth pursuing hadn't followed me around the way they would here. I can handle being judged by strangers. Being judged by neighbors? I don't want to test it out.

I should tumble into bed, but I go to the easel and squeeze

acrylic paints onto a palette. After the day I've had, I could use the creative outlet. Maybe a little progress on this cute stuffed ostrich will ease away some of my worries about the festival and Mom's romantic schemes.

If I'm extra lucky, it will crowd out every last thought about Griffin McBride.

SEVEN
GRIFFIN

I CLOCK in at Santa's workshop at eight like a good little elf, unsurprised when Hope walks in not five minutes later. Cheeks and nose pink from the cold, eyes bright beneath that crazy red hat, she looks chipper as all get-out.

"You're at it early," she says, unwinding a scarf from around her neck.

"Eight's not early." I would have been on any construction site at least an hour by now.

She bobs a shoulder. "You're at it late, then."

Her mouth curves into a teasing smile, waking up the stupider side of my brain. Eight might not be early for work, but it's way too early to be thinking *anything* about her. I need to knock those thoughts out of my head with a hammer.

I pry my eyes away from her mouth and get back into elf mode, securing boards together until the wood whines beneath my screwdriver.

On my knees over my work, I try not to watch Hope move around the warehouse. Try and fail. With any luck, she'll reassure herself I'm doing as she asked and then get gone. Doesn't look like that's in the cards, though. She puts her scarf, hat, and gloves on the workbench in a pile of red knit, and peels off her coat.

I can't help it—I crane my neck to get a better look. Her fluffy orange sweater makes her look like a Creamsicle. A soft, delicious Creamsicle.

See? Hammer time.

I run the screwdriver, telling my thoughts to line up.

She crouches down in front of me, and my thought-line goes all to crap. I do not need a closer look at that sweater. Playing with fire, I risk a glance at her anyway, and the smile she flashes is Homecoming Queen perfection.

"Silas said this would be easier as a two-person job. So I'm here to help. For a little while, anyway."

Nope. I will not be performing any two-person activities with *engaged* Hope Parrish.

"You're not dressed for it." Her outfit could be worse. She isn't wearing a skirt and heels like yesterday.

I very much liked seeing Hope in a skirt and heels.

Wrong direction, brain.

"I have to go into my shop after." She looks down at her sweater and jeans, and I force myself not to do the same. "Do you think we're going to get that dirty?"

I swallow a groan. One more reason she needs to hightail it out of here. I'm not used to distractions of the feminine variety while I work. Women on job sites are strictly coworkers, and coworkers have always been off-limits. Just like this Creamsicle should be.

"I can do it myself." I work on, hoping the sound of the drill will clue her in.

"I know," she says louder. "But like you said, it will go faster if we work as a team."

I stop the drill. "I never said that."

She takes hold of the two-by-four in my grip as though I

need her to keep it steady, her knuckles pure white like she's trying to crush it to pulp.

"Someone must have. Anyway, I'm here to help."

"Don't need it."

"There must be something I can do." She flashes another smile. This one looks sincere, or I would gun the drill to drown out her voice. "This project is kind of a big deal to me. I don't want to just sit around while you work."

I blow out a breath and put down the drill, staring her hard in the eye. "Look, I get that you want to be in control. I can relate. The thing is, I don't need a boss. In my line of work, I *am* the boss."

Or I had been, right up until I came home to work with Caleb.

"But this isn't your line of work." Her cheerful voice doesn't hide the barbs she tossed at me. "This is my Christmas festival. You're building my Winter Wonderland. I drew up the designs for the houses." Her eyebrows bob with mock-humility. "*I'm* kind of the boss."

I rock back on my heels as that sinks in. I agreed to build the Christmas houses, but I didn't agree to three weeks of micro-management. What exactly does she want to be in charge of? There's no part of these little props I can't handle.

"We'll just have to agree to disagree."

"I'm going to hang out in here with you every morning anyway." She still smiles sweetly, but her voice has an edge to it now. "You might as well let me help."

"What happens if I don't? Are you going to threaten to kick me out of the North Pole again?" Since that threat went so well yesterday.

"No."

Her smile stretches even wider, and instinct tightens something in my stomach like she's drawing back for a sucker punch.

"But I just might tell your mother."

Lord help me. She's figured out my weakness.

Her laughter at my horrified look doesn't set me at ease.

"Relax, I'm kidding. But the Winter Wonderland is my dream. I know I can't do much with building it, but I want to help where I can."

I can understand that, I guess. She must have spent a lot of time designing the houses. It can't be easy to just hand over the reins. Still. I like holding the reins.

"All right boss, why don't you bring me another one of those two-by-fours?" I point at the workbench where I left the boards I pre-cut for this section. "One of the longer ones. That'd be a real help."

She breaks into a fresh smile, apparently immune to my sarcasm. "I can do that."

I silently curse myself for letting my mother rope me into this. I hadn't expected to have a shadow the whole time. The close scrutiny irritates, especially when my audience has already admitted she has no idea what I'm doing. Now I have to let her *help*?

She walks to the workbench and examines the boards. For being so eager to be my assistant, she sure takes her time about it, inspecting every knot and imperfection.

"Any one will do," I say.

She nods and grabs the closest one. Instead of standing it up, she picks it up by the middle, so the ends shoot away from either side of her. Crab-walking across the warehouse floor, her arms hang stiff in front of her as she tries not to knock anything over within an eight-foot radius.

I run a hand down my face to stop from laughing. Delectable or not, this Creamsicle didn't exaggerate when she said she wasn't handy. She needs to get out of the warehouse before she hurts herself.

This only adds to my doubts about her festival. Does she know what she's doing with the ads and promo she mentioned, or is that like the way she carries this board—she knows just enough to get herself into trouble?

I shouldn't care. It's her business if she's taken on more than she can handle, not mine. But that question of just how disappointed she'll be in a few weeks bugs me.

She grins when she reaches me, proud of her little feat.

"Sorry, I don't have any gold stars."

Her grin sinks into a scowl. "Where do you want it?"

I hook a thumb over my shoulder. "It'll go on that side."

"Fine."

She twists to head that way. The end of the two-by-four swings in an arc toward me, and I have about one second to register what's coming before it hits my forehead with a sickening *thunk*. A white-hot pain sears through my head, sucking the breath from my lungs, and I sit back hard on the concrete floor.

I *volunteered* for this?

If I was looking for a reason to quit, here it is. Nobody in his right mind would put up with this.

"I'm sorry!" Hope drops the board six inches from my feet, and I recoil away before she can do any more damage. She kneels at my side, eyes wide and face pale, looking like she might be sick. That makes two of us. "I didn't mean to do that!"

"I sure hope not." Stars swim in front of my eyes, and for a couple of seconds, I'm not entirely sure if I'll hold onto consciousness. I cover my forehead with one hand about thirty seconds too late.

"Let me see."

Hope's hands loom large in my face. Gotta say, I don't trust her right now. I try to turn away from her, but I can't stand yet after a knock like that, and I have just enough dignity left to stop me from crawling across the warehouse floor.

"I'm fine." I try to dodge her, but she's too quick. Or that board dulled my reflexes.

"Don't lie." She gently pulls at my fingers until I let go, exposing my forehead. Her dismal groan confirms my suspicions.

I squint at her. "Am I still pretty?"

Her laughter is short-lived. "So-so."

"Bleeding?"

"A little."

She pulls a tissue from her jeans pocket and dabs at the skin over my left eyebrow—even that soft touch feels like sandpaper. She moves the tissue away, and a trace of blood stands out against the white. Not too bad, considering everything I've seen two-by-fours do.

"I'm so sorry. I wasn't thinking about you being *right there*. Obviously, I know you were there, I just didn't think about where...ugh, I should have ended at 'I wasn't thinking.'"

With our faces only inches apart, a light, citrusy smell drifts over me as she carries on apologizing. Something that reminds me of sunny summer days. Lemon, maybe, or grapefruit. Delicious.

She might be delicious, but she's still engaged. Very taken. That reminder splashes cold water on this face to face.

Staring at my head, she bites her lower lip, clearly not liking what she sees. "There's already a goose egg, and you'll have a nasty bruise."

"Right." I close my eyes against the headache pounding a rhythm in my skull. Cutting through the throb in my forehead, a thin line of fire dances where my skin is broken, aggravated by the cool air.

Not gonna lie, I kind of want a nap. Someplace in the opposite direction from this hard cement floor and this soft Creamsicle who needs to stay far away from two-by-fours.

Hope cups my jaw in both her hands, and my eyes fly open. She stares hard into my face, her nose practically touching mine.

"I think you have a concussion."

"It's not a concussion. I played enough ball in school to know." Not that I had a lot of concussions playing baseball. With her this close, I can't think about much more than how gentle her fingers feel on my skin, the warmth that surrounds her as I breathe in that citrusy smell. She looks and smells like sunshine, a ray of *hope* on a cloudy day.

I blink a few times. Okay, maybe I do have a concussion. I'm not thinking straight, that's for sure.

I try to get up, but she holds my face tighter. "Don't move. I need to check your pupils."

She peers into my eyes, and stuck as I am, I gaze back. Concern for my potential brain injury creases the center of her forehead, her eyes darting from one eye to the other as she assesses their pupil size. A few freckles dance over the bridge of her nose. Her warm brown eyes probably light up gold in the sun, shot through with amber.

"Your pupils do look kind of big," she says. "Maybe I should take you to the medical center."

"Big pupils are normal. I'm fine." I pull away from her, and she lets her fingers drop from my face. A mistake, really, but one I need to make. This close, she's making me itchy, and if I don't get some space I'm going to say—or do—something very, very stupid. "All I need is some ibuprofen and an ice pack."

The worry line between her eyes deepens. "But I think—"

"Boss. I'm fine."

She frowns at that, but I'm sure not going to the medical center over this. No part of what happened here isn't humiliating. I can just imagine what the guys on my old work crew would say if they knew I'd been smacked in the head by a Creamsicle.

"I have some ibuprofen in my purse," she finally says.

"No ice though?"

The look she tosses my way just might count.

I move to get up, but she puts a hand on my leg, holding me down. The pressure is slight, gentle even, but it sinks through me like she's riveted me in place. Not sure which is worse—her hands on my face or her hand on my leg. Both leave me spinning.

It could be the knock to the head, but right now I'm thinking it's Hope.

"I'm pretty sure you shouldn't stand up yet with a concussion."

"It's not a concussion."

"Maybe we should just pop on over to urgent care and check." She makes it sound like she suggested a fun day out playing paintball instead of enduring a medical exam.

"Why don't you go, and I'll stay right here."

She finally releases my leg, frowning hard at me. "Fine. I'll run around the corner to get you a water and some ice. Are you okay to be left alone?"

"I don't know, I feel a little amnesia coming on."

She is not amused. "I'm freaking out about you, and you're joking around?"

"Laughter is the best medicine, Hope."

She looks at least tempted to smile. I'll take it. Much better than having her stress about me.

"You're the worst."

I lay a hand over my chest. "You'd say that to an injured man? Think of my pupils."

"I'm starting to think I'd rather work with the guy who

strained his back." She goes to the door and turns around again. "If I come back and you're passed out, I'm dragging you to the medical center."

"Fair deal."

I press the tissue against my eyebrow again as soon as she leaves, wincing at the fresh stab of pain. This is some project Mom got me into. Only my second day on the job, and I already have a workplace injury.

Merry Christmas to me.

EIGHT
HOPE

I'M THE BOSS, *Griffin. I can do this, Griffin. I'm totally not going to bash you over the head, Griffin.*

I run the two blocks to the little market, berating myself the whole way for braining my only hope of finishing the Winter Wonderland on time. If word gets out I've injured *two* festival volunteers, I'll probably make front page news.

Lumber maniac strikes again.

Griffin's injury doesn't look all that bad, but my stomach crawls knowing I'm the one who gave it to him. He'd made it clear he doesn't want me hanging around, and now I've gone and given him a good reason. I'd hoped to conceal my ineptitude in the warehouse, but instead, I spelled it out in the livid bruise on his forehead.

I can't get his dazed look out of my mind. His hazel-green eyes had gazed into mine until I felt like I'd been hit in the head, too. That's the only explanation for the wooziness that had come over me when I'd stared into his face like that. My heart had raced and my thoughts had spun into an incoherent cloud as I ran my fingers over his jaw and forehead. Diagnosis: concussion by association.

It was *not* because of attraction. He's kind of being a cocky jerk about the whole *boss* thing, and I haven't missed his total disdain for my project. If he showed more non-injured moments of vulnerability, maybe...but it probably wouldn't be smart to count on that.

I pay for a bottle of water and sprint back down the alley and into the warehouse, only to find Griffin on his feet again. A good thing, but a touch anticlimactic. He's dabbing at his eyebrow with the wadded-up tissue, but tiny beads of blood stand out against his forehead when he pulls it away. My stomach curdles all over again at the darkening bruise spreading from his eyebrow to his hairline.

Welcome to the project, Griffin! Here's some brain damage.

"You shouldn't be standing up." I pass him the water bottle, but he just exhales a laugh while I fish the small bottle of ibuprofen from my purse. "You need to rest."

"I'm fine. Just a little bump on the head." He swallows a couple of pills and presses the cold bottle against his forehead.

"They didn't have any ice packs."

"I think I'm going to make it."

"You could be seriously injured."

"Is that an assessment or a warning?" His eyes stay on me like I might take another swing at him. I'd wanted to let him know I'm in charge in here, but not that way.

"Griffin, I'm so sorry." I'll probably keep apologizing until the bruise totally heals. So, for days and days. "It was a complete accident."

He tries to raise his eyebrows but flinches at the small move-ment. "You sure about that, boss?"

We've had our run-ins, sure, but I can't believe he'd truly think that of me. "I wasn't trying to hurt you."

His expression softens, and a tiny bit of that dazed look comes back into his eyes. "Don't worry about it. I know you weren't. Anyway, I've seen worse on job sites. Crushed hands, broken toes, all kinds of cuts. Saw a guy shoot a nail into his own thigh to prove it wouldn't hurt. Spoiler alert: it did."

"I guess I'm glad you didn't do that. Still, I'd feel better if you took the rest of the day off." The Wonderland can't really afford to lose another day, but it's the least I can do for him. We're both lucky I didn't knock him unconscious. The look in his eyes is still so strange, I'm not convinced he doesn't need some kind of scan to make sure I haven't seriously jogged his brain.

"You might feel better, but I wouldn't."

This man's ego never quits. Dead-set on being the boss *and* invincible. A really stupid part of me likes his determination, even if the rest of me wants to twist his arm until he admits he needs *something*. He just got hit in the head. He can take five minutes.

"You should lie down for a while at least."

He lifts an eyebrow at the warehouse floor. "Are you trying to give me tetanus, too?"

"I meant you should go home."

"Boss, I'm fine. Never better." He sets the water bottle on the workbench and summons me with a crooked finger. "We're going to have a little safety lesson."

I follow him to the stack of lumber, dreading the coming lecture even though I've proved I need one. It's like losing to him in high school debates all over again. At least we don't have a crowd of teenagers jeering at us while we verbally spar, but this isn't a huge improvement.

"This is how I want you to pick up boards." He stands one on its end so it leans against his shoulder. "I'm not knocking into anything. Safe, right?"

I nod as he lays it back down. Now is probably the wrong

time to tell him that before this project, I'd never touched a piece of unfinished wood in my life. "Got it."

He walks over to the tools he'd set out on the workbench. A drill, screwdriver, sander, and a few I don't recognize lay in a neat row on the plywood. The buzzsaw has a yellow sticky note on it that just says *No*.

"Where did you get a sticky note?"

"I come prepared. Now, if you don't know how to work any of these, don't touch them."

I'm not loving the tone of this safety lesson. "I'm not a child, Griffin."

"Which one of us just hit someone in the head with a board?"

Despite his authoritarian attitude, he doesn't sound angry, just mildly irritated, like he's more annoyed by my screw-up than his injury.

"That was ten minutes ago." I try a small smile, teasing him just a little.

He shoots me a scathing look, but there's no real bite to it. "Joking about it already, are we? I'm starting to doubt your story about how Silas hurt his back."

"That was almost entirely his fault."

"Sounds like a confession to me."

"Well, he refused to admit I'm the boss." I grin at him until he looks away, fighting laughter. "I really am sorry. I feel bad to have you just go back to work. Isn't there something I can do to make it up to you?"

His eyes do this weird thing, both narrowing and growing darker all at once. Maybe this is the pupil action I was looking for earlier. After a second, he shakes his head.

"It was an accident. Don't worry about it. Just don't repeat it, either. I don't need another round with the Homecoming Queen special."

"Are you going to kick me out of the warehouse?" He'd totally be within his rights to put up a *Keep Out* sign.

He watches me for a long minute like he just might take me up on my offer. "Would you be likely to stay out if I did?"

"Not super likely." Not even the embarrassment of cracking Griffin in the head could keep me from wanting to have a hand in my project. Plus, I'm going to have to paint the houses eventually.

I can probably do less damage with a paintbrush than a two-by-four, though.

"Then I guess I won't bother."

We go back to work, and I act as his assistant, fetching tools and supplies with perfect care for our safety. I'm not sure I've ever paid so much attention to my surroundings in my life. He doesn't talk much, but I can't work in this kind of silence.

I tell him about my plans for the festival whenever he doesn't have the drill running. His responses aren't as enthusiastic as I might like, but he doesn't criticize, and I take that as a win.

Maybe I'll get him on my team after all.

"Santa's going to be set up right out front at the Winter Wonderland. We've got some people bringing in patio warmers, and the Diaz family offered the use of one of their horse teams, along with their sleigh. We haven't had sleigh rides on Maple Street in years."

And I'll want to be first in line, but I'll do my best to show some restraint.

"We'll have carolers wandering downtown, stopping to sing songs at every corner, plus the choir to lead the audience during the tree lighting. The Christmas market is new—I already know a lot of the artists from my store, so that was the easiest part to arrange."

I hold a piece of plywood steady as he screws it into the

frame. It looks more like the little building of my dreams every hour. If he can keep up this pace, we might actually finish with time to spare. Even though I think he should rest after his injury, I'm secretly grateful for his relentless work ethic.

"The carolers used to wear Dickens-styled clothes when they went around doing their thing, but the costumes are long gone. We didn't have enough budget for a dozen new costumes, so they're all going to wear Santa hats instead. Cheap, but festive."

I'd had to make a lot of concessions, like it or not. At the moment, we're running on pocket change, but that seems like an awful lot to admit to my reluctant volunteer.

"What *is* the budget going to?" Griffin asks, plucking another screw from a box.

"Most of the ads, and any supplies I couldn't get as donations. Some of the set-up for the Christmas market, and little things like the candy canes Santa will hand out."

His eyes flash with something I can't name. "No money for you, though."

"It's a volunteer position." Just like his. If he's angling for some kind of reimbursement, he'll walk away disappointed. He'll be lucky if I don't have to ask him to pitch money in. He sure won't get any out.

"What's the endgame then? People come to this Christmas thing, they see Santa, pet the reindeer. What then?"

"What do you mean? Then the tree will be lit, and everyone will sing songs—"

"After that."

"Ideally, they would shop at the stores on Maple Street, which will be open late every weekend of the—"

"After that."

I get up on my knees and toss my hands out. "Everyone has a wonderful holiday experience?"

I'm getting shouty all over again, but his barrage of questions and constant interruptions deserve it.

He lowers the drill at the other end of the plywood sheet I've been needlessly holding down. "What happens *after* the Christmas festival?"

He isn't interested in my replies, but I can't figure out what he's getting at. "Hopefully people will come back to Sunshine to do more shopping year-round. It's a big promotion for all the businesses on Maple, and I'd be lying if I said there's no pressure to increase foot traffic. Obviously, it would be nice for the festival to be written up in local papers and magazines, too. Get pushed on some bigger apps, maybe."

I don't really care how people find out—boosting shopping dollars will help every business in town.

A look of understanding crosses his face before it settles into a smirk. "I get it. They write it up, promote what you did with your festival here, and you can use that in a portfolio, get yourself another marketing job. Clever."

He means it as a compliment, but he still manages to make that one little word feel like a slight.

"Amazing. You followed the clues to exactly the wrong conclusion."

"How? Isn't that what you're after? Get your foot in the door at some marketing firm in Bend or Salem?"

I stand up and he does the same. I'm trying to do something good here, and Mr. Cynical draws the most selfish conclusion.

"That's not remotely what I'm doing. This isn't some scheme to get a new job."

"You really want to stay here? With your degree?"

I'm not about to tell him I never wanted my degree, and never really enjoyed using it. Appealing to my degree doesn't sway me.

"Yes. I like it here."

"If you say so."

This man and his skepticism. "What's wrong with Sunshine? It's beautiful here."

He makes a face. "Kind of small, that's all."

"Yeah, well, some people like small towns, Mr. Metropolis. My store is here, my friends are here, everyone I love is here."

His eyebrows twitch, drawing my focus back to the giant bruise on his face. Man, I feel bad about that, even when he seems determined to make me angry with him for all new reasons.

"Speaking of, who's the lucky guy?"

I jerk my head back, totally lost. I should have taken him in for a brain scan when he was still wobbly. I might have been able to shove him out the door. "What guy?"

He waves a hand in my general direction. "Your fiancé."

He puts a sarcastic spin on the word, emphasizing the French. Sympathy for his injury evaporates, and something hard and cold settles in my stomach. After everything this summer, that word dredges up a deep-seated urge to throat-punch somebody.

Griffin's closest, so...

It'd been too much to hope he hadn't been part of the gossip mill. But of course he'd heard. At least, he's heard *some* of the gossip—clearly not all. Maybe he knows the rest and is just trying to be a jerk and make me say it, but it sounds like a sincere question.

"I don't have a fiancé," I say coolly.

His face contorts into something like panic. "You already got married? That was kind of a rush, wasn't it?"

This guy has no idea how close he is to getting smacked in the head again.

"I don't have a fiancé, and I'm not married."

He swallows like he's unable to process that. "I heard you were engaged."

And there it is. Sunshine's residents need to figure out a way to use their powers for good instead of evil.

"Of course you did."

I spin on my heel and put on my coat, wind my scarf too tightly around my neck, yank on my gloves, and pull my hat down so it covers my ears. Not enough to drown out Griffin trying to figure out my romantic situation, though.

"Did I hear wrong? Some guy in Bend? I heard it from like four different people."

"Stop talking." I raise a hand between us as though I can telepathically shove him against the wall. I blow out a breath, already way too hot with all these layers of knit and anger on me. "For a smart guy, you're dumb with people, you know that?"

He presses his lips together, clearly not liking that assessment, but at least it shuts him up. He's exactly like he was ten years ago—he doesn't know when to stop pushing buttons. By accident or design, he inevitably hits *detonate*.

"There's no fiancé," I say slowly. I will only go over this once. "No husband, no boyfriend, no long-distance love. Just me. And I don't need commentary on my love life or lack thereof. Got it?"

"Got it. Just you."

He stares at me for ten whole seconds, this weird light in his eyes making me itchy. Like my clarification has shifted his opinion of me, but not in the direction I'd expected. Most people find it funny, maybe even pitiable. Griffin's looking at me like he's intrigued by something.

I'm not in the mood to stick around to find out exactly *what*.

"I need to go open my store." I walk out of the warehouse almost wishing I'd let Mom make that call to her contractor.

NINE
GRIFFIN

"ARE you gracing me with your presence for dinner tonight?" Mom calls when I walk through her front door. I stop in for dinner a couple of times a week, but she still manages to make it sound like a surprise every time.

"Depends what's on the menu." I join her in the kitchen, ready to earn my keep if she needs any last-minute prep, but it looks like I've missed out. A pot steams on the stove, and she has a plate of flatbread ready on the island counter.

"What on earth happened to you?"

She pauses on her way to the pot on the stove. The familiar scent of chicken pot pie drifts to me, but with a dash of something warmer mixed in. I know those smells, but I've never known them *together*.

"Did you put curry in the pot pie?" I lean over the stove to check, but she swats my hand before I can reach the lid.

"I'm trying something new."

Culinary experimentation is one of her hobbies. Some flavors just aren't meant to mix, but that never stops her from testing out her next concoction. Also never stops me from trying them, but she's had a few close calls.

"What happened to your face?"

Oh, right. I almost forgot about the morning's mishap. The pain has dulled down to a low ache I ignored most of the day.

"I had a little run-in with my boss."

Her eyes widen. "*Caleb* did that to you?"

My stomach twists at the implication she thinks my older brother can take me in a fight, and the direct acknowledgement she considers him in charge over me. He is, of course—and should be. He'd come back to the family business after college to work his way up, and I only rolled in a year ago. It still chafes.

"Not that boss. The one you got me tangled up with."

She takes me by the chin and moves my head around under the glare of the can lights. I haven't seen a mirror yet, but her surprise when she caught sight of me says my face doesn't look good.

"Did Hope do this to you?" She gives my cheek an extra pat and lets go. "You'd better watch yourself with her."

"A little late for a warning."

"Are you working too slowly for her, and this is her way of getting you to speed up?"

Some sympathetic mother she is. Her mouth twitches while she gives the curry a stir, and the smells wafting around the kitchen double in intensity. I can't tell yet if I want a bite or if I'd rather pick up take out on my way to my apartment.

"That's not an issue."

I'd nearly finished the first of Hope's houses by the time I closed up the warehouse tonight. I got the walls set up, secured the pitched plywood roof, and used a jigsaw to cut out the decorative fronting pieces for all the trim. I'm starting to see what she has in mind for it, but it'll need a lot more work before it will enchant the little kids of Sunshine.

Did I push just a touch harder to get this done than I had yesterday? Yes. Did that have anything to do with wanting to make a little bit up to the suddenly very much un-engaged festival organizer? Also yes.

Probably a bad idea to let any interest in her take hold—especially when I know how brutal she can be with a weapon—but that didn't stop me from putting in the overtime.

"Did you make a pass at her?"

"Funny." Not that I would admit anything there. "She's just a little overzealous, that's all."

"She's got a lot of enthusiasm for the project," Mom confirms. "But people are making demands of her on every side, and not everybody is as supportive as they could be."

"Who's not supportive?" I want to track her critics down and give them a piece of my mind. Getting riled up in her defense is probably a bad idea, too, but for the moment, I can pretend it's all in the name of the festival.

We are a team, after all. Kind of.

Mom steps away to lean against the counter. "You know how people are. They don't like change. It's easier to think of her as a flighty girl with her head in the clouds than as a smart businesswoman who's trying to improve town events for everyone's benefit."

Guilt squeezes my ribcage until my breath sticks in my lungs. I've pretty much been thinking the same thing, haven't I? Maybe even worse, since I basically accused her of trying to turn the festival into a job opportunity like some cut-throat mercenary.

The amount of work she's doing for no pay and possibly negligible reward still puzzles me. I can't question her sincerity, though, not after she defended Sunshine so heartily. She truly believes in this project. That has to be worth something. Even if I can't see it reaching her desired success, I need to get fully on board with it, too.

"And the gossip never lets up," Mom goes on. "Whether Hope succeeds or fails, someone will be talking about it right behind her."

That was one of my favorite things about my life in Portland —nobody cared what I did. My coworkers wanted me to get my job done, my friends wanted me to pay for rounds at the bar now and then, but everybody else? Crickets. I'd gotten used to the anonymity. Here, my life is in a fishbowl, on display for the whole town to pick over choice by choice.

"Yeah, about that. Where did everyone get this story Hope was engaged? I asked her about it and wound up sounding like an idiot."

Mom's gaze turns thunderous. It's been a long time since I last saw that scolding look. "Griffin Thomas. You asked her about that? What's the matter with you?"

Her scolding cuts, especially since I don't have a good excuse. How many times had I endured lectures growing up about not sharing stories about other people? "I was curious. How was I supposed to know it wasn't true?"

"I raised you better than to go around repeating gossip."

"Again, I didn't know it was gossip at the time." Hearing it from four different people around town isn't quite the same as a secret whisper sharing unverified intel.

Even if it had turned out to be unverified intel.

"I'm surprised you paid any attention to that in the first place. You're not one to go in for small talk."

"I'm not." Being trapped making small talk makes my eye twitch. The twitch has become a problem since I moved back here, getting worse all the time. More than one person has suggested I have it checked out. "Usually I just ignore gossip."

"I see. But you didn't ignore it when you heard gossip about Hope?"

Even if my ears had perked up like satellite dishes tuning in whenever I heard her name through town, I won't dignify that with a response. Especially not with Mom about five seconds from laughing at me as it is. I need to keep her on track.

"Why did everyone think she was engaged if she wasn't?"

That question rattled around my head all day, splintering off into more questions I don't have answers to. Did she refuse a proposal over the summer? Did she recently break up with the guy—or get dumped? She only said she has no fiancé or boyfriend *now*, she didn't offer any info about her past.

Not that I really want to know. The thought of some mystery fiancé had left a bad enough taste in my mouth, I don't want any details about the guy. If he had, in fact, existed. Preferably, he hadn't. Just a figment of the town's collective imagination.

Mom narrows her eyes like she can see straight inside my skull. I try to clear whatever guilty thing my face is doing.

"Explaining that would be gossip." Mom sets her smirk on high. "You'll have to go to the source."

"I'm not going to ask Hope about her personal life."

"Sounds like you already did."

I blow out a breath. "Dinner's not worth this."

I stalk out of the kitchen, Mom's laughter trailing behind me. I can blame Caleb for her increased interest in my dating life. Ever since my brother got married, Mom has taken that as an invitation to poke around and drop hints.

There's been nothing to share since I left Portland—I've been too much in my head to think about dating. Right up until I reconnected with one Christmas-loving Homecoming Queen. Who may or may not have gone through a big break up a few months ago but is certainly single now.

And mad at me. That part's pretty key.

I need something to do. A task to accomplish and check off a list, and most importantly, get my mind off of Hope's mysterious love life.

I peek inside the wood stove in the living room and dump half a bucket of pellets into the hopper so Mom won't have to do it later tonight. It's become my habit in the winter months, a small thing I can do for her around the house. She doesn't let on she needs help very often, but I do the few things I can.

Then, I make a mistake. The same mistake I've made dozens of times over the last year. I never learn.

Against my will, my eyes land on Dad's acoustic guitar where it sits on a stand in the corner. My chest seizes up like all my organs are deadweight, pinning me in place. I take slow, stuttering breaths, trying to keep everything under control. Below the surface. Not out in the open, where I can't be sure I'll get that grim genie back in its bottle.

Sometimes I actually manage it now, and I can't tell if I'm more grateful or disappointed in myself. I can't live with the crushing grief forever, but moments when I can keep it in check come with a layer of guilt, like it somehow diminishes my love for my dad. Makes me less of a son when I can just breathe through it instead of needing to duck into my old bedroom and let the tears flow.

"You okay, honey?" Mom asks softly. She'd come up beside me, and follows my gaze to the corner. Reading my mind, she runs a comforting hand along my back. "Nobody played like your dad."

"Nope." The lump in my throat makes it impossible to say more. His riffs off of 70s rock songs used to fill this house, the soundtrack that played softly behind all my childhood memories.

"He left picks everywhere." Her strained laughter makes me

look away. If she tears up, that will get me tearing up, and my goal tonight is to stay in one piece. "Inside the house, out on the deck, in the car—I can't tell you how many went through the wash, clinking around in the dryer."

"He always left one or two behind when he visited me in Portland." Those weekends when our schedules lined up just right, and he'd drive north to do nothing but have a beer with me and watch a game—I hadn't known how important they were until I'd lost them. I want like anything to have just one more.

"I should have had them delivered on a subscription service. A twelve-pack of guitar picks sent to our door every month."

"There's your side-hustle."

We both laugh, but she keeps watching me. "I think you're the one who needs the side-hustle."

"No time for one. Too many elf houses to build." My cheeky grin doesn't seem to comfort her.

"Honey. Are you sure this is what you want?"

"Hey, you're the one who volunteered me for the project." I'm not complaining—aside from the bruised face, I don't mind the work.

"Not that. The business."

The weight in my chest sinks down into my stomach. I need a second before I can answer. I don't like lying to her, and I've told this particular lie a time or two already.

"I want you to do what makes you happy, whatever that is." She waits, as though if she stares hard enough, she'll see the truth hiding in my eyes.

She just might, and I can't let that happen.

I flash a bright, fake smile that would make my Homecoming Queen boss proud. "I am happy, Mom. Working alongside you and Caleb is right where I want to be."

She rubs her hand along my back and gives me a gentle pat. "You'll let me know if that changes?"

"I'm not going anywhere."

And I won't. I was off doing my own thing when Dad died. From here on out, I'm putting my family first.

She nods once. "Dinner's almost ready."

Then she slips away into the kitchen, leaving me to stew in my lies.

TEN
HOPE

I REACH for the warehouse door but hesitate like it might bite me.

I don't really want to go in there. After yesterday's game of Engaged or Not Engaged, Griffin will surely have questions for me. I don't feel like telling him anything about Mark or Mom's meddling—and definitely not everything that came after. The thought of having to brush off an interrogation about that humiliation turns my stomach, especially if Griffin is the one asking.

He doesn't seem like the sympathetic type. People mostly fall into two camps: those who think I was at fault somehow, and those who think I should have dated someone with a better sense of humor. Which, incidentally, still puts the blame on me.

Griffin would absolutely blame me.

Nope. Time to stop feeling sorry for myself and get moving. I shake off the wisps of anxiety swimming around in my stomach and pull the warehouse door open. Inside, the question of just what Griffin might think of me dissolves, overshadowed by a glimpse of pure Christmas magic.

He finished the first little building. Not just four walls and a roof, but he'd bumped out the front part like he said and attached all the trim around the door and windows. The plywood is bare, but I can imagine how it will look in the end. A brightly colored little bakery so inviting you'll wish it were real.

Griffin emerges from behind it, and some of my plywood-induced euphoria clears at the sight of his ghastly purple bruise. Even if he'd irritated me enough yesterday to tempt me to wallop him again, I hate the proof of my dumb accident.

"You finished it already," I say, stating the obvious.

"I had to make a few adjustments to your plans. I hope you don't mind."

He sounds...dare I say it? Humble. That's an even bigger shock than the completed house.

"I've made it so it can easily be disassembled for transport to town square."

"Oh. That's smart. I hadn't thought about moving them." Which I obviously should have—we can't carry six-foot-tall buildings down the street. I'd been so occupied with the design, I hadn't thought through the logistics.

"This way, we can truck them over in pieces. It's all sanded, too. All it needs is for you to paint it, and it will be ready for kids to ogle it to pieces. Hopefully not literally."

"You did a really great job." It's even better than what I'd designed.

"Thanks." He clears his throat and steps closer. "Look, I'm sorry for what I said yesterday. I shouldn't have repeated things I'd heard. You're right—it was dumb and rude, and I apologize."

For a guy who says he doesn't know the first thing about humility, he wears it well. I like this gentler side of him, even if I'm skeptical about how long it will stick around.

"Thank you."

He gives a firm nod. "Are we good?"

Are we good? Is he going to drop it? Usually, when people bring up last summer's fiasco, they ask questions. They want to know the actual dirt, like how such a big mistake had happened, maybe even dig for info on the fallout. But opting to just apologize and move on? Unheard of.

My stupid stomach dips like he's defended my honor.

"We're good."

"All right." He seems relieved, and that surprises me all over again. Does he actually care about what I think of him? He hasn't let on that he does so far. "Are you ready to paint this thing?"

"That's my time to shine." I might not know the first thing about carpentry, but I'm one heck of a painter. He's already surrounded the little house with plastic drop cloths and has the bucket of primer ready to go. I only have to peel off my parka and get to work.

"Blue today," Griffin says from somewhere behind me.

I face him, pulling on rubber gloves. "What?"

He gestures at me with the cordless drill. "Your sweater is blue today."

I glance at the navy sweater I'd chosen. "And?"

"You wear a lot of colorful clothes."

If he thinks this is colorful, I'd hate for him to see my apartment. Or worse, my artwork. "You wear a lot of flannel."

He looks at the shirt he's wearing, a blue-and-green check. Incidentally, rolled at the sleeves.

But like I'd told Wren, I'm much too busy to notice the way the muscles in his forearms shift with every subtle move he makes.

Much. Too. Busy.

"Touché." He turns back to the Wonderland bakery as though inspecting it for code violations. "Do you mind if I play some music?"

He takes his phone from his pocket and scrolls on the

screen. I wave him along, and he sets the phone down on the workbench, Queen blasting from tiny speakers.

"'We Will Rock You.' It sets the mood. I was expecting—"

He raises a hand. "Don't say it."

"Van Halen," I finish.

"Oh." He tilts his head at that. "I thought you were going to say country. Yeah, Van Halen's somewhere on this mix."

"Sammy Hagar or David Lee Roth era?"

He smiles, and a butterfly bomb goes off in my chest. I'm still trying to hold onto my irritation, but my goodness, do I love his relaxed side. Boyish and utterly disarming, that smile could convince a woman to wreck her plans for him.

Not me, though. Some *other* woman.

"Bit of both," he answers. "You're a Van Halen fan?"

"A little."

I'd become a fan after one of his debate speeches about why Eddie Van Halen was the best electric guitarist of the twenty-first century. Curious, I'd started listening through their discography that same night. I might have thanked him for the music recommendation if I hadn't been completely sure he would have lorded his triumph over me for being so convincing.

He starts framing out the next house while I slap a quick coat of primer on the first building. It doesn't need to be pretty or detailed, but it still takes forever to work the brush into all the little nooks and crannies. All this time, I've been thinking the construction would take the longest, but it's pretty clear now that the painting—and my limited availability to do it—makes me the weakest link on the Winter Wonderland production chain.

We listen through every major hit of the 1970s before I finish priming the house. Griffin comes over to stand beside me, and I get the impression he's inspecting my work. Painting primer on plywood isn't fancy, but I still hope he doesn't find flaws. He's the one with construction experience—I just like to paint.

I kneel down to reach the last few inches along the floor when my stomach growls out an aching cry of hunger. Not even Aerosmith can drown out a sound like that.

"Was that your stomach?" Griffin sounds both alarmed and impressed.

I dare a quick glance over my shoulder. "I might have forgotten to have breakfast."

He pulls his eyebrows together. "It's past lunch."

"It's no big deal." I drag the paintbrush along bare spots on the plywood. I'd planned to eat bites of something once I take over The Daisy from Abby in the afternoon. If I look extra pathetic, Wren will bring me a hand pie.

"It sounds like it's a big deal to your stomach."

I shrug. "I just forget sometimes."

"What, forget to eat?"

"Sure, don't you?" I turn in time to catch his disgusted expression. Skipping breakfast is apparently not one of Griffin's bad habits.

"No. How can you forget to eat? Do you forget to breathe, too?"

I force a laugh. "I've been pretty busy lately."

"Right. Take a break. Let's go to Delish and grab a bite."

"I need to finish this."

He holds a hand out to me to help me up. "It will still be here when you get back."

"But if I finish now, it can dry while we eat, and I can paint on the colors after lunch."

He slants his mouth, but I can tell he's got no argument for that even before he gestures for me to continue. "Prime away."

I don't have much left to do, and in a few more minutes, I've fully primed the little building. I slip the paintbrush into a freezer bag, close up the bucket of primer, and pull off the plastic gloves I wore while I worked.

"Come on." Griffin waggles his hand in front of me. "Let's get you some food."

I put my hand in his, and he pulls me to my feet. But when I stand, his strong, warm hand doesn't let mine go. He holds on, his fingers tightening a touch on my skin, and he raises his other hand to the side of my face. My thoughts crash together into a tangle.

He touches my hair, and I freeze, unsure if I want to get the heck out of there, or lean right in and see what happens.

He draws two fingers along a strand of hair, that small, slow touch rippling through me as soft as a caress. My lips part, and his eyes fall to them like a weight.

I hold my breath.

"You've got paint in your hair." Griffin lets go of me and looks away. "Let's have lunch."

My soaring stomach comes in for a crash landing, going up in a tiny whoosh of flames.

ELEVEN
GRIFFIN

YOU'VE GOT *paint in your hair?* That crack from the two-by-four must have done more damage than I'd thought.

Keeping Hope on the inside of the sidewalk where less ice collects, I try to figure out just when I became such a cheeseball. I could have pointed out the paint flecks and avoided the moment of awkwardness it'd spiraled into. But that little speck of white against her dark hair had called to me, begging me to touch her hair.

And I'd done it, like a goon. Before I could risk my status as a volunteer elf by doing anything more, I'd pulled myself together.

I'm not here for this. Since my dad's death, I've done my best to put my family first. Atone just a little bit for my years when I'd set the family business aside and gone solo. I need to be here for them for once, and that means setting aside my own selfish wants.

Hope is very much a selfish want.

Amy Ellison stands on the other side of the diner, taking down a customer's order, but she spots us the moment we walk in. "Well, Griffin McBride and Hope Parrish! Aren't you two a sight?"

Half of the people in the place turn to look at us in the doorway like we're a brand-new zoo exhibit. Impossible to go anywhere incognito in a small town, but I let my desire to feed Hope lead us straight into Gossip Central.

"Sit anywhere you like," Amy calls before turning her attention back to her customer.

Hope slips past me to snag a booth, and I slide in across from her. Her stomach grumbles again, and she covers it with one hand as though that will stop me from hearing it. I don't like that she let herself go so long between meals it turned into some sort of hunger emergency.

"How often do you—"

An older couple stops at our table before I can finish.

"I sure am sorry I won't be able to make those little houses for you, Hope." The man with the sad-looking face is Silas, her former handyman. He twists one arm to rub at his lower back like it's still bothering him. "If the doc hadn't said no lifting, I would have been right there with you every day."

I don't want to discount the guy out of hand, but given his age and stooped shoulders, no way he would have been able to handle her project, even running at full capacity. I kind of wonder why Mom didn't ask me to help Hope out sooner. Maybe she didn't realize just who had signed on.

"It's okay, Silas, I understand." Hope smiles up at him and gestures my way. "Griffin volunteered to make the Winter Wonderland for me."

Not entirely true, since my mother had done the volunteering, but I don't mind the note of praise in her voice.

The man's eyes grow wide as he looks me over. "Did he now? Well, maybe this festival will work out for you in more ways than one."

He and his wife share a chuckle, but I don't miss Hope's

tight expression. She still smiles, but I like this brittle version even less than her huge Homecoming Queen smiles. There's a spark of anger hiding behind this one—because of his pushiness, or because he's pushing her toward me?

"I think it's going to be a success for businesses and visitors alike."

Silas ignores her robotic tone and winks at me. "She's a heartbreaker, this one."

He and his wife laugh together and stroll out the door, oblivious to the chill they leave at our table like two gray-haired Jack Frosts. Hope refuses to meet my eyes, fidgeting with the salt and pepper shakers on the table instead. I've missed something here, but even my tactless butt knows that asking would be too much.

Amy strolls over and sets menus in front of us. A wasted effort, since I've been ordering the same thing here since my teens. Bacon burger with guacamole, extra fries.

"This is a pleasant surprise," she says.

It's a friendly greeting, totally in line with empty chatter, but her tone has a hint of...well, a *hint*. Looks like we're in for the full fishbowl effect this afternoon.

"Griffin's helping me out with the Christmas festival decorations," Hope says right away. "Spreading holiday cheer, you know. We're just taking a lunch break before we get back to it."

I don't love her rush to explain our showing up together as strictly platonic, like she needs to make up for Silas's over-the-top hinting. It *is* platonic, but I still don't like it.

"I can't wait to see what you have up your sleeve for us." Amy turns her attention back to me. "What happened to your head, honey?"

"Is that our Griffin?" Amy's wife Jodi comes out from the kitchen to join us at our table. Close friends with my mom, the couple's motherly affection for me always loosens a little something in my chest. It never hurts to have two honorary aunts around. Her eyes go about as wide as Silas's had. "What happened to your face?"

"I just asked the same thing."

I sit up straighter under their inspection and run my fingers over the swollen spot above my eyebrow. "Would you believe I was jumped by a seven-foot-tall gorilla?"

Hope snorts. "Your memory's a little off."

"Well, it was hard to tell. I was suffering from a concussion."

She points a finger. "You specifically said you weren't concussed. You said big pupils are normal."

I try to look serious. "They are. Big pupils run in my family."

Hope laughs but seems to remember our rapt audience. She sobers right up again, her bright smile disintegrating under Amy and Jodi's attention.

"I'm guessing we don't want to ask what happened to him," Amy says to Jodi.

"I don't know. I've got a minute."

They both turn to me, waiting for the explanation of my mangled face. See? Honorary Auntie behavior.

With a day's distance, the two-by-four story actually sounds pretty funny, but I'm not sure Hope would agree. As much as she has riding on this Christmas thing being a success, I doubt she would appreciate me sharing how helpful she's been in the warehouse so far.

"I had an accident," I tell them. "Everything's fine though. Brain function normal."

"And still just as handsome as ever," Amy adds.

"Aw." I give her my cheekiest grin. "I wasn't too worried."

"It's good to see you." Jodi's already drifting away. "I've got to get back in the kitchen before Ellie's burger chars."

"You've never burned a burger in your life," Amy tells her.

"And I'm not starting now." Jodi waves my direction. "Don't be a stranger."

"I won't."

"I'll give you two a moment to make up your minds," Amy says before she darts off to tend to the other diners.

As soon as we're alone again, Hope leans forward. "Thanks for covering for me. You didn't have to do that."

I mirror her motion. "Just trying to get on my boss's good side."

"Oh, so you're a kiss up."

My eyes drop to her mouth, the word *kiss* clanging in my head like cymbals calling me to action. But if she didn't like Silas making flirty comments about us, she probably won't like me staring at her lips *thinking* flirty thoughts.

I relax against my seat. "So how does this work? How do you forget to eat?"

"When I'm not working at my store, I'm working on the festival. I've got meetings almost every day with someone who has volunteered to do one thing or another, and if you haven't noticed, I've been working on the Wonderland with you part time. Something has to give."

"That something doesn't have to be you." Her eyes widen. That came out a little more tender than I'd intended. I need to get a handle on this before I blurt out something stupid. "Shouldn't be your stomach, anyway. What are you having?"

"Burger and fries."

"Perfect."

Amy comes out to take our orders before she heads back into the kitchen. She and Jodi haven't changed much in the years I'd been away, but this place sure has.

"It's so modern in here now." The homey restaurant of my youth has caught up to the twenty-first century. Delish's wood-paneled walls were painted crisp white, tables and chairs sanded down and stained a rich mahogany. Metal pendant lamps hang from the ceiling, and a chalkboard sign listing the specials of the day holds a prime spot behind the counter. "Wouldn't be surprised to have my burger served deconstructed on a granite tile."

I would hate the presentation, but I'd still eat it. Jodi makes the best burgers I've ever tasted.

"I like the updates."

"So do I, but it still takes me a second to get my bearings whenever I walk in. Delish used to be my home away from home in high school. My friends and I would nurse our coffees for hours until Amy and Jodi shooed us off home at closing."

"I remember." Hope laughs, then her eyes shoot to mine. "I mean, I hung out here too. With my friends. Obviously not with you."

All of her protesting today isn't boosting my ego.

"Gotta say, I don't care for the 'obviously not with you.'"

"Don't pretend we hung out together. You were the big-name baseball player, the guy who wanted to debate everyone, the..." She gestures at me but swallows down the rest.

"The arsonist?" I supply.

Her full-throttle smile shines on me. "Something like that."

"It wasn't as bad as everyone made it out to be. A total accident, and stupid for sure, but it got a lot more play around town than it warranted. I planted trees with a forestry crew that summer, so I think I've made restitution."

"Oh. I never heard about that."

"You probably shouldn't listen to gossip anyway." I *tsk* as if I've got a leg to stand on.

She frowns at me for teasing her, but I just chuckle.

"When my dad found out what I'd done, he signed me up for the work crew the same day."

He hadn't been angry, exactly, but he'd always believed in

making up for our mistakes. Words can be empty, but follow-through means everything. So—I'd planted seedlings for six weeks.

"I'm sorry about your dad," she says gently. "He was a really good man."

"Yeah, he was." I love hearing that, but I hate it, too. Soft little cuts that make me miss him even more. "Tell me about your store."

She watches me for a second like she sees the change of topic for the ruse it is. Thankfully, she doesn't push it.

"You should stop in sometime, it's just up the street next to the bakery. I sell all kinds of handmade things like soaps and lotions, jewelry, handbags, and clothes."

"I could use a new handbag."

Her smile has me grinning at her like a fool. A dangerous game in a place filled with so many prying eyes.

"Why'd you decide to start that up?"

"The store? I was nosing around at the farmer's market stalls talking to artists and realized a lot of them don't have many other places to sell what they make. A lot of businesses don't want to work with small vendors, and some have such high wholesale requirements, just one contract would turn into a full-time job. I figured I could open a shop that only sells local art."

"So you did."

She shrugs. "I researched and planned for several months while I got ready, but yeah. Think of it as a really specialized boutique store."

"What do you make? Aren't you in there somewhere?" I can't think of another reason she would set up a shop with all that handmade stuff if she doesn't have a part in it.

"No, not really. I paint, but I don't sell my stuff in the store."

"Why not?"

Twining her fingers, she looks out the window to the gray day outside. "My paintings aren't ready yet."

"What's wrong with them?"

Her eyes snap back to me. "There's nothing *wrong* with them, geez. Why do you go straight to that? They're just..."

She spreads her hands, and the puzzle pieces click together.

Her paintings might be ready, but she isn't. This is curious. She's never seemed to have a lack of confidence, but the topic clearly bothers her.

"What are your paintings like?"

"I do a lot of florals. Pets. Still lifes. Small moments in time captured in bright color. I don't think they would really be your thing."

"Why not?" She's probably right, but I don't like that she automatically assumes I won't appreciate what she paints. I have an urge to see her artwork, and that isn't a familiar feeling for me.

"You don't strike me as a floral guy. You'd have paintings of things like tractors and motorcycles." Her small smile seems designed to fire me up in more ways than one.

"You figured me out. It's all hot rods and tractors at my place. Only the manliest artwork for me."

"You'd have a framed license plate that says *The Boss*."

I lay my arms out on the back of the bench. "Well, I am the boss. I'm glad you've seen the light."

"I refuse to do any such thing."

Jodi brings our food out with a wink, and we start eating. Yep. Best burgers I've ever had.

"What did you do when you were in Portland?" she asks after a few minutes.

"I did custom carpentry for residential builders. Moldings and trim, mantelpieces, fancy staircase banisters, things like that."

It'd taken me years to build my reputation, and I'd given it up. A small wave of regret washes through me, but I will it to drain away. I made my choices, and I intend to stick with them.

"That sounds almost creative."

I like her teasing more than I should. Let's be real—I like everything about her more than I should.

"From a certain point of view." The work is partially creative, but it's also logical and mathematical. I fit those descriptions a lot better than the creative type she's thinking of. I'm a craftsman, not an artist.

She dips three long French fries into ketchup and eats the whole thing in one bite. "And here you're...?"

She leaves me to fill in that blank, but I don't have much to supply. Technically, I have an executive title, but most of the time, I act as the office manager and fill-in labor crew. I'm the guy who stepped in when his family needed him, but I don't know how to explain just what I do for them.

So I resort to my default.

"I'm the boss."

She purses her lips at that. "Of course you are. How is it working for your brother?"

"With. I work *with* my brother."

I don't really want to get into just how I feel about that experience. I need to be here long term, I know that deep in my bones. But how is the actual day to day? How is it falling into line, deferring to Caleb's judgment, and biting my tongue on every other issue?

"It's complicated."

"I can imagine. I wouldn't want to work for my sister." She shudders.

"With," I say under my breath. I don't know if I'll ever be ready to say I work *for* my brother.

"Do you get along?"

"On most things." A bit of an exaggeration, but she doesn't need the unvarnished truth.

"That makes sense. You're a really cooperative guy."

Her meaningful eye contact serves up a heaping spoonful of sass. Her mouth finally tips up, pleased as can be with her little jab.

"I can be a team player," I say, my eyes on those soft, berry lips. "When I'm working with the right team."

I'd told myself I'm not here for her, but when her cheeks wash with pink and her lashes flutter, teaming up with Hope sounds like an excellent idea.

TWELVE
HOPE

GRIFFIN PAID FOR LUNCH.

I offered to split the bill, but he just gave me a dirty look and pulled cash out of his wallet. I tell myself it's all in the name of teamwork. Even though, as the *boss*, I probably should have been the one paying. The festival doesn't have any money left and had never had that kind of discretionary cushion anyway, but still.

I also tell myself he only walks close beside me because of the damp, overcast weather, but that doesn't sound entirely believable. Or maybe I just don't want to believe it. He looks unspeakably handsome in the afternoon's hazy light, wearing his thick brown barn jacket, unzipped so his flannel shirt of the day peeks out in the middle. Meanwhile, I've buttoned my navy blue peacoat to the top, and the November air still worms its way through every gap it can find, leaving me chilled as soon as we stepped outside.

"What kind of houses did you work on?" I ask as we weave between shoppers on Maple Street. Although he'd technically answered my questions in the diner, he still hasn't said all that much about himself. I don't really think he's taciturn so much as calculated, like everything he has to say is on a need-to-know basis.

I can't say about *need*, but I want to get him to open up a little. For the sake of working together, of course.

"I started with a cookie cutter developer. They built huge neighborhoods using just a few plans, every house identical. We traveled all over the Northwest." He scuffs a tan work boot across a pile of slush. "The last couple of years, I worked for an all-custom outfit."

"You liked that better?" His voice had softened just enough to make me think so.

"The big developer was a little easier, since everything was the same. But I liked working on the custom homes more for the same reason—every job was different. More complex. Designed specifically for one family and their preferences."

Oh yeah, he definitely has a note of fondness in his voice now. That added sweetness in his low voice twines through my belly. Even when he's talking about houses, the man has appeal.

"What was the most interesting house you worked on?"

"Most interesting?" he echoes.

"You know, did you ever build a house with a bookcase that concealed a secret library or something? A two-story closet? Panic room? Oh—maybe a secret dungeon?"

"Secret dungeons. Where is your mind right now?"

I swat at his arm. "You know what I'm asking."

He grins to himself, stepping out of the path of a steadily-dripping awning. "Most of the houses were pretty standard luxury: walk-in closets, butler's pantries, wine cellars. Is a cellar as good as a dungeon for you?"

"I'll take it." I don't really care about the wine cellar, but I'd kill for the walk-in closet and pantry. "Do you miss it?"

He cuts his eyes to me but goes back to watching the side-walk. "No. I'm good where I'm at."

Hmm. He might as well have told me his dog has pneumonia. I don't buy it.

"You're good working with your brother even though it's *complicated*?"

"Family stuff gets tricky."

His careful tone reminds me of exactly why he came back, and I feel bad for being so nosy. I don't want to push him to talk about his dad or the rest of his *family stuff*.

"What's your dream house like? Craftsman, modern, farmhouse?"

"That's kind of personal, isn't it?"

The lilt of amusement in his tone tells me he doesn't really think so, he just wants to be contrary. Seems pretty typical of the guy who'd liked nothing better than a good argument in high school.

"You're the expert on houses."

He lifts a hand to his ear and leans my way. "What was that?"

I shove his shoulder. "Forget I asked."

His low, rich laughter dances up my back like he's tracing his fingers along my spine.

"If I had to choose, I'd go with a dungeon house. I hear women like those."

"I don't think you need any help attracting women."

No. *No.* I did not just say that.

His face splits into a smug smile like he used to wear whenever I'd concede a point to him in class after a long back and forth. I kind of want to slither down the drain to escape his self-congratulations.

"Don't take that the wrong way," I add.

"Explain to me the right way to take it."

I'm trying to come up with a believable way to say "I don't think you're hot" when someone calls my name.

Should I be grateful my mom just saved me or horrified?

I'm going with horrified.

She waltzes over to us, way too delighted by this chance encounter. *Oh please, let it be a chance encounter.* I don't like the idea of her spying on me, looking for an opportunity to interrupt, but I can't totally discount it.

"I'm glad I caught you."

Her eyes dart from me to Griffin, and of course she immediately notices his bruised head. It doesn't look any less awful today, and I still wince at the glaring reminder of my mishap in the warehouse.

Mom points at her own head. "Are you all right?"

He shrugs it off like the big old bruise is totally normal. "All good."

I make cursory introductions, wishing I'd stayed in the warehouse. I'd rather let my stomach start digesting itself than endure whatever must be coming.

"We're all so glad you stepped up to help Hope out," she tells him. "She was saying the other night how impressed she is with your work."

Griffin's eyes lock on me. "Really."

Not a question. More of a smug gloat. It's simultaneously mortifying, and really, really attractive. Ugh. I can't be smitten with Griffin McBride. I need to crumple all that *smit* up like old wrapping paper right this second.

"That's not exactly what I said." I can't remember *what* I said, but Mom will make it sound ten times more flattering than it was. It's all part of her "This house is a bargain at any price" attitude.

"You really came through for her," Mom goes on. "She said you're the best man for the job."

Apparently, Griffin has been keeping his smuggest smiles

under wraps until right this minute. Smirking that hard has got to hurt.

"I said you were *a* man for the job. Whether or not you're the best remains to be seen."

Mom ticks her head to the side, silently scolding me, but it doesn't matter anyway. Griffin's expression is unchanged.

"I have no problem with proving it, Hope."

My stomach swoops low, flooding with warmth. Maybe I got something fishy in my burger at the diner. It is *not* Griffin-induced.

Mom smiles away at him for another few seconds before turning to me. "I ran into Mayor Martinez this morning. He's very enthusiastic about your festival."

"I'm glad to have him on my side." He's supported me ever since I stood up to volunteer, and even pushed for a bigger budget than the original number. He's not all-powerful in this town, but it's good to have him in my corner.

"We were talking about how Sunshine needs someone focused solely on bringing in travel and tourism. You're doing so well with the Christmas festival, think of what you could do year round."

I wrap my coat tighter around me against the icy breeze. "I was really only planning on Christmas."

The festival had sounded like a great fit for me—I love the holiday and have good connections with other business owners because of my store. But year-round events? I don't have ideas or the time.

"Enrique said they're thinking about creating a permanent position. Maybe half-time at first, but I know you could make it a success."

"You mean a job?"

Mom nods. "You could really do something amazing with your degree and make a difference for the whole town."

She's so dang happy, I can't bear to burst her bubble and tell her I don't want to take on a new marketing job, especially if it means giving up my store. And I sure won't do it in front of Griffin, who's watching us like he understands what Mom's proposing even better than she does.

"I'm glad he's that excited about the festival," is all I can manage.

"I'll let you two get on with what you're doing." She grins at us, those sparklers in her eyes making her meaning painfully obvious. "I can't wait to hear what Hope will have to tell me about you next."

You'd think I'd be used to her antics by now, but my stomach aches from all the awkwardness she's heaped on me in a few short minutes. She says goodbye and carries on down the sidewalk, waving at everyone she passes like she's best friends with the whole town. Her breeziness can be a lot, but it all comes from a place of sincerity. She really wants me to be happy. I just wish she would dial it back a little.

Griffin and I share a look. Somehow, I know he gets it. The love, the encouragement, the not-so-gentle pressure. I will hope and pray he remains oblivious about the *rest* of her hints.

Who am I kidding? He ate up every word.

"It's like I said about family," he says.

"Yeah. It gets tricky."

THIRTEEN
GRIFFIN

I AM NOT A VOYEUR. I don't spy on people. But when I show up at the warehouse first thing in the morning with a box of donuts, Hope is lip syncing all the words to "Jump" while she paints the trim on the little Wonderland building.

And I watch.

She bops along, rolling her brush over the wood, one hip jutting out every time she mouths the title. I try not to stare at her hips or the careless way she sways them around, but I've never seen her quite this loose and relaxed. This discovery feels monumental, and I can't look away.

This ambitious, determined woman rocking out to Van Halen? If she breaks into an air guitar solo, I might drop down onto one knee and propose.

"I don't remember Santa singing this one."

She shrieks before I finish and flies to the workbench in a flash to stop her phone. "I wasn't expecting you this early."

Her face is pink from all the dancing, and probably just a little bit from getting caught.

"It's eight."

"Already?" She tilts her phone toward her. "Wow. I guess I lost track of time."

I set the box of donuts on the workbench and stalk closer. "How long have you been here?"

"Six-thirty. Ish."

"So, six."

She waves a hand in the air, confirming without admitting anything. If she bent over backward any further for this festival, her head would touch the ground.

"Next time you want to come in for a pre-dawn painting party, call me first. I don't like the idea of you in here alone."

"I couldn't sleep, so I thought I'd get some work done."

"Yeah, well, the door was unlocked, and you didn't notice me come in."

My skin crawls just thinking about it. Our small town is reasonably safe, but that doesn't mean everyone behaves perfectly all the time. Maybe it's a holdover from Portland, but I don't want her in here alone.

"I don't want to bug you."

"It'll bug me more if you don't call me."

She finally hears the rough edge in my voice, but instead of helping her see the seriousness of the situation, it just switches her attitude on.

"How have I survived twenty-eight years without you here to hero me up?"

This woman tries to get under my skin, I swear. Always has. Probably why I've always given her the same right back. "Don't be difficult. Just call me the next time you decide to come in early."

Yeah, that does it. Her face goes even pinker, clashing beautifully with her bright red blouse.

"I'm not being difficult—that's you. You're the one who keeps sweeping in and telling me what to do."

"Me? I'm being nice. I brought you donuts this morning."

Her face brightens, irritation gone. "You brought me donuts? I forgive you."

She rushes past me to the box of treats.

"I don't think I should have to be forgiven for trying to protect you."

Wait—those words aren't right. Or, maybe worse, they are *exactly* right. Thinking about her in here all alone when nobody's around...yeah, I want to protect her.

She turns slowly toward me, apple cinnamon cake donut in hand, eyes wide. Pretty sure I don't want to hear whatever sassy thing is about to come out of her mouth. Not when I'm already halfway to digging my own grave.

"Just say you'll call me next time." My voice goes so low it's practically a growl. We don't need to go around in circles over this.

"Oh my gosh, fine. I will call you. Are you satisfied?"

"Thoroughly."

I stare at her for a second, imagining her calling me for something other than to take part in an early-morning work crew. I don't wade very deep into those thoughts before my attention zeroes in on Hope taking a big bite out of her donut.

Eating is not an attractive activity. I don't want to hear anyone eat, and I don't especially want to see anyone eat, either. But my eyes are stuck on Hope like they've been welded there. The way her jaw works as she chews, her throat shifting as she swallows, her little pink tongue darting out to lick away a crumb at the corner of her mouth—I'm as engrossed as I was watching her dance.

I should not be tracking every move of her lips, but at the moment, I'm not sure there's anything her mouth can do that I wouldn't like.

I should have bought a bottle of water at the café so I could douse my head with it.

"This is so good," she groans. "I want to have babies with this donut."

Everything about this morning has conspired to throw me off my game. My newfound protective streak, my abnormal urge to watch Hope eat, the weird twisting thing my stomach did when she said the word *babies*. Probably best to just clock out now and call it a day.

But of course I won't. I grab a donut and set the box aside. We eat in a silent stare down, like we're waiting on someone to call "draw."

After a minute, she dusts off her fingers and points vaguely at me.

"How's your face?"

The words are sassy, but her tone is sincere.

"Not so bad anymore." If I didn't have to field "What the heck happened to you?" twenty times a day, I wouldn't even think of it.

"I'm sorry."

I brush her apology away. "It was an accident."

"Not that." She ticks her head to the side. "Not just for that. I'm sorry for being bratty just now. It's kind of a bad habit with you."

"I know what you mean." It doesn't say much about me that I've fallen back on behaviors I'd honed when I was sixteen.

"It's nice of you to think about my safety."

I'm thinking about a lot more than just her safety, but if I'm aiming for *nice*, this isn't the time to tell her.

"And—" she says, slipping past me, "it's nice of you to think about my empty stomach."

She pulls another donut from the box, a double chocolate this time.

"Even elves get snack breaks."

She groans. "Why are sweet treats so tasty?"

I breathe a laugh, unable to look away from her enjoying the donut. "I wish I'd known you were like this back in high school."

Her eyebrows furrow. "Like what?"

"You jam out to Van Halen. Whisper sweet nothings to donuts. You're..." I want to say *relaxed* but I'm trying to be nice here, and that would go too far the opposite direction.

"You didn't know me very well back then."

"I'm thinking now that was a mistake."

She watches me for a second like she's trying to decode something in my comment. She can take it however she wants to hear it.

"You couldn't stand me."

It's not quite a question, and the vulnerability in her soft voice stops me from tossing the same remark right back at her.

"Nope. I liked getting under your skin, because you were sure under mine."

She tilts her head at me like she's looking for traps. I hate that I've made her doubt everything I say. I want to think I've put my high school mistakes behind me, but they've got a long tail. Seconds pass, and my neck gets hot and itchy while I wait. When she finally smiles, all the tightness inside me loosens.

"We were pretty different. I was busy running for class president. You were busy throwing epic parties in the canyon."

"Why didn't you ever come to any of those parties?" I might have instigated them, but they took on a life of their own. Almost everyone in our class had showed up at least once. Right now, Hope's absence feels like a glaring omission, and I wonder what it would have been like if she'd ever joined in. We might have argued over the best way to start a campfire, but it wouldn't have been boring.

Her sharp laugh punctures the air. "My mother would have grounded me until college if I'd gone to one of those parties."

"They weren't that bad."

She shoots me a look that says she knows that's total BS.

"Most of them weren't that bad," I amend. Nothing she doesn't know already will make them sound better, but they weren't all wild. "Sometimes they were actually relaxing."

"A relaxing bonfire?"

"Sure. There's something about sitting under the stars when there's no other sound but the fire crackling, just you and the woods. It's peaceful. A good place to go when I need an escape."

Once again, I've confided too much. Maybe starting the day with sugar was a bad idea for everybody.

"I'll have to try it sometime."

"You should."

"I'll probably need a guide," she says. "You know—to start the fire."

We watch each other as the moment stretches out between us. If I thought seeing her dance to Van Halen rocked my world, having her open the door for me like this has it beat by a factor of ten.

"I know a guy."

Her grin presses the accelerator on my heart, revving my engines. I'm seriously tempted to see if I can crack that door a bit wider, when she snaps out of whatever had her gazing at me like that. She dusts her hands on her jeans and claps them once.

"I've got paint open." She gestures behind her at the Wonderland house. "I should probably keep working on that before it gets all filmy and gross."

She hustles over, pulls her rubber gloves back on, and starts painting away like she wants to paint over this whole charged conversation. But then she shoots a look at me over her shoulder. Our gazes collide, and her eyes are full of a fiery hope that strums through me like a plucked guitar string.

Maybe I've got a merry Christmas to look forward to

after all.

———

A COUPLE OF HOURS LATER, I've nearly got the second Winter Wonderland house done, and Hope's admiring her progress on hers, rubbing her hands together.

I admire the house, too. The plans were cute, and even the unfinished house had charm. But this? It's freaking adorable. She's painted the building a warm orange, with a pink and white awning. In the front window she painted cakes and sweets on display, and they're so well done, I feel like I could reach in and take a slice. The North Pole's picture-perfect bakery.

If I thought I was the key to getting Hope's Winter Wonderland pieces built, seeing this one proves just how wrong I was. I can build them, but she's breathing life into them. Turns out there is a little magic in here, and it all belongs to her.

"What do you think?" she asks when I've gone on staring too long.

"It's enchanting."

She lifts an eyebrow at me. I'm gearing up, ready for a remark from her on my word choice, but her smile lets me know it was the right one.

"I like that. That's exactly what I'm going for." She presses her left thumb into the base of her right hand. "You've got some Christmas spirit in you, after all."

"Maybe." I step closer. "Does your hand hurt?"

"Painting this house is different from working on a canvas. I'm just a little sore, that's all." She flexes her fingers a few times, trying to work out the stiffness.

"Here." I take her hand in both of mine, running my thumbs up her palm and across the pad in continuous strokes. I work down each finger in small, rolling motions, digging in just a bit at the base of her thumb. Her muscles are tight from holding the paintbrush for hours, but after a minute, they warm and loosen.

"That feels so good. Where did you learn to do this?"

"When I played baseball. I got massages to keep my pitching hand loose, or it could seize up on me. Even now, I do exercises so don't strain my hands. Carpal tunnel can end a carpentry career."

I go through the movements again but slower this time, massaging from the base of her hand to the tips of her fingers. My brain has finally caught up to what my hands are doing, and I'm not sure if I should stop touching Hope immediately or go on massaging her fingers until she tells me to knock it off. The second feels more likely at this point.

I work higher, running my thumbs over her wrist and up along the tendon. Her whole forearm must be sore after days of painting. I'm just trying to prevent another workplace injury.

By touching her as much as I can, for as long as I can.

"You really liked working construction," she says.

"Yeah, of course. Building something from nothing? Seeing real, tangible results of my work? There's nothing better than that." My thumb slides up along the center of her soft forearm like it's got its own definition of *nothing better*.

"Do you ever think about going back?"

I slow my fingers and drag them down her forearm, over her wrist, and along her hand until I finally let her go. Touching Hope worked like a truth serum, and I can see by the soft curiosity in her eyes I've revealed too much. Maybe to both of us.

"I am back." I toss her a smirk, even though I don't feel it. "I'm building these for you, and they're looking good, right?"

"They're better than good. That's the point. You could open your own custom carpentry business here."

My grin falters. "That's not on the horizon."

"Maybe you need to change the horizon."

"I don't think that's how horizons work."

Her little look tells me I'm pushing it. True, but so is she.

"Well, at the risk of giving you an even bigger head, these are turning out beautiful, and that's all because of you."

"Funny, I was going to say the same thing to you."

She glows, and I get the feeling she doesn't hear enough praise. On this project, on her artwork, on her store—I can't tell which, but I want to change that.

"We had signs made up for our sponsors. We could add one for you if you wanted."

"I'm sure McBride Landscaping will appreciate it."

"I was thinking of something like *Griffin McBride's Custom Woodworking*. That'd look pretty good next to the Wonderland."

She's not very subtle. All the heat that'd been coursing through my veins over my impromptu massage cools back down.

"You're obviously skilled at stuff like this. Haven't you thought about starting your own business here? Maybe if you try—"

"Hope. Leave it alone."

Her smile shrivels up, and I want to kick myself for snuffing out that light. But I can't do what she's suggesting, and I can't explain it all to her right now.

I can, however, get some of the attitude out of my voice so I don't drop us right back to the sniping square one we started from.

"Please," I add gently.

She purses her lips but seems to accept my request.

I go back to the building I'm working on, hoping the drill will smother all the thoughts she's trying to plant in my head before they can take root and grow like weeds.

FOURTEEN

HOPE

I'VE STARTED to hate the sound of my phone buzzing with text messages. *Ping ping ping.* I'm suddenly the most popular girl in Sunshine.

> Lila: Where are all your Facebook posts?

> Lila: You can't just make the page and do nothing

> Lila: You have to build interest

> Lila: I'll send you some ideas

> Mom: How are things going with the festival?

> Mom: Have you asked Lila her thoughts about it?

> Mom: Everything good in the warehouse?

> Mom: Things going well with Griffin?

> Mom: Don't forget to take breaks now and then

> Mom: Maybe you two can take a night off and get dinner together

I can't handle all of this poking and prodding at me. At least my dad's texts are normal.

> Dad: Did you happen to see my spare reading glasses when you were here last?

After texting my dad that his glasses were on the front windowsill, I put my family's messages out of my head. I'll respond to the rest tonight. Maybe.

I slip my phone back into my purse, but I wasn't very subtle about checking it.

"Do you need to take care of that?" Griffin asks.

He dragged me to lunch right at noon. I suggested the pizza place a couple of blocks off of Maple—it's a little less crowded over here, but I still feel exposed. Nobody's come up to make weird hints and insinuations about us though, and we finished our slices in record time.

"I'm trying to ignore it."

He side-eyes my purse but doesn't say more. His curiosity has a touch of something in it I'm afraid to name. But I want to reassure him...also for reasons I'm afraid to name. Too many nameless things are fogging up the air between us, but clearing that air doesn't feel like the work of this volunteer lunch date.

"It's just my family. Everyone's got advice."

And they can all keep it to themselves. Except for my dad. He can go on texting about misplaced items whenever he likes.

"I hear that. I had to leave my family group chat."

"Why am I not surprised?"

"Caleb sent one too many emojis. I did what I had to do."

Maintaining eye contact with him, I slide my phone from my bag. His gaze narrows on me while my thumbs tap around for a second. Somewhere on his side of the booth, his phone buzzes.

He levels me with a flat look. "Do I even want to know what you sent?"

I am the picture of innocence. I'm a baby deer batting my huge eyelashes at him.

He shakes his head at me, fighting a smile. "All right, boss. Let's go."

We leave the pizza place and walk up the block toward the warehouse, blasted by the cold that whips down Fourth Avenue. The weather can't make up its mind between mild, overcast days and brief bursts of snowfall that's gone the next afternoon. We're sure to get a big dump of snow eventually, but I'm crossing all my fingers that holds off until after the festival.

"Just out of curiosity—what emoji did Caleb send you that finally made you snap?"

He laughs. "Pretty sure if I tell you about the straw that broke this camel's back, you'll just send me a whole truckload of straw."

I try to look offended, even though obviously that was my plan. "Not me."

My merriment turns into full-blown nausea when I see Ada and Isabel barreling toward us. Can we hide somehow? Nope, too late for that. The two elderly gossips have their eyes locked on me, drawing closer like joy-seeking missiles, ready to snuff it out.

Okay, maybe that's an extreme reaction to two adorable elderly women approaching me in town, but I have a good reason. Ever since the Christmas festival revival was announced, people have been going out of their way to stop me on the street to voice their opinions, make personal preferences known, and air their grievances.

Mostly they air grievances.

Ada flags me down so I can't pretend I don't see them. I stop, preparing myself for whatever they're itching to say. Ada was once a warm-hearted second grade teacher, and Isabel used to be a nurse, but now that they're retired, they occupy themselves with digging into other people's business.

"I'm glad we caught you," Ada says. "We have a list of songs for the choir."

She nods at Isabel, who pulls a sheet of paper from her oversized purse and passes it to me. I scan their notes. It's a list of a couple dozen popular carols and hymns, some with green check marks, and others with red exes next to the titles.

"I'll pass your suggestions on, but I'm letting the choir director decide their song list." I keep my smile friendly to soften the blow. The Christmas festival's suggestion box has been closed for months, but nobody ever wants to hear it. "She'll have a better idea of song choices to get the crowd into the holiday spirit."

"Funny, she's the one who told us to tell you."

Whoops. I guess the choir director was trying to get out of disappointing them, too. "I'll take a look through your list and talk to her when we meet next."

"Try for *traditional* songs," Isabel says. "You don't need to modernize it."

"These are the songs people want to hear." Ada jabs at the list in my hand like she's trying to give me a paper cut. "Real Christmas music, not sad songs about romantic breakups."

It seems unlikely the choir's going to belt out "Last Christmas" underneath the tree. Unlikely...but not totally impossible. "I understand, but I can't make any promises."

"Honey, are you in charge or aren't you?" Ada asks.

A throat clears just over my shoulder, reminding me of our audience.

"You know Griffin McBride?" I gesture his way, and their eyes skate over him.

"Oh, yes," Isabel says. "It's good to see you back in town. Did you have your fill of Portland?"

His mouth twitches. "Something like that."

"I don't know about having him on your crew," Ada says to me. "Might be dangerous putting him around all that lumber."

She gives a soft laugh, totally missing that her joke doesn't land. I shift in front of him as though I can shield him from their laughter over his mistakes from ten years ago.

"Griffin's doing a wonderful job making my Christmas village. Nobody else could build them so well or so quickly. It's going to be the cutest thing you've ever seen, and I owe it all to him."

They size him up again as though they can judge his carpentry skills at a glance. But when they turn back to me, I know they're not done talking about the festival. That's the thing about airing grievances—nobody ever wants to stop once they get started.

"That festival's so much to handle." Ada's words are kind, but they don't make me feel any better. She makes a sound that's simultaneously impressed and dismayed. "And you're adding even more to the celebrations. We just want to make sure nothing falls through the cracks."

"It's a lot to get done, and there's not much time left to do it," Isabel adds. "You don't want to let people down."

The universe has rolled all of my deepest fears about the project into one well-intentioned but still supremely awful conversation. Their fears make sense, though. I don't have the best track record. Marketing, my mom's real estate firm, my imaginary fiancé—I have no shortage of stories going around Sunshine about my inability to see things through.

"Hope isn't going to let anyone down." Griffin speaking up in my defense sends warm shockwaves through me like he's switched on my own personal space heater.

"So many people are counting on this," Ada says. "We just wonder if it might be easier on you if you had more help."

"I'm sure Helena wouldn't mind lending a hand with the festival. And your sister, too. Isn't this the sort of thing she's so good at up in Seattle?"

Isabel has no idea she just landed a death blow. My brave face crumbles. Lila *is* good at it. I'd thought taking it on myself would prove I'm capable, too, but it seems like it's just making people wish my sister were here to do everything for me.

"I wouldn't underestimate Hope."

Griffin stands so close, his chest presses against my shoulder. He's warm and reassuring, and I lean into him just a little. Maybe it's weird of me, but I need it right now.

"I've seen her plans," he says in that low voice of his that doesn't bend in an argument. "Her festival is going to knock this town's socks off. She's giving her all to make this thing a success."

His support runs a glittery thread of pride through me, even if I'm not sure he believes his own words. The houses are starting to look cute, but the rest? Will it really be enough to pull in as many people as I'm hoping?

"Oh, I'm sure. Nobody doubts how much she loves Sunshine." Ada smiles at me like she still sees the second-grader I used to be.

She *doesn't* say that nobody doubts I'll actually come through for them. How could she say it, when she just suggested I ask my mom and sister for help?

Griffin glances over at me, and it's like the tumult of emotions inside me have been printed out for him to read. I never would have described him as a perceptive guy before, and really wish he wasn't starting now.

"She's got your suggestions," he says to Ada and Isabel. "But we need to get going."

He puts a hand on my lower back, and I mutter goodbyes as he steers me away. Our boots crunch up a block of sidewalk before he drops his hand without a word.

I let us into the warehouse and flip the lights on again. A tremble shivers through me, but I'm not sure if it's from the weather or from doubt spreading icy crystals in my heart. The hope I'd held that renewing the Christmas festival might change people's opinions of me just burst in my hands like a gauzy soap bubble.

Instead of going to his collection of tools, Griffin steps closer to me.

"Are you okay?"

"Sure." He doesn't seem swayed by my smile. I laugh to really drive home my *it's no big deal* attitude, but I don't think it's holding up under his close scrutiny.

"Do you want to talk about it?"

I'm tempted to make a joke about us having a heart to heart, but I can't do it. "I just wish they had more faith in me. She sounded like everyone expects me to call in reinforcements from my sister."

"That woman isn't *everyone*."

"Not the best time for a semantics lesson, Griffin." I step away, growing more agitated the longer he watches me with that soft look on his face. "I figured some people think along those lines, it's just the first time someone said it straight to my face."

"Hey." He steps in front of me before I can start pacing. "You're doing your best, and then some. You're creating this magical festival, improving every piece you touch, and expecting nothing in return. They're going to be impressed by you. *I'm* impressed by you."

My heart jolts around behind my ribs, reveling in praise from this man.

"That's the part that counts, right?" I need to poke a little fun at both of us and bring this moment down a touch. He's turned way too sincere on me, and my fingers are shaking so hard, I can't manage to undo my top coat button. "I need to maintain my image as your boss."

Griffin's eyes snag on my fingers fumbling with the button, and he closes the distance between us to stand right in front of me.

"Here." He moves my fingers out of the way like he's going to unbutton my coat for me, but he startles at the contact. "Your hands are freezing."

His warm fingers wrap around mine, shutting out the chill. I immediately forget that I wanted to bring the moment down. My focus narrows to the solid warmth of his hands like a microscope collecting the tiniest details. The calluses on his palms just below his fingers. The sheer size of his hands compared to mine. My heart beating entirely too fast.

This is apparently the day for him to hold my hands, and I don't hate it. I'm hungry for it, ready to gather up all the warm, soft touches from Griffin.

"Where are your crazy red gloves?"

He slips my hands together and rubs them vigorously like he intends to start a fire between us. *Yes, please.* He pulls them close to his face, cups his hands, and blows on them, letting his hot breath create a little oven perfect for finger-thawing.

"I forgot them here."

My voice comes out so soft, I'm not sure he heard me, but his eyes snap to mine. Flames might as well come out of his eyes. Hazel-green sparks bore into me with...I can't even name what. Or, I *can*...but like the rest of this strange "one step closer, one step back" dance we're doing, I don't know if I *should*. It's definitely something *hot*.

We stare at each other ten whole seconds, this "I'm too

much of a chicken to say what" flying between us before he squeezes my hands one last time and lets go.

"You know what we're going to do, don't you?" he says.

A dozen slightly saucy answers come to mind. Whatever he suggests, I'm ready to agree.

He tilts his head an inch closer. "We're going to give this town the best Christmas festival they've ever seen."

I like that plan.

His confidence colors me with a rosy, golden warmth. I could bask in his encouragement, just swim around in the coziness of knowing he's behind me. He's supporting me and my festival like we really are a team. Like he believes in me.

Griffin McBride found my Kryptonite.

I'm not sure my defenses were all that strong to begin with.

FIFTEEN
GRIFFIN

THE NEXT PERSON who smiles pathetically at me tonight is going to get punched in the face.

I move around in my parents' living room, collecting sad half-smiles like a magnet pulling in iron filings, each one delivering a tiny sting as they worm under my skin. Everyone means well, I know that. I still hate this.

Hate that he's gone. Hate that we have to grieve him at all, let alone collectively.

But Mom wants to celebrate him, and I never refuse her. This event is meant to be a little less somber than last year's wake, and she's invited friends, acquaintances, anybody who knew Dad to come share the moment with us.

I accept condolences without much of a thought or acknowledgement. The owner of the local stone yard claps me on the shoulder on his way to the food in the dining room. Two nursery workers shake my hand. Amy and Jodi hug me on their rounds through the family. All while classic rock plays softly from the record player I brought down from Dad's study.

People in the living room laugh over someone's story. I've mostly tuned them out. Being here at all has my heart in a vise—

listening to everyone talk about my dad just squeezes the handles tighter.

Caleb and Rowan sidle over, arms locked around each other's waists. They haven't let each other go all night. But if I had a buoy here to cling to, I would do the same thing.

Rowan flashes a sad smile. Since she's my sister-in-law, I count her exempt from any pity-smile resentment.

"It's a nice turnout," she says.

"Mom spread the word." I can't keep the disapproval out of my voice. Normally, I like gatherings of any size, for any reason...but not *this* reason. Some days, I want to be the only one grieving him. I don't want to know how everybody else misses him, too. Childish, but it's the truth.

"It comforts her to hear how much people loved your dad."

The three of us look over at Mom on the other side of the living room, where she listens to one of dad's friends tell an animated story. Fifty-eight is too young to be a widow. I know that's not how life works, there are no guarantees. But it's still wrong. We've all lost our own pieces of him, but sometimes I hate what she's lost the most.

Smiling—laughing, even—she doesn't look anything close to the way I feel. Grief tears her up, too. I never question that for a second, but sharing the burden eases the ache for her.

I'm not convinced it does the same for me.

Caleb runs a hand along Rowan's shoulder, keeping her close, and she looks up at him with pure adoration in her eyes.

Jealousy circles around my chest like a dog searching for a place to lie down. I've never seen him this far gone over anyone but Rowan. I don't need the domestic contentment he's found in her...but part of me sure wants it sometimes. I could use an anchor right about now.

Buoy, anchor—apparently, I only have water-themed metaphors for relationships tonight.

"Griffin would rather fish his feelings away," he says.

"As nature intended."

He levels me a stern look, and his silent lecture runs through my head. *It's not healthy. Talking it out is normal. You bottle up too much.* We've been through it a few times over the last year, but I haven't made much of a dent on those counts. Keeping my grief safe in a lockbox seems best for everyone.

"You'll be ready at five, right?" I ask.

"I still say the river's going to be iced over."

"Not on the section of the Olallie I want to visit."

We planned a morning of fly fishing to honor Dad on our own. Just us and the river—no sorrowful condolences from anybody. We spent so much time fishing with him growing up, every day I've been out on the river since we lost him has felt like a memorial. Tomorrow, at least, it will be intentional.

"You're both more dedicated to fishing than I could ever be," Rowan says. "Tomorrow at five, I'll be warm in my bed, sound asleep."

Caleb nuzzles against her ear. "I'll join you when I get back."

"Smelling like fish guts? I don't think so." Her eyes go wide as if Caleb whispered something spicy in her ear, but then she lifts a hand to her round stomach. "That's a big one. I don't think he liked the smoothie I had earlier."

Caleb covers her hand with his, and a few seconds later, he grins, too. "He obviously wants more of my barbecue."

"Do you want to feel him kicking?" Rowan asks me.

I raise my hands and take a step back. "I've seen *Alien*. I'm good."

She makes a face at my teasing, but getting grabby with my sister-in-law's belly—even to feel a baby kick—just feels wrong.

"His foot is *right there*," Caleb says.

"He needs more room." Rowan rubs wide circles over her belly.

"Hang in there one more month, little guy."

I'm happy for him, I really am, but I don't need to witness this sickeningly sweet display.

An odd, prickling sensation goes up my back, like I've stepped into a warm draft. I turn around, and there's Hope standing in my mother's open front door. Amy greets her as she lets her in, but Hope's eyes scan the room until they land on me. Her genuine, open smile lights her face, and my heart kicks to rival my nephew. My feet take me across the room to her before my brain can think to tell them to.

"It's real sweet of you to join us," Amy says to her when I reach them. "Kat's in the dining room, I think, and the boys are, oh—here's Griffin."

She takes me by the sleeve and moves me even closer, as if I hadn't been angling for that spot already.

Hope's smile melts into something else. Not pity, but closer to embarrassment. Like she isn't sure if I'll welcome her here and now. We've been working side by side all week, and I never mentioned this gathering. I hadn't wanted to add to this somber party, but I'm grateful to whoever asked her.

She lifts a box in her hands. "I brought a pie from Blackbird's, I hope that's okay. It's a coconut cream. Maureen said that was your dad's favorite."

"It was. That was good of you." The lump in my throat makes my words stick.

"Why don't I take that into the kitchen for you, honey?" Amy says.

"Put it in the fridge, will you?" I'm selfish, and I don't want to share this small gift.

Amy pats me on the shoulder and slips away.

I stare at Hope, trying to figure out how she knew to be here.

"I didn't invite you to this."

Her gentle smile crumples, and she shrinks closer to the door. "I'm sorry, I—"

I take her by the elbow, her thick, brightly striped sweater softer beneath my fingers than I imagined. My brain is too busy keeping my heart in check tonight to monitor the things that come out of my mouth. I do this a lot. Half the time I don't care, but this time, I need to make it right.

"No, I'm sorry. I didn't mean it that way." I lightly squeeze her arm, wanting to hold on, pull her close, *something*. But those things would probably tell her more than I'm prepared to. I let her go. "I didn't know you knew about tonight. I'm glad you're here."

"Your mom mentioned it in the store the other day. I just thought..." She looks around at the few dozen people spread throughout the main level of the house. "Well, I wanted to stop by."

"Thank you."

"There are a lot of people here." Her attention snags on the spinning vinyl in the corner by Dad's guitar. "I kind of wasn't expecting Led Zeppelin to set the mood, though."

I laugh softly. "One of his favorites."

"This explains a lot about your warehouse playlist." Her mouth pulls into another soft smile, and I feel it straight between my ribs. Her fake smiles leave me itching for something real, but this one is like fireflies soaring around in my chest, leaving sparkling trails behind them.

Is it sacrilege for my stomach to soar when she looks at me this way, here at Dad's final one-year anniversary? I decide...no. Dad would have shoved me in her direction and told me to go after her. He probably would have already scolded me for dragging my feet, and I only reconnected with her a few days ago. Halfway was never his style.

"Soon you'll know all my secrets."

She tips her head to the side. "I doubt that."

I wouldn't be so sure. I'm not one to open up much, but when she looks at me like this, I'm tempted to start.

"I'll never forget how happy James was that day," a voice says loudly, cutting into our moment.

A small group in the living room has gathered around Bill, one of Dad's long-time friends. He raises his glass toward Caleb, who still stands with Rowan near the dining room.

"You'd just graduated with a degree in landscape design and told him you were coming home to work with him. I don't think I'd ever seen him so proud. You made your dad's dream come true."

Bill shines a soggy smile Caleb's way, oblivious to the dagger he's stuck deep in my chest. I stand stock still while he goes on about how happy my brother made our dad when he joined the family business.

Working with him was the only thing Dad had ever really asked of me. And the only thing I'd ever refused him. If there's one thing I don't want to hear about tonight, it's Dad's business.

"Bought us a round of beer when he told us about it," he says with a laugh. "He couldn't get over it. Passing the business on to you...nothing could have made him happier than that."

Caleb's eyes cut to me. We have a whole conversation in the one look—a silent apology on his part, an acknowledgement he doesn't need to offer one on mine. I don't blame anybody else for the choices I've made. This poorly timed story sure isn't my brother's fault.

Bill seems to remember James McBride had *two* sons, and he finally registers me in the group.

"He was proud of you too, of course, Griffin. Building those houses and everything." He falters over his praise, clearly fuzzy on the details of what I did in Portland. "He'd have been real happy to know you made your way into his business after all."

Maybe. That'd been the goal. Too late, but the best I can do.

Bill looks as if he'd like to fade into the woodwork, but we still have the full attention of everyone in the living room. The dining room buzzes with low conversations, but in here, the mood is falling like an airplane whose engine has cut out.

"Thanks for sharing that story," Caleb says, playing gracious host.

Bill glances to me again, but if he's looking for thanks or absolution, he won't find it here. I'm not really in the mood to find some show of gratitude for how easily he'd summed up the divide between me, my brother, and my dad.

The room settles into awkward silence, searching for a way back to easy chatter. That won't come from me, either, even if, as one-third of the hosts tonight, it probably should. Can't really think of anything cheerful to say at the moment.

"I have a story about Mr. McBride," Hope says.

Most of the room turns to look at her. She swallows as if the attention makes her uncomfortable, but she flashes that perfect smile. She's had some experience with handling crowds, after all.

"It was my senior year in high school. I was on my way home from a trip to the mall in Bend and got about halfway between there and home when I..." She looks up at me, bracing me for something, before her eyes flicker over the people around us. "Well, I ran out of gas."

A titter of laughter works through the room, easing some of the tightness Bill's story left behind—and probably everything my face did in response to it.

"It was so dumb, but I was sure I had enough to get home. I called my dad's office, but he was with a patient. I called my mom, but she was at a showing and didn't answer. It was starting to get dark, and I was sitting there on the side of the highway trying to figure out what the heck I was supposed to do, when a big truck pulled up behind me."

She has everybody's attention now, mine most of all.

"For a whole minute, I thought for sure I was in trouble. I locked all my doors and just stared at the rear-view mirror, waiting. The man got out of his truck, walked around to my door, and leaned down to see me. My heart just about stopped. I don't think I've ever been as relieved in my life as I was when I recognized Mr. McBride standing there."

A collective sigh and low laughter ripples through her rapt audience. The same relief runs through me, and I'd been ninety-five percent sure I knew where her story was headed in the first place. I can picture him standing there in his work coat, salt and pepper beard, dark hair wild at the end of a long day. Probably had his hands stuffed in his pockets so he'd look a little less frightening to her.

"He was so kind to me. Said he had a full gas can in the back of his truck. He poured it into my tank for me and never said a single word about how stupid I'd been to let my tank go empty. When he was done, he followed me the rest of the way into town to the closest gas station to make sure I got there okay." Hope shrugs slightly, as if this weren't the sweetest story she could have told right now. "It was a small thing, maybe, but I've never forgotten it."

People nod and smile, confirming to each other how her story fits what they knew of my dad. The mood-airplane lifts again, raised up by Hope. She'd told a story highlighting my dad's generosity at her own expense, and I suspect she did it to ease *my* discomfort. A swell of gratitude has me wanting to pull her to me and hold her close. I've been fighting that urge for a while, but right now, I can't remember why.

"James changed my tire out on Obsidian Road once,"

someone pipes up. "I thought I was in for an hour wait for Triple A, and there he was, my guardian angel."

Conversation re-centers around the uncanny ability my dad had to find people in their cars broken down on the side of the road, the awkwardness of Bill's story forgotten. Admiration buzzes through me, but when I look down at Hope, the warmth in her eyes knocks my feet so far out from under me, I have no doubt I'll wind up flat on my back when I come down again.

And her soft smile? Not a trace of pity.

The house is suddenly too hot, too stuffy, too full of memories I don't feel like sharing. I don't want to commune with everyone else and sing Kum-ba-ya, but one person managed to bring me a spot of comfort. One bright, shining, unexpected person.

"Do you want to get some fresh air?" I ask her.

"Please."

We slip out without another word. The frigid evening air pinches at my face and hands, but it's a relief after the oppressive warmth inside from so many people crowding around. I wave her toward the porch swing on the wide patio. We sit, our thighs lightly touching on the narrow seat. This might have been my plan all along.

She wraps her arms tight around her, rubbing her shoulders. Her thick sweater can't do much against this cold. My great scheme to get her alone won't last long in weather that barely touches forty degrees.

"Here." Reaching around her, I grab a throw blanket draped across the back of the swing, and wrap the fleece around her shoulders like a poncho. "Mom watches the sunrise out here every morning, so there's usually a blanket or two ready for her."

Won't add it had been her habit with Dad. Can't.

"Thanks."

I tuck loose ends around her until she's a little burrito, her fingers curled inside the blanket layers. My gaze sticks on her mouth, and my hands slow their aimless work. Other ways to warm her spin through my head. I finally sit back, my shoulder brushing hers.

"I should thank you. You rescued me back there."

"I just filled some awkward silence."

"Boss," I say gently. "Accept my thanks."

She nods, fighting a smile. "You're welcome."

I push slightly on the swing, rocking us slowly back and forth. "I'm glad my dad was there for you that day."

Being stuck on the side of the highway could be a bad situation for anyone, let alone a teenage girl.

"Yeah. I couldn't have asked for a better person to find me in a spot like that—including *my* dad. He's more the type to call in help than to offer it. The only hands-on work he does is all the braces he puts on at his orthodontics practice."

"Did you get in trouble with your parents for running out of gas?"

She snuggles deeper into the blanket so it covers her chin. "I never told them about it."

I dip my shoulder against hers. "Hope Parrish. You were secretly a little rebel, and I never knew."

"It was self-preservation. I didn't need a lecture about how *Lila* never ran out of gas on the highway."

"You got it too, huh? Perfect Older Sibling Syndrome?"

"Textbook case. Lila's spent her whole life checking off the list of things Mom wanted for us. I'm always scrambling to keep up."

We rock for a minute, listening to the muffled hum of conversation from inside.

"I'm sorry for the way that man in there talked about you like you were an afterthought to your dad. You know you weren't, right?"

Caleb had fallen into line behind Dad a whole lot easier than I had. Dad never pitted us against each other, but the comparisons didn't have to be voiced for me to feel them. I know he loved me without question. But I also know I'd failed to do so many of the things that would have made him happy. Intentionally and unintentionally.

"I went to all your baseball games," she says.

Now that's an interesting bit of news. I spin my head to face her, but she lifts a hand out of the blanket cocoon I'd made for her.

"That's not the point. The point is, your dad was always the loudest fan in the stands. He cheered for you like crazy, yelling his head off and whistling for every pitch."

Just her mentioning it has the piercing sound echoing in my head. "His wolf whistles could damage people's eardrums."

"You guys lost your last home game. And your dad cheered for you just as hard as ever. I remember him running out onto the field to lift you up in this huge bear hug even though you weren't having it. I didn't know him, but it looked to me like he just wanted to celebrate *you*, win or lose."

Win or lose.

My lungs contract in that heavy, stuttering way that says tears are right around the corner. I suck in air as though that can protect me, but my defensive line is weak. Hope charged right through it with her memories of Dad.

She isn't wrong. He'd supported me and cheered for me no matter how things shook out. I didn't need to win to earn his proud looks and congratulations. He'd always had my back. Always championed me, always been the dad anybody would have loved to have.

It made it that much worse that I'd opted to leave him and everything he'd hoped for me behind.

This is why I hate events like tonight. Reminiscing. Sharing.

I don't let my emotions get the best of me. But a few soft words from Hope, and my eyes well with tears, my heart very nearly breaching the surface.

"Oh." Her soft breath blows a little puff of vapor between us as she twists to face me, her leg pushing harder against mine. "I'm sorry. I shouldn't have said all that."

"It's okay." I don't meet her eyes, and my voice cracks. I don't really want her to see me like this...but I don't want her to leave, either. "That's what tonight is about."

I just hadn't expected Hope to be the one to make me miss my dad with this ferocious ache.

She brushes away the tear that made a slow fall down my cheek. That smooth, soft glide of her thumb tugs like a hook in my belly, pulling me inevitably closer to her. She runs her hand to the nape of my neck, trailing the backs of her fingers there in small strokes, soothing with her slow touches. Giving me permission to cry, maybe. Letting me know she doesn't judge my grief.

Slowly, she leans closer against me, bracketing me between the hand on my neck and the other on my chest right over my heart. Those soft touches are agonizing enough, but the soft press of her lips against my jaw just about does me in. She kisses my cheek like she can stitch my heart back together, soothing the ache with a balm of her own invention.

She starts to slip away, but I don't want to lose her so quickly. I turn my face until my mouth meets hers in a gentle slide. My fingers drift through her hair to hold her to me as though if I don't, she might float away. I recognize the terrible timing, where we are—but I want this soft moment with her.

Sweet, chaste kisses pass between us, like she's giving me comfort in every one. Reminding me she's here for me. I'm not alone in this. I press my forehead to hers and breathe her in, gratitude for her tonight filling me up to overflowing.

The sound of the door latch pulls us apart. We watch each other in the dim porch light, both of us probably looking less than totally casual as the stone yard owner and his wife leave the house. They turn at the front steps, but if anything looks amiss between us, they don't show it.

"Goodnight, you two." They walk down the path to the sidewalk and are gone.

We sit for a minute, my pulse thrumming in my ears, my heart torn in two directions at once.

Hope pushes the blanket off of her shoulders. "I should probably go, too."

I want to persuade her to stay, but I need to get back inside with Caleb and Mom. I'd promised them I wouldn't hide out tonight, and I had anyway. I have no regrets, but I can't avoid our guests inside much longer.

"I'll walk you to your car."

We cross the yard and turn the corner in silence. Her hand slips against mine like a tentative question. I hold onto her even though I'm not entirely sure of the right answer.

She stops in front of a red Jeep Cherokee. "This is me."

"Thanks for coming tonight."

"Thanks for letting me share a few memories."

She moves into my space, arms wide, and I pull her to me. Has anyone else ever felt so perfect against me? I can't remember. Can't think of anything but the sweetness of Hope's arms around me. Once again, she's giving me comfort I hadn't known I needed.

She finally draws back, brushing dark hair away from her face. "You don't have to work on the Wonderland stuff this weekend, okay?"

Her offer feels awfully close to a pity smile. "Are you going to be working on it?"

"Some of the time, yeah."

"Then I'll be there, too."

Her frown almost makes me laugh, which probably would earn me something worse than just a frown.

"Seriously. You've done so much work this week, you deserve a break."

I hitch a shoulder. "My boss gave me a key so I can work when it's convenient."

After the Doubting Duo laid out their concerns about Hope's success, I can't just sit on my hands all weekend. When Caleb and I get back from fishing tomorrow morning, I plan to head over to the warehouse to get a few more hours in at least.

I'm not working on this project to satisfy my mom anymore, and it isn't for kids who still believe in Santa Claus. It's all for Hope.

"Okay, well. Don't overdo it."

"I'll be careful not to strain my back."

Her frown morphs into a laugh. "Goodnight, Griffin."

"Goodnight, boss."

SIXTEEN
HOPE

I REALLY, *really* can't wait for Abby to show up for her shift at The Painted Daisy so I can go over to the warehouse. Only because I'm so eager to see Griffin's latest progress on the Winter Wonderland, and get a few hours of painting in. That's all. It has nothing to do with our sweet porch kisses that have been playing in my head like that Mariah Carey Christmas song on repeat.

Wow. Now I'm trying to lie to myself.

But the text I got first thing this morning makes it hard to just dive right in and think about the truth.

> Mom: I heard you and a certain handyman have been having lunch together around town
>
> Mom: Bring him by the house for dinner some night
>
> Mom: Find out his favorite meal and I'll plan on it

I texted back a feeble protest that we're not dating, but Mom's favorite state is willful ignorance.

When there's a lull in Blackbird's Saturday morning pie frenzy, I wander over to their side of the pass-through. Wren wipes down the counters while Tess slices fresh pies for the display case. They both wear purple aprons with an outline of three little birds perched on a pie on the front.

"I have five dollars, and all I want in the world is an apple strudel hand pie." I wave the bill in the air like an old-timey lady waving her handkerchief at a naval captain.

Wren's sympathetic look lets me know I'm already too late. "We're all out of hand pies. We've got a couple of cupcakes left though."

"All I want in the world is a cupcake."

She sets one on the counter, and I slide her the bill. I peel away the paper, and my mouth waters at the sight of that rich chocolate cake. Their mom has the genius touch with pies, but Tess's gift is with cupcakes. She's only been selling them in the shop for a few months, but every flavor I've tried makes my eyes roll into the back of my head from deliciousness.

I take a massive bite, doing my best to avoid getting frosting all over my face. Pure bliss.

"Is that caramel buttercream?" I ask before digging in for my next bite.

Tess closes up the freshly-stocked display case. "It's my latest combination. We'll see if people like it."

I moan a little bit while I chew and swallow. "The only way someone could not like it is if they've had their taste buds surgically removed."

Tess beams at that too-faint praise. "I'll count that as a *yes* vote."

Wren eyes me. "Do you need another? You downed that in sixty seconds flat."

"Might have been less." I grab a napkin and swipe it across

GENNY CARRICK

my lips. I worked through lunch and needed the snack. Empty calories still count.

"Are you here to tell us the latest on your handyman situation?" Wren shoots me a finger gun so I can't miss what info she's fishing for.

"I heard you've got some unexpected help over there." Tess's arch look says she heard more than just that.

A spike of fear lodges in my chest, making my smile go tight. I tell it to cool it, but I need a minute. These are my two oldest friends, and I know anything I tell them won't leave this bakery. But after last summer, even that small hint of gossip among friends feels too close to being ambushed by the Spanish Inquisition.

I blow out a breath and try to play it casual. I really do. But Wren's slow grin proves my face is no better than fingerprints all over a crime scene. I can't come up with a good denial with that much evidence against me.

"Why do I get the feeling you don't hate him as much as you used to?" Wren says.

"I didn't hate him." Not even in my worst moments, but that's probably not the part I need to clarify. "We're just kind of...you know. Spending time together."

Might as well have signed a written confession.

Wren's mouth pops open. "You kissed your handyman?"

"You did what?" Tess cuts in.

"I never said that!" Clearly, I don't have the first clue about playing things casual.

Wren points at me. "Your *face* said that. And you didn't deny it."

Now I probably look pathetically smug. "No. I didn't deny it."

They make excited sounds, encouraging me to spill my guts. I tell them about last night, to a point. They get a little more serious when they hear about the subdued setting, and I don't mention how Griffin revealed his soft underbelly to me.

Everything I know of him says sharing his feelings even as much as he did is a huge deal. The trouble is, after one small taste, I've already become addicted, and all I can think about is when I can get my next fix.

"It was sweet, but it was really just a comfort thing. I wanted to make him feel better."

"So?" Wren says, her saucy smile growing wider. "Did you make him feel better?"

My cheeks burst into flame, and I throw my hands in the air. "That's all you get now. I'm going to zip my lips from now on. Consider yourself cut off."

"Aw, come on." She pouts at me. "You know I'm jealous. It's been months and months since my last kiss."

"You don't want to know how long it's been for me," Tess says.

That puts things into perspective. Single mom dating is a whole different realm from just regular small-town dating.

"But seriously," Wren says. "I like this for you. I approve."

My heart shimmies in my chest, as though her approval has any actual weight to it. But then I remember who else voiced—or *texted*—her eager approval, and my heart settles back down.

"Mom beat you to it. Somebody saw us in town and reported back to her. She's halfway to a frenzy already." Her dinner invite hints don't bode well for the next time she *just happens* to see Griffin and me in town together.

"So don't let anybody in town see what you do next." Wren winks just in case her lascivious tone didn't get her point across.

"If you really like him," Tess says, "you can find a way to make it work and avoid the gossips."

"Does anybody ever truly avoid the gossips in this town?" I ask.

Wren leans forward, her elbows on the counter, her chin in her hands, grinning away. "All I'm hearing is you didn't argue about really liking him."

I narrow my eyes on her. "You're giving strong Helena Parrish vibes right now. We're just reluctant co-volunteers who have kind of become friends."

"Kissing friends," she helpfully reminds me.

My stomach tumbles with eager butterflies. I really, *really* liked that part of our new friendship. But I'm not sure how we can pursue something without being the talk of the town.

I know already how quickly gossip can destroy a promising relationship. I'm not looking for a repeat of that humiliation.

SEVENTEEN
HOPE

IS THERE anything more satisfying than rows and rows of paint swatches? All that bright color and untapped potential just calls to me. I run my fingers over the paper strips, imagining hues and textures laid out on canvas or wood. I didn't drop by the hardware store for my own projects, but I'm tempted to get a custom color anyway. Just in case.

"Why am I not surprised?" a voice says behind me.

I jump, but my stomach tumbles because that's not just any voice. I spin to face Griffin's wide smile.

"Makes sense to find you surrounded by color."

He's looking at me like I'm the prettiest painting he's ever seen. It's hard to believe we acted so chilly to each other just a few days ago. Because right now? He's got enough heat in his eyes to melt snowmen in a twenty-mile radius.

"I want another accent color for the bookshop. Just trying to decide which one."

He nods, his eyes skimming the paint chips over my shoulder before landing back on me. My heart glitters like it's full of sugar plum fairies dancing away. The hardware store isn't usually this warm, right?

He lifts the small plastic bucket he's holding. It's full of metal pieces like he went trick or treating at a scrapyard. "I needed more fasteners. Are you headed to the warehouse after?"

"Yup. I plan to paint the rest of the day away." I hitch a shoulder. "Or at least until I have to meet with the Christmas market volunteers tonight."

His easy smile thins. "It's Saturday night."

"It's the only time everyone had available."

"When do you get more than a minute to relax?"

I flash a big smile. "Painting relaxes me."

He narrows his eyes at me, refusing to swallow my lies. To be fair, it's not a lie—I truly do find painting relaxing. But I can tell he wouldn't like to hear that the only downtime I get right now is when I'm asleep, and I'm not even getting the recommended daily allowance of that.

I'm about to reassure him I'm totally fine when suddenly, I'm very much *not* fine. My mother's voice drifts to us from the front of the store. She's greeting Luke Bridger, who was at the counter when I walked in, and probably anyone else up there. I can't see her because of the tall shelves back here, but I'd know her voice anywhere.

The warm glow my heart was basking in freezes right up. This is not good.

I grab Griffin's elbow and steer him deeper into the store. Nobody's in the moving supplies and tarps, but I can't expect that luck to hold out.

"What is she doing here?" I whisper. I try to tap into some kind of super-hearing to figure out what she's after, but I can't make it out. It'd be just my luck she actually needs a tarp and stumbles right on us.

The judgey looks Griffin sent my way over my busy work schedule have transformed into confusion. "What's wrong?"

"Shh." He's being entirely too loud for sneaking around. No stealth. "My mom's here."

"So?"

Kat must be one of those non-meddling moms. If she saw us together back here, she'd probably say hello and move on with her day. No big deal. If *my* mom sees us together, she'll turn it into something way more than just two volunteers buying supplies for the Christmas festival. It will be romantic and sweet and fill her head with all kinds of gooey scenarios ending with Griffin and I saying *I do*.

I don't want to give her a reason to sink any further into her daydreams than she already is.

"I think she's getting closer."

He tilts his head toward me and drops his voice. "Why are we whispering?"

Maybe I could slip into the bathroom until she leaves? But that would leave Griffin wide open. She'd probably double down on her dinner invite, and without me there to run interference, he'd be trapped.

Nope. The only option is for both of us to hide out.

I grab his hand. "Come with me."

We reach the end of the store aisles. There's a short hallway with three doors leading off of it. One's the bathroom, the next I discovered just a few weeks ago opens into the stockroom and lumber portion of the hardware store, and I don't know what the third is. The first two options are no good, so I open the third door.

A mop handle falls forward, and I catch it. It's a closet. There's not much here—some cleaning supplies, a small shelf stacked with things like register tape and pens. It's tiny, but it's good enough.

I wave him along. "In here, please."

His eyebrows are practically at his hairline. I get it. I do. I'm acting like a crazy person, inviting him into a strange closet for reasons unknown, but the alternative is so much worse. If Mom sees us together, she'll start an avalanche of gossip that will crush us flat. Neither of us needs that.

"Hope, what—"

I clamp my hand over his mouth and look past him into the store. I don't see anyone yet, but I have no idea what Mom's in here for, or where she's headed. She could walk around that corner any second. If she sees us, whatever hope I had of something normal with Griffin will blast apart.

"Please just get inside," I whisper.

He smiles beneath my hand that's still covering his mouth. I suck in a breath, my skin warm and tingly everywhere I touch him, but now is not the time. Thankfully, he takes two steps backward into the closet. I follow him inside and pull the door shut. Tilting my head toward the door, I listen for a second, but I can't hear anything out there. This might be worse than before.

Actually...this is absolutely worse. Griffin and I are practically pressed together in the cramped space. We have nowhere to go, and nothing to look at but each other.

Didn't I say just a week ago I wanted minimal eye contact with this man? Yet here I am, staring into hazel-green perfection for everything I'm worth.

"If you wanted to kiss me again, all you had to do was ask."

I glare at him, but my cheeks warm with the blush that must be crawling across my face. Kissing's probably the most logical conclusion when a woman pushes a guy into a tiny closet. Seven Minutes in Heaven, right? Not that I ever played that game.

"That's not what this is about."

"Are you sure?" He looks down, and I realize I've fisted my hands in his barn jacket. "I'm game if you are."

"Sorry." I release his coat and step back. Well, I try to step back—there's nowhere to go, and I just press up against the closet door. Which makes me think about *him* pressing me up against the closet door. Which doesn't help me stop blushing.

"Okay, so why are we hiding out from your mom?"

It looks like my big scheme only managed to swap one embarrassment for another. "I don't love having to tell you this."

"You don't want to be seen with the former arsonist?" He's got a smirk on his face, but his eyes aren't laughing.

"It's not about you," I say before he can go on thinking I'm worried about something he did years ago. My issue is a little more recent. "It's me. Remember how you heard I was engaged?"

He shifts like he's trying to give me more room, but we're sharing about two square feet of floor space. "I remember."

Nerves crawl up my back to settle around my ribs. I hate this story, but I can't keep it from him forever. Especially when I've forced him into *this* ridiculous scenario.

"I don't know if you noticed, but my mom is a little bit over the top. She's like that about everything in my life: work, relationships, you name it. She's way too enthusiastic about my dating life and goes overboard the second she hears me even say I met someone."

He nods, probably remembering the way she'd tried so hard to push us together for a date last week.

"Last summer, she got really excited about a guy I was seeing in Bend and told everybody I had found *the one*. And I mean *everybody*."

I'd never had a piece of gossip about me get so much traction. There were probably people in this town who had no idea I'd opened a store on Maple Street, but I doubt you could find one who hasn't heard something about Mark.

"He turned up in town for our fourth date, and someone called him my fiancé to his face. Nothing I said could convince him I wasn't the crazy one thinking we were going to get married. No surprise I never heard from him again."

I shudder thinking about the way he'd gone white as a ghost when Silas—my sweet, well-meaning, busted up handyman—had called him my fiancé. As soon as he'd walked away, Mark's switch had flipped from horrified to furious. *"You seemed like a nice girl, but you're a psycho."* He'd blocked me before he even got to his car.

"If Mom sees us together, she's going to draw conclusions no matter what I tell her, and then the whole town will be involved." I gesture helplessly, accidentally brushing my fingers across his glorious, flannel-covered stomach. This conversation isn't going right, but it probably all went wrong when I shoved him into the closet. "Whether a relationship is good or bad, everybody knows about it. Everybody has something to say. I just want something to be mine for a change."

Ever so slowly, his lips tug up into a smirk. "That almost sounds like you want *me* to be yours."

"That wasn't exactly what I meant." I must be the worst liar ever, because that was *exactly* what I meant.

He puts one hand on the closet door by my head and leans in a touch. It might have only been an inch, but that small shift turns my bones to jelly. I'm pretty sure my legs are too weak to move, but I wouldn't even if I could.

"I'm thinking we should spend time together outside of the warehouse and this closet," he says. "What are you doing after your Christmas market thing tonight?"

"Going straight to bed."

His eyebrows tick up. I laugh and grab his open coat again.

"That wasn't flirting. I mean, it's going to be a late night." But I don't want to slam the door on his would-be invitation. I'm not sure I even care what he's inviting me *to*, I just want him to know he can ask again. "Another time?"

He nods. "Another time."

But he goes right on staring at my mouth. We're competing again, but now we're waiting to see who'll cave first in the world's sexiest game of chicken. A shiver ripples across my skin. Maybe I should play to lose.

A knock sounds right behind my head, and we break apart. I bump into the shelves of front counter supplies, and a roll of register tape thumps onto the floor.

"Uh, guys?" a muffled voice says. It's Luke Bridger, the generous owner of this store who donated all of the lumber and supplies to make the Winter Wonderland possible—and now he knows I was hiding out in his closet with Griffin. "I need something out of there."

I spin around, my pride shriveling into a pathetic little prune, and open the door. Luke stands on the other side, one hand covering his eyes as he looks toward the store as if he fully expects to find us naked in here.

I have some pride left. Not much, but I'll cling to it.

"We weren't doing anything!" My blurting game is strong today. "We just needed..."

What, Hope? What could you have possibly needed that you would drag a man into a closet with you to get?

Luke peeks at me, but he's smiling a touch now. "You don't need to tell me."

"I'm so sorry, we were just...having a private conversation."

"My supply closet really isn't the best place for that."

Griffin bends down to get the stray roll of register tape and puts it back on the shelf. "Next time, we'll take it outside."

He sounds more amused than mortified. That tracks.

My plan to keep us flying under the radar is off to a great start.

EIGHTEEN

GRIFFIN

MY SMILE IS DANGEROUSLY SMUG when I see a text from Hope Sunday morning. It's not another one of the waffle emojis she's sent a couple of times. It's better.

> Hope: Do you know anything about electric trains?

Caleb and I used to have a set, but I haven't played with one since I was ten years old. I think I know where her question is headed, though.

> Griffin: Sure

> Hope: Can you help me set one up? A big one?

It's probably a good thing she can't see me as I type.

> Griffin: Just say when and where

She sends an address, and I throw on my heavy-duty flannel jacket and head out the door. Ten minutes later, I pull up in front of the old department store and find Hope's red Jeep already out front. She was probably here when she texted. Late night last night, constant early mornings—does the woman ever sleep?

I climb out of my truck and go to the department store door. It's propped open with a block of wood, and I knock on the glass as I pull it open.

Hope appears, her dark hair pulled up into a loose bun, wearing a grotesque orange Oregon State University sweatshirt with a pair of tired jeans that have gone ragged at the knees. Seeing her in something so casual, my brain pops and fizzes like she's poured water over my hard drive.

"Are you ready for this?" she asks. With her looking like this, I'm ready for just about anything. She pulls me through the door and into the huge, empty space. "Look."

I struggle to draw my eyes away from her when she's so relaxed and delectable, smiling at me like we're old friends. Or new, very close friends.

I want the second option.

Finally, I look where she's pointing, but I don't know what I'm seeing. A dozen boxes dot the empty department store's ratty old carpet, each with a picture of a vintage electric train on it. The boxes look at least as old as the department store itself, the aging cardboard criss-crossed with yellowing tape.

"What is all this?"

"Fred Deckard's trains." Her voice is low like we're in a museum. "These are just the ones he was willing to loan me."

"He's got more than these? That's dedication."

"You have no idea. He has an insane amount of trains, some in glass cases. His basement has a very creepy Smithsonian vibe to it."

"What are you doing with these?"

"*We*," she says, gesturing between the two of us, "are going to set up a Christmas scene in the picture window. I got permission from the bank to use the storefront during the festival. I convinced them it was free advertising for possible buyers of the building."

"Smart."

"My mom's the agent, so it made sense. Anyway, I have this whole classic Christmas toy store idea in my head, and New to You has offered some of their vintage toys to display in the window, also up for sale." She frowns at the array of boxes spread across the floor. "But I've never set up a train before, and I don't know the first thing about it."

"That's where I come in," I deadpan.

"Exactly."

I've never had a little white lie bite me in the butt so fast. I probably know less than she does about trains at this point, but I kneel in front of one of the boxes and start to open it. "Might as well see what we're up against."

"Wait!" Hope grabs my shoulder and kneels down next to me on the shabby carpet. This floor has seen some things. "Mr. Deckard has ground rules about the trains."

"Ground rules," I repeat, wondering what possesses a man to spend his life collecting trains nobody's allowed to use. Mostly though, my thoughts focus on Hope's warm hand resting on my shoulder and the way her arm drapes casually against my back. In this moment, I'm not thinking much about rules of any kind.

"Yes, ground rules," she says, oblivious to the direction of my thoughts. "All the boxes are catalogued, so anything we take out of one has to go back in the same box when we're done. There's no mix and match. Also, he's very concerned about them getting damaged, so we have to be ultra-careful or I think he might sue me."

"Why didn't he set them up himself if he's so worried?"

"He said he doesn't have the energy for it. But *you*," she says, gently shaking my shoulder, "you've got loads of energy."

"You don't have to keep buttering me up. I'm already here."

She puts one hand to my forehead. "Are you feeling okay? It doesn't seem like you to turn down praise."

My smile is probably the smuggest. "I am feeling warm."

She shoves my shoulder and carries on.

I'm feeling warm? I sure hope my brain is in one of these boxes.

We open each box to assess the contents and decide which trains will be best for the display Hope has in mind. Along with the assortment of train pieces, Mr. Deckard loaned her bins full of little buildings, trees, and tiny figurines to complete the scene.

There's no halfway with Hope. I can't help but be drawn to that.

The big display window is about fifteen feet across and three feet deep, giving us plenty of real estate to fill. Using the window during the festival is a clever choice on her part. Sitting dark and empty, it would just accentuate the vacant spaces downtown, but bright and filled with Christmas-themed spectacle, it can only add to the magic.

Sunbeams cut across the floor, peeking through tiny strips between sheets of craft paper taped to the windows. The department store has been vacant for a while, but the paper is crisp and new.

Now that I look at it, the entire display area is freshly scrubbed. The woodwork shines, and although I'd expect a network of cobwebs to lace the upper reaches of glass, the corners are spotless.

"Did you clean all this?"

"Yeah." She pulls a bundle of green felt out of one of the bins. "It was pretty disgusting. I don't think anything has been touched in here since Henderson's went out of business. Just pretend there weren't mouse droppings all over the floor up until eight this morning."

No wonder the carpet looks so rough.

She gasps and pulls something out of the bin. Hurrying over to me, delight dances across her face. "He has a tiny Christmas tree! We have to use this."

"A Christmas scene within a Christmas display within a Christmas festival. This is getting too meta for me."

"It's perfect, and you know it."

"I have to say, boss, I'm starting to enjoy your sassy side."

"It's one of my better features." She smirks and returns to the box of tiny treasures, bending over as she searches. I ponder her other fine features for a minute before she turns around to show off another find. "A truck hauling a Christmas tree!"

"If anything goes missing out of that box, I'm ratting you out to Fred Deckard in a heartbeat."

I'd hoped touching the electric trains would recall some long-forgotten muscle memory, and I would set them up without hesitation. The reality is, I'm fumbling track pieces around and have no idea if the train sets can all be run together, or if they're even compatible types.

Hope picked out two red engines that look the most Christmas-like to her and laid out her selection of cars off to one side. I don't have the heart to break it to her I'm not sure I can maneuver multiple trains on the same tracks without crashing them in a tiny ball of electric fire.

Her eyes stay on me as I try to lay out a fancy loop. No matter how I put the track together, I can't make it work. The pieces just don't seem to fit snug enough to keep the trains from derailing, and I don't want to risk a trial run that seems doomed to failure.

She leans against the windowsill, staring hard at me. After a few minutes, her amused scrutiny gets the best of me.

"What?"

"You don't know what you're doing, do you?"

I try to look offended. "Excuse me?"

"This." She gestures with a piece of track at my poor progress. She has grand dreams of interlacing tracks with tunnels disappearing into snowy, toy-covered mountains, and I don't even have half a figure-eight laid out yet. "You don't know how to set the trains up."

"What makes you say that?" Answering a question with a question—the last resort of a cornered man.

"Your face," she says with a laugh. "Your mouth is all twisted, and your eyes are scrunched up like you're trying to do calculus problems in your head."

"They are not." I relax the muscles in my face, but it's too late now.

"Oh, your concentration face is cute."

Cute. Not my first choice of description, but I'll take it. "Is it so different from my usual face?"

She squares off against me, looking me full in the face. Her gaze roams over my forehead, sticking an extra second on the bruise, then down my nose, until at last she lingers on my mouth. Under the harsh fluorescent light, I can't miss the sweep of pink on her cheeks. My pulse ticks up a notch.

This is not the place for a kiss, with the musty odor and the slight risk of Hantavirus.

Doesn't stop me from wanting one.

"I think it's pretty much the same face." The twist of a smile on her teasing mouth has me ready to lean in and go for broke, when her eyes snap back to mine. "Should I call Mr. Deckard to give us some pointers?"

"No, we can do this." I'm not about to have her call Mr. Deckard for help. Asking an old man in a recliner for help from across town is anything but cute. And I want an upgrade to *sexy*.

"I like that *we*, teammate." The flirtatious spark in her grin again makes my heart go wild, urging me to do something about it.

"Oh, there's a hierarchy here," I say, leaning a touch closer. "Never doubt you're in charge."

Her cheeks go so red, I'm tempted to check *her* forehead for fever. But touching her will lead to kissing her, and I just promised her we can sort this out. Getting sidetracked won't get us any closer to her goal of a magical Christmas display.

Even if, at this point, kissing her again is the only goal I have in mind.

NINETEEN
HOPE

OKAY, so maybe my big plan of multiple trains passing each other on interlocking paths in a perfect Christmas scene was a little too ambitious for our skill set. Some of the train boxes have instructions in them, but they don't cover the elaborate project I had in mind. We have three instruction booklets opened up in the window and no idea between us how to make the simplest combination track.

Griffin agreed to meet me awfully quickly for someone who doesn't know the first thing about electric trains. It could just be his Type A, Mr. Manager personality shining through. Boss Griffin, come out to take charge of the project. But I'm hoping he agreed for the same reason I'd asked him in the first place.

"This doesn't look right."

He frowns at the tracks in his hands, trying to get the ends to snap together. He shakes his head at the results as though this train is serious business. Maybe he hadn't liked me using the word cute, but seeing him so disconcerted is adorable. In the warehouse, he's always so tough and in control. I like seeing this glimpse of uncertainty.

"Let's see if we can get a little assist from the good old internet."

He pulls out his phone and calls up YouTube. After a quick search, he finds some videos for beginner vintage train enthusiasts. I huddle next to him, trying to keep up as Engine&Tonic77 talks trains.

I can't focus on much of anything beyond his body against mine, all hard muscle that sends my thoughts drifting. He smells good, too, the lightest hint of mint and spice, with a trace of sawdust from his work in the warehouse. Griffin McBride is just straight-up sexy, even when standing in the middle of a somewhat dank, mouse-infested department store.

I need to remind Mom to do something about the mice before she tries to show the store again. A vermin infestation would kill interest pretty quickly.

"This one looks good." He thumbs a video for a compressed figure-eight, with the track crossing in the center of the scene and loops running parallel to the window. The layout would make good use of the space and shouldn't outreach our limited time and abilities. Once we have a couple of trains weaving in and out of vintage toys, it should be reasonably impressive, even if it isn't the dream window I'd originally imagined.

We keep the video on repeat as we lay out each track piece, double-checking where everything goes. When we finally have it ready, Griffin sets both engines on the tracks in preparation for our test run. If all goes to plan, they'll circle the tracks and cross in the center with plenty of room to spare.

If things don't go to plan, Mr. Deckard will add our heads to the display shelves in his basement.

Griffin rests his hand on the train switch, ready to get the party started. "Do you want to say a few words?"

I look to the ceiling, pressing my palms together in front of my chest. "Please, God, bless these crash test dummies."

"Amen."

He throws the switch, and the trains come to life with a spark and a whirr of electricity. They jostle along the tracks, pulling their cars behind as they navigate the straightaway and the first curves. I squeeze my hands together as they pass each other and switch tracks, completing the figure-eight.

Griffin lets out a whoop and holds his hands up for a double high-five. I slap them, and he curls his fingers around mine as we bask in the glow of our hard-earned success. He lowers our hands to shoulder height, and the high-five shifts into something else.

His gaze zeroes in on my mouth like we have unfinished business. We did kind of leave things hanging after the closet fiasco. He leans closer, the breath between us slowly shrinking in a tantalizing dare. Will I give in?

That's a resounding *yes.*

I stretch up to reach him and my eyes nearly drift shut, but before we make contact, a tinny sound of metal hitting metal breaks us apart. Both trains lie on their sides across the tracks.

"I guess we celebrated too soon." Griffin switches off the trains, and we examine each car, searching for any evidence of the crash. "They look okay, though."

"What was that you said earlier about ratting me out to Mr. Deckard?" I run one finger along the side of one of the engines but can't feel any scratches. If Mr. Deckard gets out a magnifying glass, all bets are off.

"I'll keep this one just between us."

"Maybe we should just do one train." It's a bit of a letdown, honestly, but it will still look pretty cool.

"We can get it." He goes through the video again, making slight adjustments until the trains go around the track without threat of collision. This time, we just make jazz hands over the tracks.

Griffin switches it back off. "That's lunch."

"You really like being the lunch break police, don't you?"

"I really like eating lunch. How about sandwiches?"

"Perfect. Um...do you mind if we eat them here?"

His low opinion of this idea twists his mouth as he looks around the empty store. But when his eyes land on me again, I'm practically begging.

"I can keep working while you're gone, and we'll get more done that way," I add.

His eyes soften, and I know he's thinking about my confession yesterday. There's only so many work lunches we can take together before people start making pointed commentary. Well...*more* pointed commentary.

"Sure."

When he leaves, I move to the treasures I'd set aside from the tiny houses, trees, and figures. For all his fears, Mr. Deckard gave me plenty to work with. I'd almost expected him to lend out the most beat-up items in his collection, but I suspect he's shared some of the best. Maybe they aren't glass case-worthy, but I have no shortage of fabulous little buildings to choose from.

When Griffin returns with sandwiches from the deli, I have the makings of a town coming to life in Henderson's window. Tiny brick buildings line up on either side of the split train tracks, but it isn't anywhere close to finished.

"What's all this?" He glances it over and gives me a funny look. "You're making Sunshine?"

"If I can't have interlocking trains and mountain passes, I'll settle for a tiny replica of Maple Street, complete with town square at one end."

"Where we're going to put that Christmas tree you found."

"You know it."

We lean against the window and eat our turkey and cranberry sandwiches in a hurry, careful not to get anything on the collection. A crash was bad enough without adding mustard stains to our list of infractions.

"What gave you the idea to do this?" he asks between bites. "You said you're trying to recapture the old magic, but we never had a toy display window like this in town when we were growing up."

I'd love to entice a toy shop to open up downtown, but that's a task for another time.

"Don't laugh."

"No promises."

I glare, but he just grins back.

"I won't laugh, tell me."

"I love the opening scene in *A Christmas Story*, when all the kids have their noses pressed against the glass of the toy shop window. I always wanted to see a window like that, and I never have." When I was little, I wanted to *live* in a window like that, but seeing one will be a close second.

"So you're making one."

"Pretty much. Is that weird?"

"No, it's..." He looks like he can't light on the right word. "I think it's just like you."

"I'm not hearing a no to *weird*."

"I'm impressed. What you're making will be better than we ever had."

Oh. Okay, then.

Finishing the town with its minuscule decorations and inhabitants turns out to be a painstaking process. For every tiny fir tree I add, I knock two more down. I move in slow motion to avoid collisions, filling out the scene piece by agonizing piece. Griffin is less meticulous, and when I look over, he's nearly finished his side.

"How are you doing that?"

"I've got some experience with building neighborhoods in record time."

He moves closer to help with my side of mini-Sunshine. I'm painfully aware of him, afraid I might bump into him and start a chain reaction. First the little trees will start falling—then I will start falling. That near-kiss is under my skin, and I can't shake it.

Eventually, we climb out of the completed window and stretch. His work might be fast, but nothing is out of place. He even put the truck hauling the Christmas tree in a prime viewing spot at the front of the window.

"What else do you have planned for the display?"

"I'll wrap some empty cardboard boxes with Christmas paper and bows to put in the back of the scene, and string lights overhead. I've got my eye on some vintage toys from the antiques shop, and a few felt dolls from my shop. I found a couple of room dividers at the thrift store, and I'll drape them with black fabric so when people look in the window, they'll only see the wonder of Christmas, not the sad, empty department store behind it."

"Good idea. Keep the mouse droppings on the down low."

"Mice are only cute at Christmas when they're ruining and then fixing singing clocks for Santa."

"I have no idea what you're talking about, but sure."

I shake my head in disappointment, because that cartoon is a classic. "I feel sorry for your childhood."

He watches me with that odd look again, like he's trying to add something together and he's coming up short.

"What?"

"You're not skipping any details. It's more than a lot of people would do for a volunteer position."

"I don't know if it's enough." That question hasn't stopped hounding me. I wanted it to be this rousing success, something that will spread to all the stores in town, but right now, I can't be sure of anything. Like Griffin said when he first signed on—maybe I should have aimed lower.

He gently takes my elbow like he needs me to listen. Tilting his head down to capture my gaze, his eyes burn into mine like flames. "Hey. Take a compliment. You're working hard on this, and it shows."

His praise blooms through my chest, drowning out the whispering critiques that have followed me around since I started this project.

"I guess if I'm winning over your skeptical heart, it's high praise."

His mouth quirks up. "You're winning over my skeptical heart, all right."

Unfair of him to burst *my* heart into a cloud of pixie dust like that. Wren's advice to "run with it" swims through my mind. I plan to, just...maybe not in this specific building.

He drops his hand and gestures to the train display. "Is that it for the Window Wonderland for today?"

"I think we're good."

We step out into the brisk evening, and I lock up the store. With our trial and error, plus the YouTube videos, it took longer to get everything set up than I expected, and the light has faded to a deepening purple. We spent all day together working on the trains when I hadn't meant to make him work weekends at all if I could help it.

"Thanks for being my angel of electric trains. I'm sorry I took up your whole day."

"I'm not."

Funny how the cocky tilt of his mouth drove me crazy a week ago, and now I want to kiss it.

"Do you want to come over to my place?"

He freezes. My invitation sounded a lot more suggestive than I'd intended it. My husky voice didn't help, and the words themselves hold any number of meanings. I need to narrow it down a bit.

"Just to hang out. You know, have dinner. Maybe watch *A Christmas Story*. I kind of owe you for helping me today."

"You want to hang out?" His voice is low and mock-sultry.

"Don't make me take it back." Even though, when he talks to me like this, I'm not likely to deny him much of anything.

"You're not taking it back. I accept your invitation to hang out." He steps closer, and his eyes go dark in that freshly-whacked-with-a-two-by-four look. "But not because you owe me anything for today."

Pretty sure I have the same look in my eyes. "Then just come over because I'm asking."

"Lead the way."

TWENTY
GRIFFIN

HOW MUCH CAN I think about kissing Hope's mouth without being obvious about it?

The answer turns out to be—not very much.

I followed her Jeep through side streets until she pulled up in front of a big old Victorian house. We get out and take careful steps up the uneven walk to a big wraparound porch. Up here, I see the Victorian has been partitioned out into multiple apartments, and she leads me to a door with a rust and red wreath hung beneath the window. She glances over her shoulder at me, and I get an odd feeling about being invited into her home, like not just any guy gets to see this side of her.

Or maybe I'm just standing too close to her on the porch.

"This is it." She pushes the door open and flips on the lights.

I blink at the sudden shock. It looks like a paint set exploded in here. In a good way, but it's a lot to take in. Bright paintings line every wall, a blanket with rainbow zig-zags splashes over one end of the dark blue sofa, and a wildly colored area rug sits beneath a vivid teal coffee table. The colorful apartment is like a physical manifestation of the cheer Hope spreads everywhere she goes.

"Wow." I'm at a loss for more.

"I like color."

As if an explanation is necessary. My apartment is...well, nothing compared to this. I've got a couple of framed photos of mountains around the Pacific Northwest hung up, but I didn't put much thought behind it. It's not exactly a spark of life. Maybe I need a hot pink ceramic llama on my coffee table.

"This is great," I say once I get my bearings. "I like it."

She shrugs out of her coat and hangs it on a hook by the door, so I do the same with mine.

"It's not for everyone."

I *tsk*. "No tractors on the walls, though."

"Not yet, but you never know."

I step closer to one of the canvases. I don't want to admit it, but she'd been pretty much on the money with her first assessment of my tastes—I'm not an abstract guy. I like facts and figures, tangible goals and clear end results. This painting is all color and no *thing*. I don't know how to judge something like that. The colors are nice enough, but what can you say about splotches of paint? But knowing Hope had made those splotches, I can't help but like them.

An easel stands on the other side of the small living room with a painting propped on it. This one I can appreciate a bit more—it shows a deep burgundy armchair with a floppy stuffed ostrich sitting on it. The scene is simple but soft, and I get the feeling that ostrich has been loved on by a very special little kid.

How did she capture that? I would barely be able to describe that kind of feeling, let alone paint it.

"What do you think?"

She has one corner of her bottom lip in her mouth worrying it, and I have the urge to take her lip in my mouth, too. I wouldn't be nearly as rough as she is with those soft lips.

She bobs her eyebrows at me. Right. She asked a question—and I've been staring at her mouth again, being obvious.

I nod interest and pretend like I have some knowledge of art. "They're colorful. Interesting. I feel like I could give this one a hug."

I gesture at the stuffed ostrich.

Her answering smile makes my chest heat, like just making her happy is a massive win. Maybe I should go around the room and compliment every painting until her true smile stays on her face for good.

"What do you think of spaghetti?"

It takes me a second to follow her question. She pulls a pot out of a cupboard, and I remember the point of this visit. Not art appreciation, and not kissing.

Well...that wasn't the point of her *invitation*. What we do with the rest of the evening remains to be seen.

"Spaghetti sounds good."

"Normally, I'd make something a little more complex, but lately I've been resorting to the classics." She sets the pot in the sink and fills it with water. "Some nights, I hardly have enough energy to make a peanut butter and jelly sandwich before I fall into bed."

I move into the small kitchen to stand right beside her. "Don't tell me you forget dinner, too."

"No, but sometimes it's not much more than toast and jam."

It's too easy for her to overlook her own needs like that. "You need to take better care of yourself."

She shrugs off my advice and puts the pot on the stove. "I'm fine."

She admitted to regularly missing meals, and she put in a full day's work today, even though it's the only day her store is closed. I don't want to think about how many days she's up at six doing something for the festival. She's working herself too hard, all for the sake of an event that might end in bitter disappointment. Even if the Christmas festival were a raging success, it wouldn't be worth this level of self-sacrifice.

"You're running yourself ragged. Sit down."

Her sweet smile holds a spark of challenge. "This is my house, you know."

Groaning, I pull my fingers through my hair. Here I am trying to take charge of her, even off the clock. I don't want to order her around. I want to take care of her, protect her, get some food into her so she can relax for a solid minute.

I...am deeply grateful I didn't say any of that out loud this time.

"It is your house," I agree, taking her gently by the elbow and leading her to the small dining table. "And you're going to sit down. Please."

She makes sure I don't miss her eye roll, but she sinks onto a dining chair. She still looks like she's running through all of her festival tasks in her head, but at least she's sitting. That's a step in the right direction.

"I salute your selflessness, but you deserve to eat meals, too."

"It's not selflessness. This could bring in a lot of revenue for downtown businesses, mine included. This was a calculated move. I'm not stupid, Griffin."

"I never thought you were stupid."

As fast as her eyebrows dart up, I know I've given her the impression I did. She's a lot of things in my mind, but stupid has never been one of them.

"Sincerely. That was part of why I liked challenging you so much back in school, because you *are* so smart." I throw my hand over my heart like I'm in the habit of making vows about stuff like this.

"Like the time you won the *Number One Debater* award out from under me? Because you think I'm so smart?"

"I said I like a challenge. I never said I like to lose."

She twists her mouth, shaking her head at me.

"The potential revenue is huge, but that's not the only thing." She grimaces, but that frown dissolves again in an instant. Her face is like an Etch-a-Sketch, and all it takes is a little shake to erase her emotions away. "We haven't had a really big Christmas celebration in almost fifteen years. Tourist dollars will be great, but even if it doesn't bring in a ton of money, it's going to be *fun*."

Doing it for fun is a terrible business strategy, but listening to her talk it up the last week has spread a little of her enthusiasm my way. Sunshine could use a celebration, and if she wants to be the one to give it to them, I can't argue. She's right, local businesses will benefit. Even a little bit could turn things around for a struggling small business owner.

"You still shouldn't have to work yourself into the ground."

"I'm not."

It's a testy response, like we've switched right back to our old dynamic. I lift an eyebrow at her, because if she thinks she can lie to me that obviously, she can think again.

"I have eyes, Hope. I've seen how much you're doing."

"Yes, I'm putting a lot into the festival, okay? It's just...I don't have a whole lot of successes behind me. I only stayed in Portland a couple of years before I ran back home. Then I worked a few jobs around here, but nothing stuck. I even got my realtor's license and tried working with my mom. When that didn't last, I couldn't walk three feet in town without people giving me these sad, judgmental looks. I think everyone expected The Painted Daisy to close up in the first six months."

Taking time to figure out what she wants to do for work shouldn't equate to being a failure, but I know as well as anyone it can be hard to shake the role people want to put you in.

"I thought, if I got this festival right, maybe I could change people's minds, and—" She groans, and shakes her head like she's edited her thoughts, crossing them out before she can say them. "It doesn't matter. The point is, I am going to give this town an amazing Christmas festival."

She smiles again, but it's empty.

"Why do you do that?" I ask gently.

"Do what?"

"Smile when you don't mean it. You flash fake smiles all the time."

The corners of her mouth fall. "Old habit, I guess."

"I'd rather know what you're really feeling than watch you play pretend." When she shows me the real Hope hiding behind the plastic smiles, I want more.

"The feeling is mutual."

The air in this small apartment feels too thick, too charged. I need to reroute this evening before we both reveal things we'd rather not admit. I rifle through her cupboards and finish preparing our dinner. I drain the spaghetti, pour warmed sauce into a bowl, and call it a meal. It's lucky she has simple tastes, or I would have been out of my depth when I commandeered her kitchen.

I set a plate in front of her and bring glasses of water to the table.

"I think this is the first time I've ever been served dinner in my own house."

"No boyfriend ever made dinner for you?" I don't know why I asked. I don't want to know a thing about it. The idea of some other man fixing meals for her doesn't do much for my appetite. I want to be the one taking care of her.

It's like being around her switches on my Neanderthal brain, and I can't think beyond the basics. Protect, provide, care. *Kiss* goes on there, too, but I'm trying to be a gentleman Neanderthal.

"Nope. There haven't been a ton of those to begin with."

Neanderthal that I am, that sends another shock of warmth through my chest. "What about wildly helpful handymen with dashing good looks?"

And there it is—her real smile. I can't stop staring at those pretty pink lips, so soft and full, like they're just waiting for me to grow a pair already and kiss her again—kiss her for real.

"There's only you."

I might tell myself I want to protect her, but my desire for her now speaks of something else entirely. I'll leave if she wants me to, but if she wants me to stay...

"Do you want to watch the movie?" she asks.

"Absolutely."

TWENTY-ONE
HOPE

I COULD GET USED to the caring side Griffin's shown me these last few days. He went out of his way to help me with the trains. He recognized I'm dead on my feet and fixed dinner for me—I could get in over my head with him.

Maybe I'm already halfway there.

I put on the movie, and we get comfortable on the couch. Not *too* comfortable—I leave space between us but can't decide if it's too much or too little. Secluded in my cozy apartment, *hanging out* isn't quite as straightforward as it'd seemed in front of the department store.

The movie starts up, with the old-fashioned cars driving through town, eventually zooming in on the children with their noses pressed up against the toy store window. The wonder, the awe, the barely contained joy—that's what I want for the festival.

"Okay," Griffin says. "I see the magic you're going for."

"See? You've got some nostalgia in you, after all."

He holds up his thumb and index finger a centimeter apart.

"What's your favorite Christmas movie?" I ask.

"*Die Hard.*"

I've got my hand raised between us before he can get out the second word. "Nope, *Die Hard* doesn't count. You can only choose from holiday movies where nobody gets shot in the head."

"Uh, it absolutely counts. *Die Hard* is the best Christmas movie there is."

I am incredulous. I should have expected it, but I'm still incredulous. "Buddy the Elf would disagree."

"Buddy the Elf would have been the first to go at Nakatomi Plaza."

He starts to put a foot up on my coffee table but glances over the debris spread across it. Library books, an empty water glass, an old set of oil pencils. He makes a harsh sound in the back of his throat, and I follow his gaze to my ceramic OSU coasters.

"I get the feeling you're not a Beavers fan," I say.

"University of Oregon Ducks all the way."

I make a sour face to match his disappointment. His warm laughter presses a nerve deep in my belly. It might be the best sound I've ever heard.

"So you have a disgusting Ducks fetish?" Yeah. If only the word "fetish" hadn't tumbled out of my mouth, that would be great.

"Something like that." His eyes are too bright, too intense, too focused on me. "What took you up to Portland after you finished at OSU? You don't really seem like the city type."

"You're saying I'm too small town?"

"Yes."

My mouth drops open. "You're not supposed to just answer straight out like that."

Not that I should expect anything less from him.

I consider bending the truth, but he's already called me out on my fibs, and fake smiles tonight. "I wanted to study art, but my parents didn't think that was a good career choice. Lila studied public relations, so I did marketing. When Mom pushed moving to Portland, I promised her I'd give it a try. She had such high hopes for me. She was sure I would hit my stride and blow everyone away."

I watch him carefully, but his expression doesn't change.

"This is where you say something sarcastic about me making career choices to please my parents," I prompt.

"I'm on shaky ground there myself. Some would say I went too far the other direction. My parents wanted me to go to OSU like Caleb did."

"Ah. So you chose their rival."

"It seemed like a good way to ease Dad into the idea of me going into construction. Sophomore year, I wound up dropping out and getting an apprenticeship, and then there was no way around it."

"Your dad didn't want you to go into construction?"

He leans forward to grab one of the coasters off the table, turning it in his hands. "Dad wanted me to stay right here and run the landscaping company with him and my brother."

"But you wanted something else."

He nods, watching the coaster. "I thought I wanted to do my own thing."

"Because you don't like letting anyone else be in charge?"

His eyes lock on mine. "Maybe."

"You've gotten used to having me in charge. You're taking my orders pretty well now."

He sets the coaster down and relaxes back against the couch. "You're a special case."

"I had to rough you up a little first. Prove who runs the show."

His eyes go all dark and hazy. When they drop to my mouth, my stomach breaks into cartwheels.

"You did do that, boss."

That short word was never meant to be so sexy.

He draws his thumb and forefinger along a lock of hair that's fallen from my bun. My body sparks to life beneath that soft touch, practically purring for more.

"Do I still have paint in my hair?" My voice sounds light as a breath. I am *not* subtle, but I do not care.

"No."

He traces his fingers along my jaw to my hairline, drawing nearer until all I can see are his eyes, intent on my mouth. That slow shift closer is a delicious tease that sets my skin on fire with want. Just before he reaches me, he pauses as if asking a question. I give him my answer by tilting my chin, urging him closer.

Yes, yes. One hundred percent.

Personal space, rational thought, hesitation—it all leaves my body when his lips meet mine. His mouth is decisive, guiding the kiss like he's leading a tour of all my favorite things. His fingers slip through my hair, cradling my head as he angles my chin, devoted to his task of leaving me totally unraveled.

I want to remember this moment, imprint it on my synapses to recall and savor a million more times, but my mind is too scrambled by everything we're doing to do more than experience it and hold on.

This kiss is unprecedented in my life—maybe in the history of time. I've never kissed anyone and thought *Yes! I was made to kiss this man!* But with Griffin, nothing has ever been so perfect. No one has ever left me so content yet wanting so much more.

My left hand moves along his arm and across his shoulder, my right trapped between us, pressing over his heart that races beneath a layer of buttery soft flannel. He likes being in control, but now I realize I much prefer him *out* of control. Knowing I've affected him as much as he's gotten to me? I think I'm drunk on it.

Somewhere in the background, Ralphie plots ways to get his BB gun. Flick gets stuck to the light pole. The bully gets what was coming to him.

Griffin and I don't watch a minute of it. Nothing else matters but right now, right here, his mouth on my mouth, his hand on my hip, his breath just as ragged as mine.

My phone pings with a text message, an unwelcome intrusion bringing us back to reality. If it's my mom or sister, I might murder them in their beds.

We slow our kisses, loosening our hold on each other. He strokes stray strands out of my face and curls his fingers in my hair. His eyes are dark and heavy-lidded, and I fist my hand in his shirt, ready to pull him back for more.

He swallows. "You should probably check that."

Inhaling deeply, I breathe in his soapy scent while the rational side of my brain flickers back on. "It's probably nothing."

Honestly, I'm surprised I can string three words together when all I want to say is *more*. I kiss him again, nibbling at his mouth, and his grip tightens on my waist.

Because I can't have nice things, my phone pings again.

He releases me, shifting himself back on the couch. "It might be important."

"Is there something more important than this?"

His eyes still have that happy, sleepy look, but his mouth slants. "You should probably check."

All at once, I remember he has good reason to fear bad news out of the blue. I reluctantly get up to check my phone. It had better be *really important*.

Lila: Festival plans going okay?

Lila: Sure you don't need my help?

"It's just my sister." Helping, as usual. I turn to Griffin, but all hope of going back to where we'd left off disintegrates like a snowball exploding on the ground when he crosses the room.

"Everything good?"

"She's checking up on me. Making sure I can handle the Christmas festival. It's like she knows everyone thinks she'd do a better job at this than me."

"I can see one big defect with Lila."

Sure. Nobody has ever found a defect with Lila. "What's that?"

He levels me a look that sets my heart fluttering. "She's not you."

I open my mouth to say that isn't much of a mark against her, but he goes on.

"Has she ever put on a Christmas festival to benefit a whole town? Has she designed a Winter Wonderland to make hundreds of little kids happy? Does she paint pictures that make you smile just looking at them?"

He moves closer, his eyes blazing into me. "Does she shine so bright she makes you feel lucky just to be around her? Lila's got nothing on you, Hope."

My heart fizzes like an overflowing champagne bottle. "My art really makes you smile?"

His soft laughter ripples through me, a caress I want to lean into. "I knew that would get you."

"I never imagined you were such a sweet talker."

"I'm not usually. I think it was that knock to the head."

"Maybe I should whack you again."

He looks down at me like he's trying to decide something. Fingers crossed for the outcome that leads to more kissing.

"It's late," he says. "I should probably go."

My brain knows this is a reasonable choice, but my heart isn't feeling all that rational right now.

Griffin pulls on his jacket slowly, as if he doesn't really want to. Stepping into my space, he runs his big hands around my waist and kisses me, sweet and gentle. "See you in the warehouse tomorrow?"

"I'll be there to boss around my Christmas elf."

TWENTY-TWO
HOPE

I'VE NEVER SEEN SO many cute clay charms. Tiny mugs of hot cocoa complete with minuscule marshmallows, little pumpkin pie slices with dollops of whipped cream, gingerbread men complete with gumdrop buttons—I love a good food theme. I've been unwrapping and setting out the perfect little replicas dangling from earrings, necklaces, and bracelets. They're a new item, but they fit right in at The Daisy.

One set of earrings catches my eye, and I immediately buy the pair for myself. I try not to do it too often, but sometimes I can't help myself. Really, it's good business. Free advertising and all.

Now I just have to figure out the right time to wear these tiny waffle earrings.

That reminds me. I text Griffin another waffle emoji. He hasn't mentioned them yet, but he will eventually.

"You're sure happy about something."

I jerk out of my daydream, and just about drop my phone. Abby walks up the store aisle, smiling at me as she pulls off her sleek white puffer coat. We first met when she brought me the journals she makes out of vintage book covers. *Pride and Preju-*

dice always sells out first, no surprise. When we discovered she could use a part-time job and I needed extra help in the store, I hired her on, too.

"It's nothing." I tuck my phone away on that believable lie.

"Oh. I thought maybe my grandma texted you. She's not terrible at it, so it's in the realm of possibility."

I go still, my hands splaying on the counter. "Did she decide?"

Her grin goes wide. "They're all yours if you want them. She said she's home anytime. You can get them whenever you want."

"You are an angel! I'm going right now."

"They're big, though. They won't fit in your Jeep."

"That's okay. I think I've got a ride for them."

I gather my things and head over to the warehouse, the good news Abby just gave me putting an extra shimmy in my step. Or maybe it's the three inches of snow that fell last night that's making my boots slip around on the sidewalk. Either way, it's exciting stuff.

I burst through the door and into the quickly growing Winter Wonderland. Griffin's working on the third building, a cute little townhouse with shutters around the windows. I can't wait to paint this one.

Okay, fine, I can't wait to paint all of them. I'm easily pleased that way.

He notices me and sets down the drill. Moving closer, he holds his hands out to the sides in a little *ta-da* move. The glittering delight winding through me proves I'm easily pleased by a lot of things this morning.

"Pretty good, right?" Cocky Griffin sure hasn't left the building.

"It looks amazing. The kids are going to eat these up."

"I've got a few things left to do, but you should be able to start painting this afternoon."

"I'll be ready. Hey, quick question—how much can you lift?"

He blinks at that randomness. "Like in a gym?"

"It's probably a lot, right?"

The ghost of a smirk touches his mouth. "I'm flattered. Why are you asking?"

"I need to go get something, but I'm pretty sure they'll be too much for me. Can we use your truck?"

"Sure. What are we getting?"

I toss him my sauciest look. "I think it's the kind of thing you need to see for yourself."

"Should I be excited or scared?"

"Can't it be both?"

Fifteen minutes later, we're standing in front of Abby's grandma's open garage, staring at two seven-foot-tall nutcrackers. They're painted like red and green soldiers, and I know from years of seeing them at the end of Cherie's driveway each holiday season that they have lights in their buttons, along their swords, and in their hats.

"Thank you so much for offering these to us," I say to Cherie. "They'll make a great addition to the festival decorations."

"I'm just glad you're taking them off my hands now that Henry decided he doesn't want to wrestle with them another season." She laughs and waves a hand at the garage. "Help yourself. I'm going to nip back inside and warm up."

"Thanks again."

When she's gone, Griffin leans closer. "What's the plan for these?"

"I'm thinking they can guard the main entrance to the Christmas market." It'll be an extra step for set-up and tear-down every weekend, but a great touch for the overall look of the festival.

"I'm thinking they're creepy."

"What? No, they're festive." I draw out the word as though if I say it right, he'll agree with me.

"They're menacing."

I stare at them for a minute. Their faces are painted like any nutcracker—huge black eyes, always-stylish handlebar mustaches, wide grins showing off big, square teeth. "Maybe they're not exactly friendly, but they're *not* creepy."

Griffin's lips tug into the smallest smile. Probably because I agreed with him.

"You're just messing with me." I step over to the nearest one. It's almost a foot taller than I am, and up close, it does feel kind of threatening. I blame the wobbling in my stomach on Griffin's power of suggestion, not the innocent nutcrackers.

"I've never liked them." He moves closer to me, putting the giant nutcracker between us. "Caleb convinced me the one my mom used to keep on the mantel came to life at night and spied on us in our beds. It had a fuzzy head and beard that made it look sort of wild. I'd wake up and find it staring at me from my nightstand."

"Like an Elf on the Shelf? Now *those* are creepy." I always thanked my lucky stars my parents never introduced that partic- ular tradition to our house.

"I was afraid of that thing for years before I realized it was all an excuse for Caleb to pull pranks on me."

"Aw." I reach up to pat the nutcracker's cheek. "Is this guy making you nervous?"

"No. I don't get nervous." He holds eye contact with me, that smirk back on his mouth. This man and his swagger.

"All right, Mr. Cool as a Cucumber, let's haul this guy to your truck."

I brace myself to take the nutcracker's weight as we lean it back in an awkward three-person dip, but the shift never comes. Griffin's eyebrows tug together.

"I thought you said these things were heavy." He tilts it all the way back and into his arms like a light-as-a-feather, stiff-as-a-board bride.

"Cherie told me they were." Although, given her age, maybe I should have taken her description with a grain of salt.

He gives me a disappointed look and carts the nutcracker off to his truck, maneuvering it into the bed with ease. When he returns to me in the garage, he's got a teasing scowl twisting his mouth.

"*How much can I lift?*" he grouses, his eyes bright. "These things weigh forty pounds, max."

Apparently, the nutcrackers only *look* like wood.

"Don't blame me," I say. "I have to be careful. My last handyman had a very delicate back."

"Nothing about your new handyman is delicate." He sweeps the second nutcracker into his arms, showing off.

"Be careful with it. You don't want to knock it into something." The garage is filled with all kinds of disused items, and it probably wouldn't take much to punch a hole right through that deceptive plastic the nutcracker's made out of.

"You know that from personal experience, do you?"

"Ha ha." I trail behind him down the driveway, a tiny but very loud part of me wishing he would bridal carry *me* around like that. I'd probably weigh nothing in his arms, too.

When he gets to his truck, he sends a saucy look over his shoulder like my brain is an open book and he just dogeared his favorite page. He hooks a bungee cable across the nutcrackers' legs so they won't tumble out on the drive back to the warehouse. "If you're hoping to keep this under wraps, you'd better get that look of yours under control."

I straighten. "What are you talking about?"

He grins even wider, because we both know what he means. The hearts in my eyes are bright shiny beacons outing me as totally smitten with the man.

He leans closer and drops his voice. "You look like you want a little fire in your life."

Oh, he did not just say that. And it did *not* make me shiver like poor Karen riding on the refrigerated car with Frosty. He closes up the truck's tailgate, smirking so hard, I'm surprised he doesn't pull something.

I gather a big handful of fresh snow from the pine trees along Cherie's driveway and pack it tight. Griffin turns toward me, and I debate for about half a second before I chuck it at him.

The snowball hits his left shoulder with a satisfying wet smack, half of it raining down onto his boots. He looks at the clump of snow on his jacket and then looks at me, that fiery *something* back in his gaze that makes my insides flutter. This was either the worst mistake...or the best. I'll know in another minute or two.

"Are you sure you want to do that?" he says low. "I was a pitcher, Hope."

I have horribly miscalculated. I'd wanted to get him back just a little, but the light in his eyes is all confidence. The fluttering inside me cranks up to something frantic, and I take a step back. "I think we can agree it was an innocent mistake and we should just move on."

"I don't think so, boss."

He stalks toward me, and I shriek with laughter. I try to run down the sidewalk, but if I pick up any actual speed, I'll just slip on the slushy cement. I scamper along, trying to keep my footing and get out of snowball range. From everything I saw in his old baseball games, I can't run that far.

Three seconds later, a snowball hits the center of my back, and I laugh even harder.

I peek over my shoulder, but instead of prepping another snowball, Griffin's chasing after me, his boots kicking up fresh snow. My stomach dips and floods with heat even as my fight-or-flight instinct has my feet scrambling for purchase on the sidewalk.

"As your boss, I command you to cease and desist," I shout at the sky.

"You picked the wrong guy for a snowball fight."

He's right behind me now, and I shriek again, knowing I'm doomed. What will it be? A few more snowballs to the back? Wash my face with snow? Worse?

His arms wrap around me from behind, and he lifts my feet off the ground. I cackle like a witch—it's not a bridal carry, but he's lugging me around like nothing, and I love it.

"Do you want to rethink this?" His voice is at my ear, his warm breath playing over my neck until I shiver again.

I'm not sure I'm thinking at all, to be honest. I only know I've never been good at backing down from anything when it comes to Griffin McBride.

"I'll never surrender." I sound pretty jaunty for a woman being carried to a guy's truck for some unthinkable snow-related retaliation.

"I know." His voice rumbles through me, but it's practically a whisper. "I've always liked that about you."

He has? I want to pepper him with questions about that, but I'm a little too busy squirming in his arms to ask for specifics.

At his truck, he sets my feet back on the ground, but he keeps his arms locked tight around me. I can't think of many things I like more.

"Look at all that snow in the bed of my truck." He sounds like a nature documentary narrator commenting on the lion that's caught sight of a baby gazelle. "It'd be a shame if some of it went down the back of your coat."

"You fight dirty."

"You fired the first shot." Keeping hold of me with one arm, he scoops up a handful of snow with his free hand. His hands are already pink from cold, but it's obvious he won't let a little thing like finger frostbite stop him now.

I squirm more, but he's got me braced firmly against him. My fight would be a lot more believable if I weren't laughing so hard. And, you know—actually trying to get away. "You wouldn't dare."

"Oh, I would dare."

He brings the snow closer, and I'm practically burrowing against him, preparing myself for the icy shock. He flicks a few flakes at me, the pinpricks of cold fanning over my face and neck. Before the rest reaches me, he drops the snow and shakes out his hand, then slides it back around me. He nuzzles against my neck and I wish I could say I didn't sigh, but I'm a weak, weak woman.

"Maybe we can work out some kind of a truce."

His voice is practically a purr. That's not normal. Neither is the dizzying dance my insides are doing in his honor. I'm about to ask a question that will surely lead to even worse trouble than this snowball fight, when Cherie comes out onto her front porch.

I fly out of Griffin's arms so fast, I slide on the slushy street. My heart thunders in my chest, and my face immediately flushes with heat. I throw on my best innocent smile and wave, like that will prove how normal and not-flirty things are out here.

"I forgot about the power cords!" Cherie holds black cables over her head. "You won't get very far without these."

"Thank you." I take them from her when she reaches the

sidewalk. "I wouldn't have thought of them until we set every-thing up. I really appreciate it."

She nods. "You're welcome. Bye now."

I stand perfectly still as she heads back up the walk to her house. If she saw all the heated snuggling and unnecessary carrying going on between Griffin and me, she didn't make it obvious. Still, I can't help picturing her going straight to her phone to call up the Sunshine gossip crew and describe our moment in excruciating detail.

I spin to face Griffin, brandishing the cords. I try to look like someone who's capable of being in charge of a Christmas festival and couldn't possibly flirt with a volunteer, just in case Cherie's watching us out her window. "We would have been sad without these."

"That must be where the missing weight went. Do you need help lifting them?" He holds his hands out as though I need him to spot me.

I toss them his way, and he catches them easily. I'm still thinking about the potential terms of the truce he offered a few minutes ago, but the moment for asking is gone. He drives us back to the warehouse, and I dream of a world with fewer inter-ruptions.

TWENTY-THREE
GRIFFIN

OBSESSING IS NOT MY MO.

I can get single-minded, but usually over plans and goals, not a woman I'm fast realizing might be the best thing that's ever happened to me.

But here I am. Obsessed.

Streetlights glow in the deepening dusk as I walk up Maple Street, looking in windows. I've clocked out for the night and locked up the warehouse, satisfied with another completed Winter Wonderland piece.

Hope had left late in the afternoon, and I already itch to see her again a few hours later. In the last twenty-four hours, I guess I've gone about seven minutes without thinking about her. Sleep doesn't even count, because she visits me in my dreams, too.

Wearing bright orange OSU gear, which kills whatever sexy mood the dream might have otherwise taken.

My breath puffs vapor as I pass shops. Up ahead, next to the bakery, a small storefront painted bright red with a golden yellow door calls to me. The Painted Daisy. Wouldn't take a genius to figure I'd wind up here on my walk.

I look in the window, my face aching from the cold. Hope

moves around inside the little shop, checking stock and adjusting items. With the store empty, she should be sitting down at least, but she keeps making needless checks like it's physically impossible for her to stand still. Always on top of things, always making improvements. A stupid smile splits my face.

I let myself through the door. She turns at the sound of the bells tinkling on the handle, and her warm smile banishes the cold that followed me inside.

"This is a surprise. I didn't expect to see you in here." She comes closer until she stands toe to toe with me.

"Was I not supposed to leave the warehouse?"

"You know what I mean." She makes a show of looking around the store. "It's awfully frilly in here."

She isn't kidding. From shiny jewelry to floral bags and T-shirts with actual frills on them, the place gives off a distinct vibe. Whimsical and cozy, it feels more like she's invited me into a busy, stylish home than a store. Reminds me a lot of her apartment, actually.

"I wanted to see what all the fuss is about."

"See for yourself." She gestures at the short rows of shelves. I could take inventory of the whole place from right here.

"Show me." My chest tightens. She might put on her sassy cap and tell me to use my eyes, but a smile curls along her mouth.

"If you like."

Hope leads me around the store, showing off scented lotions and creams, coin purses and handbags, and all sorts of fussy items I can't name. I try to pay attention, I swear. But it isn't easy to keep my focus off of her: the shape of her as she walks, her delicate fingers pointing out objects, the way she has nothing but enthusiasm for every artist she showcases in this store.

"I still don't understand why your art isn't on this wall." I nod at the blank space on the back wall, a glaring omission in the crowded store as though she's subconsciously made room for her artwork.

"It's complicated."

"Sounds pretty simple to me. Slap a price tag on some of your paintings and hang them up."

Sarcastic laughter bubbles out of her. "So simple."

"Isn't it?"

"No." She looks around as if the nearby assortment of tiny clay moose might help her explain. "My art isn't for everybody."

"You'll never be able to please *everybody*. Some people won't be pleased no matter what you do, and you'll just make yourself smaller and smaller."

"People will talk about it, and dissect it, and you saw the other day—the ones with a negative opinion always have the loudest voice."

"You care too much about what people think." From her art, to the festival, to who and how she dates, other people's opinions have too much sway in her life.

She scowls up at me. "I can always count on you for a blunt hot take."

"Hey." I take her by the elbow and pull her closer. She's still got the scowl on, but she rests her hands on my chest, so it's a win. "I'm just saying, do what makes *you* happy. Bring all that art you've got locked away in your apartment out into the light. Give people a chance to love you."

Her brow furrows at the same time my stomach drops like somebody pushed me out of an airplane.

"Your art. Give people a chance to love your art." Man, I'm getting as bad as she is with blurting things out. "It should be in here."

"People might hate it."

She whispers the words almost like she doesn't want me to hear her deepest fear. I hug her to me and stroke her back, wanting to soothe any way I can.

"I'm no artist. I've never shared a vulnerable piece of me like that with anybody. But I know passion when I see it. You can feel your love for your art in every brushstroke." I drop my voice lower. "Don't settle for less than what you really want just to make someone else happy."

My mom flashes in my mind, and I remember all the ways I'm settling to make *her* happy, but this isn't about me right now.

I point at the blank space above us. "You should put one of your paintings right there. With a big price tag in the corner."

Her smile grows wider little by little, lighting me up like one of her bright paintings come to life. "I think you missed your calling. You should have been a Little League coach."

A light scent of citrus wraps around us, and I fight the urge to press my face against her neck to breathe it right from the source. I've never known this kind of yearning for someone right in front of me before. I think about her all the time, and now that I'm with her, even that isn't enough.

I lightly trace one palm down her back until my hand rests on her hip. She looks up at me, and I'm pretty sure neither of us is thinking about Little League anymore. We have nothing close to privacy in her store, with its glass storefront and an open doorway that looks straight into the bakery. I know she doesn't want to be on display...but I don't want to let her go, either.

I can show some restraint. My hands aren't listening, though. One skims up her arm and over her shoulder to rest where it meets her neck, my thumb grazing her pulse point. The other hand is locked on her hip, but that's almost worse, since that hand has no intention of going anywhere.

Hope's hands are equally wayward, caressing my chest in a way that makes me wish I weren't wearing several layers of clothes. Every time her fingers move, her goal of zero PDA feels further and further away. She might be rethinking that goal, too —her eyes watch my mouth like she's ravenous.

"Griffin."

My name on her lips unravels all my good intentions.

Our mouths meet, and fireworks explode in my brain. A chorus of angels belt out Hallelujah. Last night's kisses were a slow torture as we felt each other out. Tonight cranks that up to eleven, a tangle of hot breath and ready mouths, hands exploring because we're racing against time.

How can someone *taste* like sunshine? She's so sweet, with a hint of citrus, like lemonade on a bright summer day. That knock to the head really did a number on me, but I can't help it. She's delicious, and I want to eat her up.

My breath comes out a soft moan over that tempting thought. I hold her close, storing away the feel of the curve of her lower back, the scoop of her waist. One of her hands fists my shirt at the back of my neck, pulling me closer. As if I'm going anywhere.

When she sighs against my mouth, I'm lost.

So lost, I'm utterly bewildered when a loud "Caw caw!" echoes around us.

Before my brain can register we've stopped kissing, Hope leaps away from me like she did when the woman donating the nutcrackers saw us playing around this afternoon. She smooths her hands down her sides, casting a look next door.

Over in the bakery, Wren Krause grins away at us, her elbows on the counter, her blond ponytail swinging.

I look at Hope. "Was that a secret message, or—"

The bells over the door to her shop jingle. Ah. An alarm system.

"Welcome in." Hope's husky voice makes me wonder what other sounds I can get her to make.

I turn to see an older woman unwinding a long scarf from around her neck. At least it isn't Ada or Isabel, but she looks like a close second in the Opinionated Old Lady Brigade.

When I look back at Hope, she's put another couple of feet of space between us. Her eyes are still a little glazed over from our kiss, her lips pink and rough, but her body language betrays something like guilt.

Is it because we almost got caught, or because she would have been caught with *me*? I don't care much about the whispers that sometimes trail me around town, but she might.

After a lifetime, but probably only three seconds, her mouth eases into a smile. Relief floods through me at that gorgeous sight. It isn't the showy fake one. Seeing her pretend self after a kiss like that would have hollowed me out.

This one telegraphs a clear message: *Act natural.* Too bad for her. Kissing her is the most natural thing in the world now.

"Did you find everything you were looking for?" She's gone all prim and proper on me, likely to throw off her beady-eyed customer.

"No, not quite," I say in a low voice. "I think I'm going to have to put in a special order."

Color rises on her already pink cheeks. "You might have to wait for a special order."

Her lip twitch proves she knows exactly what she's doing.

"I'm a very patient man."

She raises one perfect eyebrow.

"I don't have the patience of a saint or anything, but I'm in no rush." Not that I would put up a fight if she wanted to run every red light through town to her apartment right now.

"Why don't you come back tomorrow, and we'll see if we can work something out?"

"I'll do that. Thanks for your help, ma'am." I tip an imaginary hat. "I'm much obliged."

Her eyes narrow, but her smile ruins the effect. What I wouldn't do for those lips. I might have ignored the woman wandering around ten feet away and kissed her again, but Hope is pretty clearly not here for the PDA. Her mouth drops open—possibly to shoo me on my way—but her customer cuts her off.

"I hate to interrupt," the woman says. The playful turn of her voice says that even if she didn't witness anything, she's connected the dots between Hope and me. "But do you have any other colors of these pretty crocheted hats?"

Hope gives her an indulgent smile. "I'll find them for you."

"I'll see you tomorrow, boss."

"I look forward to it." Her voice comes out almost chilly, but the look she shoots my way holds nothing but heat.

I won't get any sleep at all tonight.

TWENTY-FOUR

HOPE

MY FACE IS PROBABLY REDDER than Santa's suit.

I show Mrs. Howell every variety of crocheted hat in the shop before my heart slows its frantic race—first from that incredible kiss, and then from mild panic. I want to believe Wren's goofy warning kept Griffin and me from getting caught, but the way Mrs. Howell keeps smiling at me, I don't count on it.

"I'll take these two." She opts for a variegated plum version and a bright teal. "My nieces are visiting for Thanksgiving, and I wanted to get them early Christmas gifts."

"These are perfect." I ring them up for her, and she slips her credit card into the reader.

"I hear you're cooking up something special for the Christmas festival this year."

"We really are. I can't wait for everyone to see it." I tuck the hats into a small paper bag and hand it over. "I think you'll like the Christmas market."

"And what's this about a secret project with a certain McBride who just left?"

The arch of her eyebrow is impossible to ignore.

"Oh." A sound somewhere between a laugh and a cough escapes me. "It's not exactly a secret...but I think everyone will like that, too. I'm lucky to have Griffin on my team."

Teammate isn't remotely how I want to describe Griffin right now, but I can't possibly say anything more to Mrs. Howell, of all people.

Her eyes twinkle as if I've given her everything she needs to know anyway.

"If I were you, I'd cook up something special with him, too. That boy's a heartthrob."

I snap my mouth shut at this sweet elderly woman describing Griffin as a heartthrob. Accurate, but still unexpected. She flashes a knowing smile like my silence confirms my agreement, and heads out of the store.

I manage to follow her to the front door and lock it for the night before I notice Wren leaning in the pass-through opening. Gloating movie villains should be jealous of her grin.

"Oh," I say. "Hi."

Real smooth.

"Next time you're going to kiss Griffin in your store, warn me. Half our pies melted over here."

"Shut up." After that kiss—and Mrs. Howell's saucy advice —I can't come up with a better retort. I go through my closing up routine without looking at her. This is already embarrassing enough, but Wren won't quit until she multiplies that by a factor of ten.

She joins me at the counter and squeezes a dollop of lavender hand cream into her palm from the tester tube. "I didn't have the best view from behind the counter, but it seemed pretty hot to me."

Hotter than a barbecue stuffed into an incinerator dropped into a volcano. That kiss will be the five-star I compare every other kiss to for the rest of my life.

"You don't have to gloat so hard."

"You're right. But please rate his quality of work with a thumbs up or a thumbs down."

I turn off the overhead light, leaving us in the glow from the bakery's lights. "You're a brat, but...two thumbs up."

More like a hundred thumbs up. That kiss deserves all the thumbs.

"Nice. Happy for you."

"I'm...happy for me, too."

Her grin freezes. "Wow. That pause doesn't support your *happy* claim."

"It isn't that." I don't know how to explain it, but Wren is probably the only person I can explain it to. "It's been a long time since I've had feelings like this, and I really didn't expect Griffin to be the next guy I'd try to date."

She bounces on the balls of her feet. "I love that you said you have feelings for him, but go on."

"Remind me again why I love you?" Even though yes, feelings are happening. They're messier than the string lights I spent days untangling, and I sure don't want to nail down labels for them right now, but...yeah. Feelings. "It's just...this is Griffin. We irritated each other all through high school. I used to wish inexplicable, painful accidents on the guy. This is a big shift, isn't it?"

"For you or for him?"

"Both."

It's still a little weird to think the guy who made me want to stab him with a freshly sharpened pencil ten years ago is the man who makes my stomach flutter like it's filled with seven swans a-swimming today. Well...there are a few similarities left. His ego is fully intact, even though I suspect he's trying to tone it down. He's still got some attitude to him, and his blunt criticisms haven't gone anywhere.

But the man behind all that? The one who steps up to volunteer, who shows up no matter what I ask of him, whose smiles make me feel like I'm Taylor Swift in the middle of a cheering stadium?

My heart's in danger from that man. It's got a great big bullseye on it, and Griffin is on a mission to reach it. I just can't tell yet if he'll cherish it or smash it to smithereens.

TWENTY-FIVE
HOPE

I PARK my Jeep along the curb, thin clouds stretching across the morning sky out the windshield. I hate to get to the warehouse after Griffin does—I *am* the boss, after all—but I'm running late. My usual routine went on the chopping block this morning down to the bare minimum, and I'm still rolling in thirty minutes behind my normal schedule. My excuse isn't that great. I'd slept in fitful starts, woken by dreams of one hunky handyman.

I can't remember flannel ever making an appearance in my dreams before.

In my rear-view, Griffin pulls up behind me. Looks like my dreams have come true. My heart starts going so fast, I start to worry I might have a coronary right here in the driver's seat. I take a deep breath and climb out of my car into the freezing dawn.

"Morning," Griffin says. "Here I was thinking I was going to be late."

"So was I."

"Rough night?" His saucy glance beneath bunched eyebrows says he has his suspicions about what kept me up.

"I might have tossed and turned. Why? Did you have trouble sleeping?"

"I don't think I slept all night." He steps closer. "I was thinking about my special order."

"Do you have something in mind?" *Anything. Anything.*

"I don't think I'll be able to choose one thing."

His glorious smolder works its way through my bloodstream, heating me up from inside.

He tones down the sexy look after a minute and takes my hand. "You're wearing your gloves today."

He massages my fingers through the thin knit, gently rolling each one until he holds my hand tight. His touch pulses through me like an electric charge. With a greeting like this, who needs caffeine?

All these delightful touches first thing in the morning makes my breath hitch in my throat. Unfortunately, his sidelong glance wakes me out of my daze. He doesn't need to be *that* proud of himself.

"Okay, come on, we have work to do."

I spin on my heel and move to the warehouse door at double speed, wishing my brain wasn't short-circuiting over sultry looks and gloved touches.

"I'm all yours, boss."

Nope, definitely short-circuiting.

We spend the morning working closer together than is probably necessary. In theory, I'm helping him steady the other half of the roof supports as he secures them onto the house walls. In reality, I'm just waiting around for our next kiss break.

He fastens on a corner support and lowers the drill, a smile tugging at his lips. I've got those soft, full lips memorized, and want them pressed against mine again at the earliest opportunity.

"You're shaping up to be a good helper."

I squint my eyes at him. "How dare you?"

"My mistake, *boss.*"

His voice drops on the last word, setting off an explosion of glittery confetti in my chest. I'm gearing up to attack him and prove just how good a boss I can be when a voice says, "Well, look at all this."

Is this what a heart attack feels like? I scramble away from him in an effort to reach my mother. She stands in the middle of the warehouse in her black quilted trench coat, surveying our progress. My stomach sinks as I wonder just how much progress she's seen. Peeking to where I'd been mooning at Griffin just seconds ago confirms my fears—she'd had a clear view of our coziness for who knows how long before she decided to speak up.

Pretty sure she wouldn't have kept her joy to herself if she'd witnessed an actual kiss, but that doesn't bring a lot of comfort.

"Mom," I say, dusting off my jeans for no good reason. "What are you doing here?"

"I was meeting with Carl Perez on Oak. They're looking to lease the Kerr building. I thought I'd stop in to see how you're getting on."

Her pushy little eyebrow bob says she's not here to find out anything about the festival. She's here to snoop. Of course. She glances around the warehouse she secured for me, but she's barely looking at the buildings. Her eyes keep skating over Griffin like she's trying and failing not to peek at Christmas presents.

"We're doing great. There's not a lot to see yet, though, so—" I sweep my arm to escort her back out, but she just walks farther into the building, zooming closer to my helpful handyman.

"Oh, don't be modest, these are impressive."

She skirts close by the little bakery and then the bookshop. Although they can technically be broken down, we're keeping everything set up so the paint doesn't get damaged. Eventually, Griffin's going to add a coat of *something* to make them ready to withstand the elements.

"These will be a prime spot for photos. I can tell already."

"That's the hope." I want to see kids gathered around the Winter Wonderland, parents snapping pictures, and whole families laughing away. Isn't that usually the point of making art —to spread a little joy?

She finally wanders over to my handyman, where I know she's been dying to go since the second she walked in. "Griffin, I'm glad to see your injury's doing better."

He runs his fingers over the mark on his forehead. "It was never very serious."

He cuts his eyes to me in a silent *I told you so*. I would stick my tongue out at him if my mother weren't standing right here. A sarcastic smile will have to do.

"You've done so much work for Hope already." Mom waves around at the buildings like she's standing in front of the Taj Mahal. They *are* adorable and beautifully made, but she's still laying her enthusiasm on thick. Although, I'm not sure Mom has a *thin* enthusiasm setting. "I hope she's treating you right."

She gives me a blatant look of disapproval. I know what she's hinting at—I haven't given her any details in response to her never-ending texts about Griffin. Unfortunately, she's not above going straight to him for her info.

"Hope's a good boss," he says, eyes on me. "Very hands-on."

I might have to murder my new handyman. How can his smile look this boyish and innocent when his eyes are radiating pure sexiness?

"Is she?" Mom looks positively thrilled by this.

"Oh, yeah." He drops the smirk, thank goodness. "She's helped me with some of the construction, and her painting is beautiful. I'm impressed by *all* of her work."

Aw. Maybe I'll hold off on the murder.

"Since you're doing so much, you should be treated to a good meal. What do you say to dinner with our family one night this week?"

Okay, so murder's still on the table.

"Mom." I exhale a breezy laugh even though nothing about me feels breezy right now. More like hurricane-force gusts of irritation. "Tomorrow's Thanksgiving."

"Right." She seems to come back down to reality. I must be a clown, because I actually believe she's going to drop it, right until she smiles even wider. "Do you have plans for the holiday, Griffin?"

His eyes flick to me, but I am *not* going to let him answer that. It's way too much. She can't just spring an invite to a major holiday function on a guy with one day's notice. Also, I don't want to hear Griffin turn her down.

"Of course he does, Mom. He's spending the day with his family."

His mouth twitches the tiniest bit, and my heart sinks right down into the sawdust on the floor. Is he going to accept her invite? If nothing else, he'd do it to be contrary, solely because I'm against it. That would be a very Griffin thing to do.

He has no idea what that dinner would be like. I've endured a few family dinner-dates she's arranged, and they all go the same way—Mom pushes us together like she's playing with dolls, flirts by proxy until things get seriously uncomfortable for everyone, and I eventually go home to Google how many people die of embarrassment in a typical year. Then, I never hear from the man again.

I can't let that happen with Griffin.

I'm begging him to read my mind with his secret telepathic powers and understand how deeply I do not want him to accept this invitation. His ESP must be working, because he manages to look disappointed.

"I do have plans with my family, Mrs. Parrish. But I appreciate the gesture."

He looks at me again, and there's almost a scolding in his eyes, as if he did this against his will. He couldn't *want* to come to our holiday dinner, right? We're barely together—if, in fact, we even *are* together.

I can't shake the sense he would have accepted if I hadn't stepped in, though.

"Then I'll take a rain check," Mom says, clearly delighted he's left that window open. "Come any time. Hope will be happy to have you over with us. She's enjoyed working with you so much."

See? This is why I banned her from my personal life. Even knowing nothing about me and Griffin, she's putting words in my mouth.

They are true and accurate words, but she still doesn't need to put them there.

"All right, Mom, we've got work to do, so let's get you going." I tug on her coat sleeve like a little kid. "Thanks for stopping by to see the progress."

"It's lovely to see you again," she says to Griffin, her heeled boots resolutely *not* moving toward the door. "You're obviously a very good carpenter. Do you happen to do any work on the side?"

"No, ma'am. This is just a one-time thing for Hope."

There's no trace of emotion in his voice, but I'd bet money he's not entirely happy about that. Not a lot of money—I've only had hints to his true feelings on the subject. But I suspect he's not as settled at McBride Landscaping as he claims. Unfortunately, cracking open Griffin's head to get information he's not already willing to give is impossible. And, in front of my mother, impractical.

"Too bad. I could send a lot of business your way if you did. I'm in need of a skilled carpenter in town."

"What about Andre?" I ask.

"Oh, it never hurts to have more contacts who are good at what they do." She turns back to Griffin. "Let me know if you change your mind about that. And tell me when dinner works for you and Hope. We'll have you two over anytime!"

Oh, goody, we're "you two" in her mind now. I'm doomed.

"All right, how about I walk you out?" I practically have to shove her, but she finally gets going.

We cross the warehouse and exit onto the side street. I'm buzzing with a tangled combination of nerves and irritation, but Mom's huge smile flattens some of that out. She has my best interest at heart, I remind myself. Even if her good intentions often lead to horribly embarrassing situations.

"Looks like things are moving along well in there." She lifts an eyebrow at me, the Queen of Subtlety.

I refuse to crack. I am cool and calm. I am an ice cube. "The Winter Wonderland is really coming together."

"That looks good, too. Let me know when he's ready to take me up on my offer. Your dad will love him."

I make a series of inarticulate sounds. "Dad's not going to meet him."

Even though...she's probably not wrong. Dad's social, like Mom, but he spends a lot of time in his head. He'd rather hear honesty than flattery any day—Mom excepted, of course. He'd probably like Griffin's decisive, straightforward nature. Two composed men enduring the antics of two highly emotional women.

No, wait. What am I doing imagining Griffin meeting my dad?

Mom needs to cool it with all the *Power of Positive Speech* classes she takes. She's clearly an A student.

She doesn't reply to my denial, just smiles like she's practicing for a toothpaste commercial. "See you tomorrow, honey."

She saunters toward Maple Street, her perfectly curled dark hair fluttering in the breeze. Meanwhile, she's left me an emotionally disheveled mess.

Griffin's not going to meet my dad. He's not.

Even though now, I kind of really want that.

TWENTY-SIX
GRIFFIN

MY BROTHER HAS ABSOLUTELY LOST his mind. I've wondered a few times in the past, but today seals it. He fusses over his wife, arranging cushions beneath, behind, and around her, determined to make her the most comfortable woman on the planet.

"Think you've got enough pillows?" I ask.

"This is probably good, but if she needs—" He shoots me a dirty look over his shoulder. Taking that long to hear my sarcasm proves just how distracted he is. "Get lost."

"No way, this is highly entertaining. You good, Rowan?"

She cranes her neck to see me over her hovering husband's back. Her usually plump and rosy face turned pale a couple of minutes ago, when Caleb leaped into action. "I'm good."

He straightens and hits me with a flat look. "She said she was feeling woozy."

I nod like a doctor on a medical drama. "Yeah, I get it. Wooziness calls for all the pillows."

Rowan snickers softly in the plush armchair made even plusher with the addition of something like sixty-five throw pillows. She'd protested just a touch when he led her out of the kitchen and straight into the living room to sit down, but after a minute, she'd fully surrendered to his care.

"Let's talk again when *you've* got a pregnant wife to take care of."

I lift my hands in defense. "No need to make threats."

Even if that word sends my thoughts spiraling in one particular direction. Which is crazy. I haven't even taken Hope on a date.

Crap. I need to take her on a date.

"When it's his wife, he'll be just the same." Mom joins us in her living room and throws an arm around my waist. "Or I didn't raise him right."

"I don't know," Caleb says. "His wife will have enough to deal with taking *him* on, let alone adding a literal infant into the mix."

"I bet he winds up being *the most* protective." At least Rowan feels well enough to add to the color commentary against me. "He's not going to let his wife out of his sight."

"Can we all stop talking about my imaginary wife?" An itch works between my shoulder blades every time they lob that word at me. Even if that's exactly how I see myself being—one day, far off in the distant future—I'm not about to admit anything for this group.

"Sure, honey." Mom rubs my back for a second like I'm a cranky toddler. "Why don't you come help me in the kitchen?"

I follow her into the next room, but Caleb stage whispers behind me. "Someone's sure touchy about his imaginary wife."

The smell of turkey roasting in the oven would normally have my mouth watering, but this doesn't feel like a holiday. It feels like the memory of one, with the most important parts blurred out. It's a wall that's been stripped of sheetrock, leaving the supports exposed. Celebrations without Dad are just one more piece of the new normal I don't want to get used to.

"Want to help me make the rolls?" Mom asks.

I roll up my sleeves and jump in, hoping the task will distract me. Ground me. Something.

She stands at the counter next to me, and we take turns tearing off chunks of the risen dough to form into easy tear-apart rolls like I've been helping her make since I was a kid. It's both comforting and jarring to do something so familiar when everything feels a little off-kilter without Dad around.

"Have you seen those lots for sale down by the lake?" she asks. "Signs just went up this week."

I make a sound of acknowledgement. I'd had to stop myself from driving by and nosing around. "They're too small. They're going to be skinny two- or three-story jobs. They'll have nice lake views, but no space on the sides from their neighbors."

I'd built plenty of houses like that, but I wouldn't want to live in one. When I build a house for myself, I want some land to go with it.

"Maybe they need someone to tell them."

"Pretty sure they wouldn't be interested." Anybody selling lots that small knows exactly what they're doing and wouldn't be talked out of getting a couple of extra houses out of the land.

"I heard a custom home builder out of Salem is looking to expand to Sunshine in the new year." She leaves that there, but I can't tell if it's a test or a dare.

Either way, I put it out of my head.

"Where did you get that information?"

"You might be surprised to know I'm well-connected in this town." She says it like she's a mob boss making threats.

"Remind me never to cross you."

She laughs, nudging me with an elbow. "I think we're past that. You seem to have forgotten your teen years."

I frown, pressing two dough balls into a muffin tin. "We don't need to rehash that."

"You grew through it. I think you're doing all right."

I like to think so. I still don't love authority figures, and tend to ask more questions than I answer, but I've lost that teenage rebellious streak. I'd put Mom and Dad through more than they deserved, but their patience never wavered, even if I'd sometimes taken Dad's to its limits.

"I haven't even set any fires lately."

If Hope's claim to fame is her run as Homecoming Queen, mine is that one bonfire that got away from me. It'd taken years before I stopped hearing about that on the daily. Coming back to town has just reminded everyone to mention it again.

"A little spark's not a bad thing." She hums to herself, rolling balls of dough between her hands. "How are things going with Hope?"

More than a little spark. But after her plea to keep things between us quiet, I can't say anything to Mom. I'm not the chattiest about my personal life on a normal day, but the reminder sits heavily in my gut.

I might be a private guy, but that doesn't mean I'm a *secret* guy.

"We'll have everything ready for next Friday. Be prepared to rock around that Christmas tree."

She smiles, but I get the feeling that's not the kind of update she was hoping to hear. Have I been that obvious? I've barely mentioned Hope. But Mom's side-eye speaks volumes, and I'm not prepared to crack open that book.

"What do you want for Christmas?" I ask instead.

"Oh, probably anything from The Painted Daisy. You can't go wrong in there."

"I'll write you down for a little ceramic moose then."

She doesn't look at me this time, but her smile grows wider. Because apparently I *am* that obvious—I just admitted that one, I've been inside Hope's store, and two, I actually paid enough attention to know what she sells. I might as well recite a poem about how good she smells, and just get it all out there at once.

Caleb walks in before I can reveal anything else incriminating.

"Guess who asked me to confirm that his patio is level for the fourth time?"

I groan, glad that man doesn't have my number. Mr. Lang hired us to install an elaborate herringbone patio when we renovated his back yard over the summer, and he hasn't stopped calling about it since. Caleb's design blends perfectly with the surrounding hillside, and our crew did a fantastic job on the hardscape and the plantings, but Mr. Lang is convinced the patio slopes.

"I brought out the laser level and showed him with string ties, but he still has his doubts."

"Better you than me." That's why I like having a buffer between me and the customer. I need someone else to deal with all the pointless little calls. As I'd proven pretty thoroughly the few times they'd sent me out to deal with things like that.

"Better get ready. After this baby comes, I'm taking two months off, and *you'll* be the one crawling around on pavers trying to prove a point."

I focus on rolling the last of the dough into balls. I should be relieved I'll have some breathing room at the first of the year, but his reminder makes my chest tighten like the kitchen walls are shrinking around me. The responsibilities aren't the problem, but I can't—or don't really want to—define exactly what is.

"How's woozy doing in there?" I give him a hard time about how he's turned into a mother hen, but I care about Rowan's health, too. I wouldn't joke around if she was really dealing with something serious.

"Resting. She's been getting light-headed more often lately, but the doctor says it's normal at this stage. I still don't like it."

"I'd be more worried about her stomach."

Caleb is suddenly *right* behind me. "What about her stomach?"

His voice is a low-key threat. I shouldn't poke the papa bear, but I've never been great at laying off my big brother. I see an opening, I take it. I just didn't mean it the way he's taking it.

"It could be a symptom from eating that teeny tiny fish you caught her on Saturday."

He exhales a laugh and moves away from me, threat averted. "Yours wasn't any bigger."

"It was bigger."

"You released it without measuring, and we all know how accurate eyeballing it is."

I rinse my hands while Mom covers the rolls to rise one last time. "You just don't want to admit your fish was barely a centimeter over the legal limit."

Mom raises her hands between us, exasperated. "Boys, are we back to fighting over whose fish is bigger?"

Caleb and I share a look. We're both trying not to burst out laughing at her unintended innuendo.

"Mine's bigger," I say before he can open his mouth.

He shakes his head at me. "You're a child."

"Stop, you two," Mom says. "Or I'll put you both in time out chairs like I did when you were little."

I have a lot of memories of being in that chair.

She takes each of our hands, looking from me to him with shiny eyes. "You two were always trouble, but we never wanted it any other way."

A lump leaps straight into my throat, my eyes stinging. I slow my breathing, but if her tears fall, I'll crumble away.

"I'm grateful you're my boys." She smiles at each of us, but her gaze sticks on me. "No matter what you do or where you go."

"We're not going anywhere." Caleb leans down to wrap her up into a hug.

"You're stuck with us." I hug her, too, but when she pulls away, she's got so much meaning in her eyes, I feel like I might need to sit down in the living room with Rowan.

I've never said a word about missing my old job, never hinted I wanted anything other than what I've got with them and McBride's. But the way she's watching me, it's like she's peeked into my head and sifted through my thoughts.

I hit her with my own serious look. If she thinks I plan to do anything other than prove my love and loyalty to this family, she can go right on thinking. I'm sticking with them, no matter what.

TWENTY-SEVEN
HOPE

IF SOMEONE WERE to dust my back, they'd see my mom's fingerprints all over it.

I showed up early to help with the Thanksgiving cooking. We peeled, sliced, and prepared all morning. We ate a meal of too much food split among too little company. And Mom has kept the conversation going all day with her never-ending questions about Griffin, my work, and my festival.

At least when Lila's here, she helps divide some of that relentless focus.

"I've been nosing around a little," Mom says.

I snort into my glass of wine, because *has she ever*. We're lounging around in their living room, absently watching the parade rerun until our stomachs have room for dessert. Dad's half asleep, God bless him, but Mom's wide awake.

"Crystalline isn't renewing their lease," she continues. "Thea's moving to Ashland this summer to be with her family. You might be in a position to take over that space by then."

The gift shop-slash-reiki practice sells a huge collection of crystals, incense, and salt lamps. I stop in once in a while to browse their unusual tea collection, but I had no idea she was thinking of closing her store, let alone leaving town.

"It's in a great location, but I don't think that space is right for The Painted Daisy." Crystalline has at least three times the floor space I have now, plus one or two treatment rooms in the back. "I kind of like being small."

"It wouldn't hurt to have a little breathing room, at least. I don't see how you have space for new merchandise as it is."

True, I don't have much extra room. But I also get to hand pick everything I opt to sell, and so far, I haven't had a problem making space for anything I wanted to bring into the store. Anyway, I might waste away into nothing without the steady stream of treats from Blackbird's.

"I don't know what I'd do with that much floor space." Not to mention the price tag that must come with it. I'm well aware I sublet my space from Wren's mom at a steal. Crystalline's lease amount would probably give my savings account a heart attack.

Kind of makes me wonder why more people don't go into reiki.

"You could spread out what you have now. Make it less..." She waves a hand in the air. "Cluttered."

Given the rest of our conversations today, this isn't the battle for me to pick, but we have very different ideas of what makes good style. Mom likes mid-century modern—clean lines, everything useful and necessary. No farmhouse ceramic roosters for her. I'm of the philosophy that more is more. I want to be surrounded by as many colorful, pretty things as possible.

"How can we petition to get a toy store to take over that space? Or a book shop?" I'd kill for a good bookshop in Sunshine. Right now, we have to drive into Bend for new releases. No offense to the thrift shops in town, but mildewy books that haven't been popular for a decade just don't cut it.

"Maybe it'd make a good space for a general contractor. Or a custom carpenter."

Her eyes are on the television screen, but her hands are on my back.

"I can't imagine something like that needs a storefront." I down half my glass of wine in two big gulps, waiting for her to pounce.

"Maybe ask Griffin and see what he thinks."

I stare at the Broadway actress on television lip syncing to an upbeat Christmas song while the parade pauses. *Do not take the bait. Do not take the bait.*

"Or I can ask him when he comes to dinner," she adds.

My heart jumps up into my throat. I should have just mumbled something about Griffin and left it at that.

Dad startles awake. "Who's coming to dinner?"

"Nobody." I'm maybe a little too serious, because his eyes widen like he's aware "nobody" means "please don't let Mom invite my handyman to dinner." He's sympathetic, but he finds her romantic meddling more amusing than anything else. He should try it from my place sometime.

"He said he'd take me up on the offer," Mom says. "You two get along so well. Why shouldn't he come to dinner?"

She watches me like a cat who's trapped a mouse. What can I say to that? *We're just friends?* Wren comes to family dinner all the time. *We don't get along?* Everything she's seen proves that's a big fat lie. *I don't want him to come to dinner because you'll go overboard and mangle everything and he'll call it quits with me on the spot?*

Too honest.

"I guess if you're not interested, there's always the new pediatric dentist in Bend. Your father met Dr. Brendan this week. He's tall, handsome, never married." She gives me a satisfied smile. "I could invite him to dinner next weekend. What do you say?"

"I don't want to be set up with some strange man Dad just met."

"He works with kids," Mom coaxes.

"So do clowns." Which is exactly what I am for getting myself stuck in this mess. "I don't want you to invite him to dinner for me."

"Why not? If you and Griffin are just friends, what can it hurt?"

I down the rest of my wine, scrambling for a delicate yet firm answer to the trap she set for me. Something that reveals nothing. Something she'll actually listen to.

I've got nothing.

Out in the foyer, my phone rings. I leap up—I don't even care if it's a spam call. I will gladly talk about my car's warranty right now.

"Gotta get that," I toss behind me as I go. "It might be important."

Scurrying out of the room, I grab my phone along the way. Lila. Honestly, I might prefer the car warranty call.

I duck into what used to be my childhood bedroom. Once a purple ode to all things sparkly unicorn, it now boasts a treadmill, a stationary bicycle, and a rack of free weights complete with a ballet barre on one wall.

I lower myself onto the treadmill track. "Hey, Lila."

"Happy Thanksgiving."

"Same to you." I imagine her somewhere in the recesses of her in-laws-to-be's mansion, lounging on a velvet stool or whatever wealth like that thinks is cozy.

"Why aren't you updating the Christmas festival's Instagram page every day? You can't just create it and leave it, you have to post daily so people can see it. Now, I've got some ideas for your Stories because you obviously aren't doing that, either—"

"Wait, what's going on? What are you doing?" This is not the "I'm in a marble bathroom and you're not" call I was expecting.

"I've come up with a social media plan for your festival." She says it so matter of fact, she might as well add *duh* at the end. "Since you aren't doing it."

Again—duh. But...she's not wrong. I haven't thought much about the social media stuff since I made the first few posts, and marketing used to be my *job*. I've been having too much fun with the Winter Wonderland, and I've been too busy wrangling all the volunteers.

But if I admit that to Lila, I'm just proving her and Mom—and Ada and Isabel, and goodness knows how many other people in town—right. And I can't do that.

"Are you feeling okay? You sound phlegmy." It's true, but I also suspect appealing to her vanity might help wrap up this call ASAP.

"Just a head cold."

"Maybe you should get some rest." She could stop doing other people's work, at least.

"I've been resting. Now, with Facebook you want a different approach, because that's where you're going to get the grandmas, and they've got the cash to spend in the shops. I was thinking—"

"Lila. No. I've got it."

"Just send me permissions to your pages. I'll take care of it."

I'd need another glass of wine before I can deal with her overeager assistance. "I don't have all that here."

"You've only got a week! If you're not on top of this *daily*, it will fall apart."

My stomach cramps right up. Probably a good thing I

haven't had dessert yet. I picture town square practically empty, just a few hardcore locals there to enjoy the tree lighting. A meager crowd wandering through the Christmas market, my artist friends disappointed at the turnout. Tumbleweeds blowing through when the tree lights up.

"I'll post something tonight." I'll add reminders to my phone to update the accounts a few more times over the next week.

"What?"

"What do you mean *what*?" Her tone is too pointed to mean she didn't hear me.

"I mean what are you going to post?"

My silence over the line is better than any lie detector test. I have zero ideas.

"Maybe something about Santa." Everybody loves Santa.

"Hope, I can do this stuff in my sleep. I don't mind helping you."

"Shouldn't you be writing up press releases touting the latest in self-driving cars?" It's not exactly what Josh's company does, but my brain struggles to wrap around the tech stuff. "Running damage control on the latest malfunction?"

"I'm more likely to write up an exposé for TMZ right now."

"What do you mean?"

"Nothing. It's just a joke. Think how bad that would look for Josh." Even her laugh sounds phlegmy.

"I just don't have the brain space for this right now. Mom's doing her usual over-enthusiastic push about work and guys. I can't go through all your social media ideas at the same time."

"Who's the guy?"

Argh, of course she caught onto that. I almost want to tell her. But Lila usually takes Mom's side on the "Hope needs to find a decent guy" convo, and I'm not prepared to deal with questions about Griffin. Also, that glass of wine I chugged is kicking in.

"It's a figure of speech."

"No, it isn't. Are you seeing someone new?"

"What? No. What's that?" I call, as though talking to someone else. "Oh, Dad's cutting the cheesecake Mom made. I have to go."

"You're such a liar—"

I hang up on my sister. That's going to cost me. She'll have a whole new subject to grill me about in her text messages. I sit on the treadmill for a while, wondering how one goes about securing a burner phone.

Between my sister trying to horn in on my festival and my mother trying to take the reins in my social life, I'm having a smashing Thanksgiving. I want to go home, slip into pajamas, and watch *Scrooged*, but I just killed my escape route by drinking a full glass of wine in five minutes. I need another way.

Maybe the problem can also be the solution. Or maybe the solution will create an even bigger problem, but my thumbs fly on my phone before I can think it through.

> Hope: Rescue me please

Laughter rolls around in the next room. It's early yet—maybe they haven't even had dinner. Maybe he's engrossed in some McBride family Thanksgiving tradition, like football out on the lawn. Maybe he's having a nice, normal family meal and doesn't have time for—

> Griffin: Where are you?

> Hope: Holiday horror show

I type in my parents' address.

> Griffin: Be there in five

Chaotic flutters spin through me, like a parade balloon that's sprung a leak. I send him another waffle emoji before I can think better of it.

I waffle you, Griffin.

I start giggling, because I'm a mature woman. I really need to ration my wine next time. At least I'm sober enough not to send that one. Barely, but I do stop myself.

I walk back into the living room, where my parents have snuggled up on the couch. When they look over at me, I try to sound as disappointed as possible. "I need to leave for a while."

They both start asking questions at the same time.

"There's a problem with the Christmas festival." From their concerned faces, I'm dimly aware I'm playing it too somber. My excuse needs to be serious enough to get me out of here, but not so serious I wind up with a worried escort. "It's just a problem with the lights, but if we don't get on it right away, it could be a bigger problem later."

A problem with the lights? Am I really using the Grinch's line to Cindy Lou Who?

"Isn't that something they can take care of tomorrow?" Mom asks. "It's a holiday."

"Technically, I'm the boss." I clamp my mouth shut to stop the giggles that want to burst out. I never thought I'd love being called that, but I really, really do. "I'm going to go with one of the volunteers to check it out for a bit."

"Which volunteer?" Mom asks at the same time Griffin's truck pulls up out front.

This was quite possibly a disastrously stupid plan, but I blame the wine. Maybe the flimsy lights story will be enough to hold off more questions, but right now, I don't care much. Sober Hope can deal with that later.

I grab my parka out of the hall closet, wave to my parents, and dash out the front door without answering Mom's question.

I stomp down the snowy drive and toss myself into the passenger seat before Griffin has a chance to even turn off the engine.

"You're in a hurry today," he says dryly.

I grin at him. "Just drive."

TWENTY-EIGHT
GRIFFIN

PLAYING hero for Hope isn't a bad gig, even if I'm just helping her escape a family dinner. She didn't let me so much as get out of my truck, though. I tell myself to let it go. Hard to work up much of a bad mood when she's right here next to me.

"So, Thanksgiving was good?" I say. She laughs, and something about the husky quality rings a bell. "Good Lord, you're drunk."

She sits taller and turns her cute little nose up. "I had one glass of wine, thank you."

"I don't know how I feel about you drunk-calling me."

I do know. I want her to call me every time she gets buzzed.

"If you don't like it, I can always call someone else. I know a guy with a magnificent model train collection."

"Okay, Tipsy Sue. Where do you want to go?"

"Anywhere."

I have to convince every cell in my body not to turn my truck straight to her apartment. She's been drinking, and that leaves certain detours off the table. Another place comes to mind to take her while she burns off her alcohol. I glance her over—strictly to assess her clothes, but thankfully she's dressed warm enough for what I'm thinking.

Then, I look her over a second time, just for me.

Sunshine in the middle of a holiday is just about as dead as the town gets. The empty, snow-filled streets remind me of something out of a zombie movie...or one of those Christmas movies where the blue-collar guy wins over the sassy business-woman. Let's aim for that one.

I head out on the old highway that winds through the National Forest. Welcoming hills surround Sunshine, but these are just the snow-dusted baby sisters of central Oregon's true mountain peaks. One thing about living in the Northwest, you can never get too far from mountains, rivers, or lakes. I haven't been out here in years, but I drive on autopilot, the backroads calling me home.

"How did your family dinner go?" Hope clamps a hand over her mouth, then speaks through her fingers. "I didn't interrupt, did I?"

"Dinner was over. We were good. It's...harder. Without Dad here."

Every time Caleb and I laughed over something, I'd turn around half-expecting to see Dad walk in to join the fun. By the time I got Hope's text, I'd been ready to bolt just to get away from the memories for a minute.

She slips her hand over to rest on my knee. "Do you want to talk about it?"

"Not really." I appreciate the gesture, but I can't have her hand on my leg, talk about my grief, and navigate snowy roads all in one go. We'll wind up in the ditch.

After a few more miles, I turn down a fishing access road that on any other day would have at least three other trucks parked on it, their drivers out on the river, hoping for a bite. Today, even the most dedicated anglers are taking a break—or have already come and gone. I stop at a turnout and cut the engine.

"Do you mind taking a walk?"

She pulls her bright red hat on and flashes a grin. "I'm ready."

I help her slide out the passenger's side, wishing it wasn't so cold. My hands can't make any satisfying contact with her waist through her thick parka. At least she's wearing her gloves, and I don't have to worry about her fingers going numb today.

"Did you bring your fishing pole?"

"Nah." Our boots crunch through the thin snow as I take the lead. "Caleb and I went fishing Saturday morning."

"I was kidding. Can you actually catch something in all this?"

Hers is not the face of a fisherman, all wide-eyed surprise and a touch of disgust.

"They're still out there. You just have to find the right spot."

"You're more dedicated than I would be."

I laugh at the way she slurs *dedicated*, giving it a few extra syllables.

She tosses her hands on her hips—or where I assume they are beneath that bulky parka. "I'm not drunk!"

"The call of the drunk woman."

She huffs at me, but we keep walking.

"My dad used to fly fish all year round. We went to honor him."

It's more than I expected to tell her. I don't offer details about my emotional state that day, and I sure don't tell her about the tears Caleb and I cried at the river. But she takes my hand, understanding enough.

The gravel peters out at a well-worn path leading down to the riverbank. Some of the trees here still cling to their yellowed leaves, but most are bare. Finally, the path opens onto the

Olallie River's silver waters. The hills beyond are white, the sky a hazy gray. Even like this, I never get tired of the view.

"Oh." Hope gives a delighted little gasp I want to hear again, in a much warmer location. "It's so beautiful."

The river curves in a wide bend, perfect for catching steelhead on a fly. It's shallow and only fifty feet across at most, ideal for wading. On a busy day, you could walk up the whole river on the tops of fishermen's caps and never get your feet wet.

I pick up a smooth, flat stone from the icy bank. Curving one gloved finger around its edge, I throw it over the river, watching it skip one, two, three times before it sinks to the bottom.

Hope picks her way to a beat-up old picnic table somebody carted down here years ago. She swipes her hand to clear the layer of snow and sits down. Squeaking like a mouse, she leaps up again.

"That cold?" I ask with a sly grin.

"I think I got frostbite on my butt."

"Not butt frostbite." I sit down on the wood and pat my legs. "You can sit here."

She looks sideways at my lap like she's tempted. "It's too cold, even for you."

That's the truth. I'm not wearing thermals, and the bench is numbing me on contact, but I'm not about to give up on her so easily. I take her hand and pull her closer. "You can keep me warm."

Her lips twist, fighting a smile, but she lets me pull her into my lap. I wrap my arms around her, snuggling as close as I can, since my hands can't reach her at all. Her parka is my least favorite thing she owns.

"That's better, isn't it?"

She nods and slides one arm around my shoulders. "Let me know when your butt is frozen solid."

"I'll keep you updated on my butt."

She squints at where the river disappears in the distance. "You've been out here a few times, I'm guessing."

"This is where I learned to fish. Dad used to bring Caleb and me all decked out in rubber waders so we could practice our casts."

I can see the three of us tossing our lines in the clear sunshine. Today couldn't be more different, the sky shrouded in dark clouds and a bite in the air reminding me why I rarely fish in the winter. Even in insulated waders, the cold on Saturday had nearly neutered me.

"Those must be some good memories."

"They are. They just about make putting up with Caleb worthwhile." My laugh sounds as brittle as the ice along the riverbank, and Hope hears it. She watches me too long.

Even slightly drunk, she sees more in me than I expect her to. Most people don't. They see the confident veneer I want them to see. Hope cuts right through to the quick. I don't like it. Can't escape it.

But I don't want her to stop.

"Do you like working with him?"

"I don't hate working with him." My thoughts on that range across a spectrum from disgruntled to tolerance, but don't usually veer into anything like happiness. It's probably more to do with the work itself than him, but talking about all that isn't the point of being out here.

"Can I ask you why you're working with them?" She drops her voice to a gentle whisper, like I'm a skittish colt she's trying not to scare away.

"It's...complicated."

"Things with you usually are."

The fondness in her voice makes me want to tell her everything. I don't understand this urge to pry open my heart and show her what's inside, but I don't question it, either.

Hugging her closer, I lean my forehead against the smooth surface of her coat. I spent the whole morning pretending I don't have feelings, and she pulls them to the surface as easily as if they were only waiting for her to ask.

I sit up again and watch the river flow by on its long run south from Jasper Lake.

"Dad never put pressure on me to join the family business. When I went off to college, and later started working in construction, he never let on that he wanted anything else for me. I knew, down deep, he had this dream where both Caleb and I worked with him, but there was never a demand. He never would have. And when he did ask..."

I let the cold air on my face keep the tumult just below the surface in check. Lock it all down. There's a big difference between sharing *something* and sharing *everything*. The river gurgles and churns, catching on rocks as it runs by. Hope caresses the back of my neck, encouraging me to keep going.

"Last fall, he came up to Portland for a weekend. Asked me if I'd ever consider joining them to take on the managerial side of things. I'd only been working for the custom outfit for a couple of years then, but I was content with it. I told him no. That I'd never seen myself working the family business long-term. It'd been a casual conversation, but I still felt like I'd slammed the door in his face. We moved on, and that was that."

I suck in a breath, wishing I could leave the story there.

"A month later, I got the call from Mom that he'd..." I can't say it. Even now, I rarely put those words together. "No warning, no time to say goodbye. He was just gone. Mom and Caleb were reeling just as much as I was. And all I could think was how badly I'd let him down, that he'd...gone, and I'd refused the one thing he'd ever asked of me."

"Oh, Griffin."

"So of course I came back. Too late, maybe, but I'm here. And no, it's not always easy, but this is the only way I can make it up to him." To him, to Mom, even to Caleb. I have debts all the way around.

"Don't you think your dad wanted you to be happy, too?" Her gentle question soothes and cuts at the same time.

"I am happy." It's an automatic response after a year of practice. But I've already admitted plenty for one emotional afternoon. I haven't talked so much or so openly in years, and I can feel that cracked-open heart closing back up again. I hug her tighter. "Maybe even happier since my mom guilted me into working on this Christmas festival of yours."

She slants her mouth like she wants to convince me to go back into sharing-my-feelings mode, but I've already switched into *showing*-my-feelings mode. I slide one hand along her heavily parka'd back, urging her closer.

"I'm hearing that you're loving every minute of working on the festival," she says.

"I'm loving certain minutes." I drop my gaze to her soft, full lips. Waiting. Urging.

Hope leans down, her eyes intent on mine as she closes in. She presses her warm mouth to me and draws back to look into my eyes again. Before I can argue, she pulls off her gloves in a quick motion and cradles my face in her hands.

Her fingers caress my jawline, my temples, the taut skin that lightly aches beneath a still-purple bruise, and finally rake into my hair. I can't help the groan that tumbles out of my throat at the sensation of her nails over my scalp. She presses another soft kiss to my mouth and again pulls back. I tilt my chin, desperate to reach her.

When her mouth returns to mine and she opens up to me, I die a little inside. There's no teasing pulling away this time.

Wine lingers on her mouth, but mostly, I taste her. Sunshine. Summer. Bright, vibrant Hope.

I run a hand along her leg until I reach the parka. I've got a growing urge to be anywhere other than an ice-cold fishing spot. If I were as smart as I think I am, I would have planned this unplanned afternoon more strategically.

She smiles against my mouth, and that open affection staggers me. When has a woman ever taken so much joy from just being with me out on a riverbank? It isn't much. Isn't anything close to what she deserves.

She finally pulls away again and gazes down at me, grinning like this moment means something for her, too.

Please don't let her be tipsy anymore. Let this be all her. All us.

I press my face against her warm neck, breathing in her bright, happy scent. Heaven on earth. "What did you need rescuing from today?"

"My mother."

I try to shift beneath her, but my butt's too numb. "What did she do this time?"

"She's..." Hope seems to debate the right answer. I pull off my gloves, too, and run my fingers through her soft hair, trying to share the same encouragement she gave me. "She means well, but she's always trying so hard to get me to do more."

"More what?"

"Anything. Everything, as long as it's *more*. I can always aim higher. My store could be bigger. The Christmas festival could become a full-time job. She's always setting me up on dates because I obviously can't get that right, either."

"Is that what you needed to be rescued from, a Thanksgiving date?" I'm joking, but the laughter dies in my throat when she gives me a funny sideways glance. "You were on a date just now?"

"No!" She bites her bottom lip. "She was just...sort of trying to arrange one for me."

I drop my hands to my sides. "Who's the guy?"

She shrugs. "Some pediatric dentist in Bend."

I can't remember hating anyone as much as I hate this guy. "What's he like? Good guy?"

My voice is stiff and weird, but I can't fix it.

Hope stands, and for a split second, I think that's it. She's realized her mistake and is going to ask me to take her back to whoever her mom's so excited about. Instead, she tosses one leg over mine and straddles me, climbing into my lap. My brain malfunctions as she runs her fingers in my hair again, her legs warm against my hips.

"He's not you." She holds my face, her fingertips sending tendrils of heat across my skin. "He's never done carpentry for a Christmas festival just because his mom asked him to. He's never defended me and my dreams when nobody else would."

She strokes the sides of my face down to my jaw, her eyes stuck on my mouth. "He's never made me feel the way you do. He's got nothing on you."

I'm still processing her sweet little speech when she kisses me so tenderly, I'm not sure if I should tell her to run as fast as she can or hold onto her and never give her up. She kisses me like she's giving me something precious in every touch. I pull her to me hard and kiss her the same way, like I can share all those pieces of myself I can't explain in words.

Every piece of me that needs this woman.

When she breaks the kiss, I press my mouth to her neck. I want to eat her up. I want to cuddle up with her for days. I want to number a list of delicious things to do to her and tick through them one by one.

She gives a sidelong glance at the darkening sky. "We can't stay out here all night. We should probably go back soon."

I grumble but don't fight her. I'm already frozen to the bone. As soon as the sun goes down, the temperature will dip below freezing, and there's no sense in staying out so long in the cold and dark. Now, someplace warm inside, maybe...

She crawls off my lap and holds her hands out to help me up. I can't walk straight, frozen like I am, and I wince with every step. I look like a cowboy who just got off a sixteen-hour ride.

"Does your truck have heated seats?" Her mouth curls into a delectable smirk. I shake my head, and she wraps an arm around my waist. "You're a true gentleman to sacrifice for me that way."

"You have no idea." I nuzzle the top of her head.

We ride back to Sunshine with the heat on high, driving slowly in the twilight.

"So, your mom sets you up a lot? On dates?" I've fooled exactly nobody with my attempt at casual curiosity. I didn't mind her mom's hints about me, but the idea of her on a date with another guy is wedged under my skin. I don't like it at all.

"Sometimes. It's embarrassing. I wish she would trust me to make my own decisions."

"Why don't you just tell her that?"

"It's not that easy."

I want to argue, but I don't have much to stand on. I'd told my dad what I felt, and I've never regretted anything more.

I pull up in front of her parents' house, relieved there's no extra car here, as though maybe her mom invited that dentist over to wait it out until Hope got back. But then a thought worms into my head, and I can't shake it.

"Are you going to see him?" I sound reasonably calm, considering everything that's riding on this question.

She looks like I just started a whole new conversation. "Who?"

I toss a hand toward the house. "Your mom's dentist friend."

She leans closer and plants a kiss on my cheek. "I'm only seeing my handyman."

"Good."

"I have to go into the warehouse early tomorrow. Should I call you or the dentist or...?"

I grab her around the waist and tug her across the seat to me. "You enjoy baiting me too much."

She presses another kiss to my cheek. This one's almost on my mouth, but not quite. The tiny sliver of lip that caught hers feels like it's on fire. "But you like it when I bait you."

I really do.

"What time tomorrow?"

She moves in closer to kiss in front of my ear as if she knows I want her mouth to land there, but she's refusing. Because now, she's loving this.

"Seven." Her whisper skates over the shell of my ear.

I'm not a strong man, and I break after a few sultry kisses. Crushing her to me, I kiss my way up her neck, loving her shiver beneath my mouth.

Eventually, she slips away, but before she closes my truck door, she gets in her parting shot.

"You're cute when you're jealous."

TWENTY-NINE
HOPE

WHEN I GET to the warehouse Friday morning, Griffin's truck is already out front. I think it's a little bit overkill for him to be here so early, but I love that he's worried about me. It's not the most modern take, but his jealousy yesterday made me all fizzy inside. I'm not sure I've ever had someone care that much about me.

Not that I *know* he cares about me. I need to keep that clear in my mind. This is Griffin. He's smart and calculated, and as outgoing as he can be, he's not an open book. I used to think he didn't have much of a heart. Now I realize he's got one, but it's locked away in the biggest, sternest fortress around. I'll just have to find my way in, that's all.

Inside, he walks straight over to me with a coffee. "Caramel something something for the boss."

I accept his offering. "You are by far the best volunteer I've ever had."

He takes a sip of his coffee, watching me over the rim of his cup. "I aim to please."

It's freezing in here this morning, but I need to fan myself from all the heat in his eyes. Something hot and strong and extremely tempting holds there like a silent dare. He cocks an eyebrow, fully convinced I'm going to give in.

Apparently, I have no willpower when it comes to Griffin, because I do give in. I lean up and kiss the side of his mouth. "I like that about you."

His mouth twists. "You make it real hard to focus on work, boss."

"I'll try to be more professional." I nod once, as if I'm taking him very seriously.

He exhales a laugh. "All right, what's on the agenda today?"

I take a step back and sip at my macchiato, trying not to be too ridiculous over him remembering my coffee order. "I'm going to get a couple of hours of painting in this morning, thus —" I sweep a hand down my body. I'm in jeans and an old sweatshirt, but I'll change into something a little nicer in Blackbird's restroom before I open The Painted Daisy.

His eyes follow my movement, and that flame in them goes back to high. Really? Old jeans and a sweatshirt I've had for at least ten years do it for him? Guess I'd better note that for later. *But not today, Hope.*

"It's going to be wild in the store for the next two days, so this is it for me until Sunday. But when you have a minute, I thought you might help me figure out how we're going to string these garlands up."

We set down our coffees and walk over to the bins of light strings. It'd taken extra time to follow Griffin's advice and sort the strings by bulb type, but it's worth it to keep the lights from blowing up. I've already got detailed maps in each one so volunteers know where everything goes. They're for trees in town square, a few of the city buildings downtown, and several lengths will cross over Maple Street.

Truly, it's a crapton of lights, but what's Christmas without a jolly glow?

I show him the heavy-duty wire wrapped in fake pine garland in bins I'd set aside. "These secure to the tops of the lamp posts, but whatever hardware used to connect them isn't here anymore."

A lot of the generic Christmas festival supplies have gone missing. Nothing obvious, like the light-up snowmen or candy canes that hang from the lamp posts, but smaller things like pulleys, wires, and clamps that no one would notice until the last minute, as I discovered.

"So I've got to figure out a way to string a dozen lengths of lighted wire over Maple Street." He assesses the coils of garlands like he's up for the challenge. "Any guess what the load weight is on these?"

"Not a clue."

He chuckles. "Looks like I'll be paying another visit to Bridger Hardware. Want to meet me in the closet?"

My heart pops and fizzes over his devilish grin. Next time we do that, there'll be less talking. "I wish."

"What's my deadline?"

"I've got a crew to work on the smaller lights all week, but we won't do Maple until Thursday. That's a special job. I happen to have a contact with a landscaping company that can help us."

He pulls me straight to him, snuggling me close. "A contact, huh?"

"Just some handyman I know."

He presses soft kisses up the side of my neck. All the dials in my body go haywire over every gliding touch of his lips. He reaches a spot behind my ear, and I grab a handful of his barn jacket, no longer caring about Black Friday, my store, or the festival. There is only Griffin's mouth on me, and I need *more*.

"I heard he's skilled with a cherry picker," I breathe.

He laughs against my neck, and his warm breath makes me cling even tighter to him. "I can't wait to show you all my skills."

I have died. Burnt up to a crisp, leaving nothing but an ashy pile of want with a little sign that says *Here lies Hope Parrish, killed by too much flirtation.*

Pushing against his chest, I try oh so hard to bring my thoughts back together. "I have to start painting."

He doesn't move. "Right now?"

Those luscious hazel-green eyes are *doing things* to me. I resist for about three seconds before I melt against him.

"Five more minutes."

———

I NEVER THOUGHT I would count down the minutes until I closed up my shop, but I've got my eye on the clock, ready to punch out. For two days straight, the little bell over The Painted Daisy's door hasn't stopped ringing. I scurried around like a grinning whirlwind, ringing up sales, replacing stock, and talking up our local artists. Griffin popped by both days, but it's been too busy for me to break for lunch, even with Abby in the store.

Is it wrong that I like how he's checking up on me? He wants to make sure I'm taking care of myself and eating right, and it's the most adorable thing. I text him another waffle, just because I'm a dork.

Black Friday and Small Business Saturday have refilled my store's tills and rejuvenated my confidence that this little shop has staying power, but I'm wrung out. All I want is a steamy bath. More likely, I'll collapse in bed with my clothes on like I did last night, but I'll dream of a sudsy soak while I've got the energy.

I've just left the counter to lock the front door when I spot a woman on the other side of the glass. It doesn't happen often, but I get the occasional straggler who keeps me open late by squeezing in just before closing. I know I should be grateful for the business, but tonight I'm tired all the way down to my boots.

The woman pushes the door open, and I can feel that hot bath slipping away.

"Welcome to the Painted—Lila?"

My sister stands just inside the door, a vision of loveliness, glancing around like she's not sure she's in the right place. Finally, she meets my eyes, and her lost look morphs until she's beaming at me. "Surprise!"

Um...no kidding. I'm both excited to have her here and absolutely confused that she is.

We hug in the middle of the store. "What are you doing?" I ask when I step back.

"I'm here to help." She grins even wider, like she's congratulating me on my good fortune.

"Help?"

"With the Christmas festival. You never sent me those permissions, so here I am."

"Here you are." My enthusiasm doesn't quite match hers.

She zooms over to one of the jewelry displays and lightly touches a delicate chain dotted with coral-colored gemstones. "What are these bracelets set with?"

"Sunstones," I say automatically. I can't believe my sister is standing in my store. Impulsiveness used to be her norm, but Lila hasn't *dropped in* since she started dating Josh three years ago. "When did you get in town?"

"Just now. I've been driving all day, and I'm starving. What do you say to dinner? My treat."

I can't stop staring. Only Lila could drive six hours on winter roads and still look flawless, with her dark hair in a sleek updo and her stylish wool jacket over her neat jeans. Her sweater is probably cashmere, and a hint of her fresh, green perfume wafts over me. I would have looked and smelled like a swamp monster after driving down from Seattle.

"You drove here? Why? Is Josh with you?"

"Josh stayed in Seattle. He knows I wanted to be here with you and see the big Christmas festival you're putting on." She snatches up one of the handbags Wren's been admiring. "Is this real leather?"

"No, it's vegan. What about your job? You can just leave for the week?"

She waves a hand like this conversation can't hold her interest. "Don't worry about it."

"But what are you doing here?"

Her eager enthusiasm crumples. "You're acting like it's a crime to visit my family. Don't you want me here?"

Normally, Lila would fire back a sassy response to my continued questions, but she almost looks like she's going to cry. Maybe I could have welcomed her better. I haven't seen her in a couple of months, but I'm just so surprised, I still don't know what to say.

"Of course you're welcome," I say, softening my voice. "It's just unexpected, that's all. Mom and Dad didn't say anything about you coming for a visit."

"They don't know yet. I thought it would be more fun if it was a surprise." Lila seems to snap out of her funk. "Let's pick up pizza at Mario's. Can I stay with you for a few days?"

"Sure, but there's not a lot of room."

"I don't mind the couch." She grins again, but it doesn't reach her eyes. In fact, it looks a little desperate. "I don't want to stay with Mom and Dad. You know how they can be."

"Yeah, and they're going to be pissed with you for waiting until after Thanksgiving to come down for your little surprise visit. Why didn't you come for the holiday?"

"I wasn't feeling well on Thanksgiving. I'm all better now, though, so don't worry about germs."

I see what Griffin said the other day—the Homecoming Queen smile isn't genuine at all. How many times has she smiled like that, and I never recognized it? "Lila, is everything okay?"

"Of course. I just wanted to come see the big event in person." Her smile vanishes, and she shifts into her serious business look. "I've already got social media posts ready to go. I can't wait to show you. I'll take pictures around town this week, maybe post some behind-the-scenes shots of what you're doing. Give a glimpse of the magic. We're going to get this little Christmas festival to go viral and get everybody in the state headed this way. It will be *the* event of the season."

Oh. It all clicks into place now. She's not dropping in to see *me*. She's here because of the festival. I didn't let her get involved from a distance, so she's here in person to make it impossible for me to refuse her.

She smiles even wider again, and this one looks more natural. "Are we going for pizza or what?"

"Right. Pizza."

I pull my purse from behind the counter, flip off the lights, and flash my own fake smile at her as I lock up. I haven't decided if her eagerness to help out stems from a sudden sense of hometown pride or if Lila is just as convinced as everyone else that I can't make it a success without her.

THIRTY
GRIFFIN

I MUST BE crazy if I'm looking forward to working all day on a Sunday. But considering who my coworker is, I can't get to the warehouse fast enough.

I've got the final Winter Wonderland house to make, and she's still painting. This afternoon, we've got a light-stringing party planned with a bunch of volunteers in town square. Hopefully, by the end of the day, Hope will have enough done she can take it easy the rest of the week until tree lighting.

And by take it easy, I mean do the fifty *other* things she has to do before the festival.

She's got Christmas music going, and Bing Crosby's voice croons from her phone like melted caramels. Maybe I should have worn Caleb's elf hat today and really fit the theme. Decked out in her painting outfit of jeans and a sweatshirt, she looks like she's ready to snuggle up on the couch with me and watch Christmas movies. Not something I usually daydream about... but if we pay attention to them like we did the last one, I'd be game.

"I brought coffee," she chirps when she sees me. "And donuts, since we'll be here a while."

"I knew you were a superior boss."

She finishes getting her painting supplies ready and walks over to me. "You'll never guess who turned up in my store last night."

I will *not* say the dentist her mom's trying to get her with, even though that's the first person who popped into my mind. A rich, handsome jack-in-the-box I'd like to punch in the face. "I give up."

"My sister."

"You weren't expecting her?"

"Nope. Lila just showed up as I was closing up The Daisy, ready to help out with the Christmas festival marketing." Her nose wrinkles like something about that explanation smells off.

"That's not a bad thing, right?"

She examines the closest Wonderland building. "I guess."

"Why don't you want her to help? There's plenty of things to do." Frankly, I think she can stand to spread her responsibilities to a couple more people, but it's a little late for that now.

"She just swept in with this whole game plan. You should have heard her talk about what she wants to do. I think she's been working on it for weeks, just waiting for me to break down and ask her to help. Only, I didn't ask for help, so she's barging in anyway."

"What's the harm in letting her do it? You've delegated plenty of tasks already. Besides, anything that brings more people in to see the incredible festival you've got planned is good in my book."

"Now you're just sweet talking me."

"Doesn't mean it's not true."

She walks to the Wonderland house she's been painting. This one's going to be a toy store, but right now she's still getting the main building colors on the primed plywood.

"It's just...accepting Lila's help will prove I can't handle this project on my own. That I need my big sister to take over and rescue me like everyone thinks."

"Hey." I turn her around to face me. "Anyone who thinks that doesn't know you and doesn't matter. Sometimes you have to accept a little help, sweetheart. Even from your family."

She grumbles but settles into my arms and runs her hands over my chest. "I wanted this festival to distinguish me from Lila. Now, people will say I can't do anything without her help."

"You know what I say to that?"

She rolls her eyes. "'Who cares?'"

I hug her closer. "Not quite. Could you have made this Winter Wonderland by yourself?"

She laughs, but already sees where I'm going with this. Her little grumble is adorable. "No."

"But I'm not taking over, right?"

"I mean, you've tried."

I dip my head down to get her to look at me. "I made suggestions. There's a difference. But you can't do everything. Just because it takes a whole crew to do it doesn't take away from the end result, boss. Everybody working together just makes it better."

"Is that the same at your work?"

"Of course. The cement crew lays the foundation, the framers get the bones up, and the drywall crew comes in to smooth it all out. Then a dozen more crews come in to do all the finish work. Everybody does their part to make a beautiful custom home in the end."

She smooths her hands across my chest, looking up at me with soft eyes. "Every time you talk about your work, you talk about construction, not landscaping."

Her voice is gentle, almost a whisper, but it hits like a shock to the solar plexus. I let go of her and slowly slip out of her arms. "Habit. I'm still adjusting to the change."

True. I just don't expect to get used to it until somewhere around retirement.

She lays a hand on my forearm, stopping me from going too far. "You obviously love doing custom woodwork."

I clench my jaw, because I can't get into this. After everything I told her at the riverside, she knows my reasons. Whether she understands them or not is out of my hands.

"I'm not saying you have to make a change, but it's okay to miss it."

Maybe. But admitting that I miss it would involve admitting I'm not happy doing the thing my family needs me to do. I need to be here for them, and that includes at the business.

"Look at me," she goes on. "I worked with my mom for almost a year, and I was miserable. Can you see me selling houses and locking down leases on retail properties?"

"Actually, I can." Her enthusiasm and dedication would win over anybody on the fence. Or maybe that's just because I'd buy anything she tried to sell me.

"I was good at it, but I didn't enjoy it. I needed to follow my heart." She squeezes my forearm where she's still holding onto me. "I just want you to follow your heart, too."

If I followed my heart right now, it'd lead me to wherever Hope was. I'm ready to lock this thing down with her, and I still haven't taken her on a first date.

"Do you have time for a night out this week? Maybe a pre-celebration celebration?"

She smiles, but her eyes narrow on me. "What do you have in mind?"

"I've got a few ideas." I already know what it's going to be—providing the weather holds.

"Of course you do. How about Wednesday?"

"Wednesday it is."

THIRTY-ONE
HOPE

IF GRIFFIN SURVIVES STRINGING up lights on the courthouse, I'm going to kill him.

My heart seesaws in my chest as he teeters on the top of a ladder slightly too short for the job. Moving up to tiptoes, he stretches to reach the hooks embedded in the brick courthouse's mortar. I hold the ladder and try to ignore the panic that bubbles inside me every time he shifts his weight. One misstep, and he'll be on the pavement.

"We should have waited for a taller ladder. Or one of those grabby things." My volunteer crew is using the other ladders and gear to decorate buildings along Maple Street, leaving us with the smallish ladder nobody else wanted—and no extender pole for reaching the hooks.

"I, too, can be used as a grabby thing."

He's looking down at me with a rakish grin that both makes my insides go wild and makes me terrified he's going to get distracted and fall. And the man is definitely distracted.

"I'm pretty sure you're not supposed to stand on the top of a ladder." I'd tried holding his feet in place, but he said that only made him feel more likely to fall.

"I'm almost done." With one last effort, he stretches to tuck the light strand behind a hook. "But," he says, slowly lowering himself until he gets a foot on the top rung, "it all worked out."

He climbs down and hops the last two feet to the ground. "Ta-da!"

I release an exhale. His impatience to get the decorations up is sweet, but he doesn't need to risk his neck over it. "Don't ever do that again."

"Whatever you say, boss."

We step back to admire his handiwork.

"It's really starting to feel like Christmas." Businesses started decorating storefronts and shop windows even before Thanksgiving, and now it's impossible to walk down Maple Street without seeing red and green glory in every window. "I can't wait for all the lights to go on Friday night and make the whole town sparkle."

He looks over at me. "Why do I get the feeling I'm in for an overdose of Christmas cheer this season?"

"It's impossible to overdose on Christmas cheer. Your body can always take more."

Right now, though, *my* body is going nuts over his hint we'll be together for Christmas. We don't have some deadline hanging over us where we have to stop seeing each other after the festival on Friday, but we've very much been in one day at a time mode.

He narrows his eyes on the courthouse. "A more ambitious man would have strung up lights all along the gables, too."

"That man would have been fired by his boss for giving her a panic attack."

He chuckles low. "You can't fire me. I'm a volunteer."

"You're right, I can't fire you," I say sweetly. "But no guarantees a two-by-four doesn't go astray again."

"I knew you did that on purpose."

I put a hand over my heart as though he's mortally offended me, but that just makes him laugh outright. He folds the ladder and hoists it onto his shoulder.

"I'm going to take this to the warehouse and get a little more work done."

He leans closer like he's coming in for a kiss, and I shift away automatically.

His jaw clenches, and the moment drags horribly. "Are we still doing this? Hiding out?"

I make a helpless sound, unsure of what to say. We're so exposed on the courthouse steps, nothing we do here could be considered private. People have probably already reported seeing us together again to my mom. I don't want her calling Mimi's Bridal "just to check" on appointments.

And...I want to keep him to myself.

"No, I get it. Rumors." He doesn't quite meet my eye. "I've got to finish sanding that last Wonderland house."

He walks down the steps strewn with rock salt. I follow, ready to stop him and explain, when someone calls my name.

"Hope!" Ada's approaching me from the opposite direction. Bundled up in her big black coat, she takes careful steps on the shoveled sidewalk.

I turn for a second and watch my handyman slash would-be boyfriend get farther away before I give Ada my full attention.

"What can I do for you?" My smile feels too tight, my mind distracted, but I can't just walk away and be rude.

"Do you have an activity list for Friday night on you?"

My heart warms to see she's wearing a crocheted scarf that came from my store—or at least one of my artists. It's wrapped up high against her chin, her gray wisps of hair brushing along the top.

"I don't have anything with me." I'd left flyers in several businesses, but I don't have anything handy to give out.

"My granddaughter plans to come over from Salem with her babies, but she said she couldn't find the event schedule online, and I must have recycled the notice in the paper."

"The festival has a website, and the event's on social media if she searches for it."

"And the entire event schedule's on there?"

I drop my mouth open to answer but have to close it again. I...don't remember exactly what I posted where. Everything's on the website, but did I put the same detailed graphic on all the pages across social media? Or did I just plan to?

My stomach caves in like an igloo that can't hold up to its own weight. I've been scrambling around, trying to keep so many plates spinning. Did I completely forget about one of the most important ones? My cute Winter Wonderland and the full booths in the Christmas market won't do much good if nobody knows they're going to be there.

"I'll double check," I tell her when I've got my voice again. "I'll make sure everything's listed and easy to find. For now, I'll take a picture of the flyer when I get back to my store and text it to you."

She nods. "I appreciate it. My great grand-babies are looking forward to Friday night."

With that sweet reminder, she walks away, and I pull out my phone to scroll through the festival's socials, hoping against hope I haven't sabotaged my own plans.

———

It's late in the evening when I finally drag myself home. Between lights and painting and nine thousand last-minute phone calls from volunteers, I haven't had a minute to myself. I want a little space to unwind before I crash into bed.

My house is blazing bright, every light on in the house. Lila huddles over her computer at the kitchen table, her phone resting on top of a notebook covered in her neat handwriting.

"Good day?" she asks.

I shrug out of my coat and hang it up, sifting through my possible answers, but when I turn around, I stop cold. "You cleaned."

She looks up from the computer. "Just a little."

"*Just a little* is straightening the junk on the coffee table and putting dirty dishes in the sink. You did all the dishes. The counters are spotless." I point an accusatory finger at the floor. "You mopped."

She's not a neat freak, and her attention to detail today feels weirdly suspicious. "What's going on?"

Lila shrugs it off. "I'm a conscientious guest."

I narrow my eyes at her. "Thank you?"

"I've been researching other Christmas festivals across the country and checking out their socials all day. Now get over here and look at my week of planned posts."

"Can we do it tomorrow?"

"No. No more blowing me off. I've worked really hard on this."

So have I. But I shuffle over and pull a chair around to Lila's side. She opens a folder on her computer and clicks through page after page of colorful, Christmas-themed cheer. Peppy posts describing festival events, thoughtful posts about the importance of family time during the holidays, notes from Santa and Mrs. Claus. Lila's description of her plans over pizza hadn't come close to conveying this level of detail.

"When did you do all this?"

"The last few days. When I saw you hadn't updated the festival's socials, I knew I needed to step in."

Well. That's cold water on my appreciation. "Why don't you send them to me, and I'll post some this week?"

"Just give me all your permissions, and I'll take over." She picks up a pen like I'm going to spill all the passwords here and now.

Her offer makes me shrink a little, like tinsel too close to a fire. "Lila, I can do this."

"Can you? What are you doing this week?"

"I'm going to paint the last Winter Wonderland house, help string up lights through town, and work with the crew decorating the big tree on Friday."

She raises her eyebrows. "Is that it?"

I sag against the chair. I'll also meet with the choir director, the Christmas market set up crew, the volunteers manning the refreshment booths, and finish my toy display in Henderson's window. Plus about a hundred other tiny little things that don't seem like much but add up to one huge commitment.

"And don't forget your store," she adds. "You'll be spending some time there, too, I assume."

My smile is faint but genuine. It means a lot that she included The Painted Daisy in my responsibilities.

"When we start posting all of this, you're going to get messages. Lots of them. Question after question asking for specifics. Are you going to have time to answer them all? Do you really want to blow people off right when you're catching their attention?"

Like Ada's granddaughter who isn't sure what time everything starts. My sigh sounds a little too much like a wailing Jacob Marley. Lila's right. So is Griffin, and Mom, and Ada and Isabel, and half the town—I can't do it all by myself. Not well, anyway. Not the way I want to.

"Just let me help," she says in a small voice. "I'm kind of invested in this thing now."

"Really?"

"Yeah. I've been trying to make tech nerds sound cool and professional for years. Working on this is actually fun."

Lila's true, happy smile sweeps away the last of my resentment. Letting her work on this with me won't take away from my success. It can only make the festival better. She knows social media better than anyone else I could ask. I shouldn't be fighting something that will ultimately bring more people into town.

"Okay," I finally say.

"Okay? You'll let me help?"

I'm not sure how working together will go, and Mom will probably go bananas when she finds out Lila's on board, but it's the right thing to do for the festival.

"Yes. You can help."

She squeals and throws her arms around my shoulders. "Finally! Give me all the permissions, I want to get started tonight. I've only got a week to turn things around."

I remind myself she means well and start writing everything down.

THIRTY-TWO
GRIFFIN

CRIBS ARE a lot harder to put together than you'd think.

Caleb's collapsed in the rocking chair, and I'm sitting on the floor against the wall, sweating through my shirt. He wouldn't admit how long he'd wrestled with the crib pieces before he called me for my opinion. Frankly, it's embarrassing how long it took both of us looking at the instructions before we finally got the thing together.

"I still don't like that." Caleb points a finger around the beer he's holding at the lone washer on the floor in the center of the room.

I take a long pull of my beer, my supposed payment for my supposed help tonight. "It's probably fine."

Was it an extra? Or did we miss a step somewhere, and the crib's going to fall apart one day with his baby in it? I'd be worried, too. I'm not eager to tear the whole thing down to double check, but it'd eat at me if that were my kid.

"It would have helped if the instructions were written in anything like English. Just pictures would have been fine, too." He taps one boot over the page of single-spaced instructions. "But those were worthless."

They read like they'd been washed through a few different language translators. *"Use the main tool to rotate the piece head.* Couldn't be clearer."

"Rowan loves the crib, though."

Yeah, he didn't have much choice there, whipped as he is.

"This room used to be cool." A year ago, he had a mini-man cave with an expensive gaming set up, his vintage Lego collection, and his prized Galaxy Quest poster signed by the cast. Now, it's soft and muted, with a crib, a dresser with a soft pad on top, and a rocker. There's a plush blue rug on the floor and a lamp that barely throws off light.

At least the Legos are still here. He installed narrow picture shelves around the room to display his old mini-figures.

A stuffed giraffe slumps in one corner, waiting to be loved by the room's future occupant. Maybe in a year or so, when we know what he likes, I'll ask Hope to paint the little man's lovey for Caleb and Rowan.

"What are you smiling about?" he asks.

Because a big brother can never let a guy have a minute.

"Just thinking that I'm going to be an uncle. Feels strange."

Now he's the one wearing a goofy smile. "Just wait until you try on *daddy.*"

I do not think about creating a nursery with Hope. I do not think about her pregnant with our child. And I absolutely do not picture her holding a baby in a room just like this.

I do not.

My heart squeezes with crazy, never before heard of wants anyway.

"Are you ready for it?" I ask.

"Who is, right? I don't know if I'm ready, but I know I want it." He takes another drink of his beer. "Are you out of your dating slump yet?"

How to answer? I just had a brief but vivid vision of a

woman bearing my child, and I haven't taken her on a date yet. Does that make me invested or a creep? Little from column A, little from column B.

"Hopefully here soon."

"Anyone in mind?"

I feel like Indiana Jones trying to navigate my steps across a booby-trapped floor, knowing if I put one foot out of line, I'm sunk. Caleb's not a gossip, but after the way Hope shied away from my kiss this afternoon, it doesn't feel right to say much about her. I'm not entirely sure she'd want me to say anything at all.

"There's someone, but we're keeping things quiet."

His brows drop into a scowl. "Is she married?"

Beer goes down my windpipe, and I have to cough it out like a lunatic. I wipe my face and glare at my brother. "No! Why would you think that?"

"Why would you keep things a secret?"

I don't like that word, and I like *being* that word even less. "It's not a secret, it's just early. She doesn't want the town to talk about it."

He goes on watching me until I have to change position on the floor. "I don't like it, okay? But I'm trying to let her take the lead here."

Lord knows I've tried to steamroll her on enough already.

"How early?" Caleb asks.

I've lost the thread of our conversation. His brief accusation I would date a married woman kind of threw me off. "What?"

"How early is this relationship?"

I hitch a shoulder. "A few we—"

I catch his smirk too late. That's enough. He knows exactly who we're talking about.

"Say nothing. Seriously, man. Don't even breathe a word unless I give the all-clear."

He dashes one finger over his heart in an X. "I won't say anything. I'm pulling for you, though."

I nod, and we go back to drinking our beers in this soft, cozy room.

"Maybe she'll help you work through your feelings," he says.

"Don't."

His mouth twitches. "It'd be nice to see you get in touch with your softer side."

"I'm going to leave."

He points at me like I need to stay where I am. "You just drank a beer."

"I'll walk."

Still, I don't get up. I don't want to talk through my feelings, but I like this conversation where Hope and I are almost something real. Something real and out in the open.

"I'm glad you're here," he says after a few more minutes. "Truly."

My heart thumps hard against my ribs. "Me, too."

We visited each other when I lived in Portland, but not often enough. Nothing like being right across town from each other. Even if I hate the circumstances that brought me back, I'm glad I'm here. Our days in the office can be strained, but evenings like this remind me just how much I like the guy.

"Wearing that elf hat for her would probably seal the deal," Caleb says.

"That's it. I'm done."

So much for brotherly love.

THIRTY-THREE

HOPE

I LOCK The Painted Daisy's door and zip my parka up to my chin. Forty-eight hours to go until tree lighting, and everything's pulling together. A few meetings, a lot of calls, and a little chaos, but it's really happening. I have confirmations from all the vendors in the Christmas market, the choir director finalized their songs, and my volunteers for our drinks station more or less knows how to add powdered cocoa mix to hot water. I've done just about all I can do.

And now I've got a date with Griffin.

My heart glows and soars like Rudolph because it always does when I think about that man. He's turned out to be completely unexpected but absolutely right. His calm determination makes me feel like anything's possible, and his fierce protectiveness makes me feel safe like no one else ever has. If I could go back in time, I'd whisper to my high school self playing Kiss, Marry, Kill that she was wiping out the wrong guy.

I touch a finger to the clay waffle hanging from my ear as I turn the corner to the warehouse and see the man himself. Joy shimmers around inside me like a disco ball. And—

"Is that an elf hat?" I draw closer, and sure enough, he's

wearing a bright red and green hat complete with long tail. I flick the end to make the bell jingle. We both had secrets up our sleeves tonight.

He grins. "Seemed appropriate."

"You really are such a kiss up."

His eyes heat as they trace my mouth. "I've got so much kissing up left to do."

"Why are you standing out here?"

"Waiting for you." He succumbs to temptation and kisses me, way too briefly. "There's something I want you to see."

He pulls the warehouse door open to reveal the Winter Wonderland in all its glory. My heart explodes in a series of holly jolly fireworks, each bigger and more magnificent than the last. I clap my hands together and make inarticulate high-pitched sounds.

"I thought there'd be squealing," he says.

"You finished them. I knew you would, obviously, but you finished them."

I'd had to leave the last house for him to paint this week because I just didn't have enough time. A simple townhouse, it didn't need the details I added to the others, and I left him an intricate paint color schematic he obviously followed to the letter.

He laughs as I walk around each building, complete and perfect on the warehouse floor. A bakery, bookshop, toy store, and two houses that would fit right in at the North Pole. They're better than I'd dreamed—and I have a good imagination.

I throw my arms around his shoulders, burrowing my face into his neck. "I can't thank you enough."

"Hey," he says softly. "I wasn't expecting tears, sweetheart."

I pull back and run a finger beneath each eye. "I'm not crying. My happiness just went all watery, that's all."

"Don't, or you'll make me all watery, too. They're just pretend houses."

Really? He's trying to claim modesty *now*? Now that I've seen these festive, adorable houses in all their glory? Nice try.

"They're not, though. They're my Winter Wonderland, and you made them come to life like Frosty." I give a hearty sniffle, but I make myself stop crying. That's ridiculous. And a little bit unavoidable. "I can't wait to see them in town square."

"You're going to make a lot of little kids happy." He says it like that's an accomplishment, like that's living the dream.

And I think maybe I love this man. This confident, cocky man who swept into my warehouse like everything in it was beneath him, who now talks about my goals like they're his goals, too. My heart buzzes like I've got a whole beehive in there, every one humming confirmation of this love.

This is...maybe bad. Maybe very bad indeed. I can't *love* Griffin McBride after a few weeks of spending every single day together. Can I?

My buzzing heart maintains I can.

"You've made me so happy." I grab the lapels of his barn jacket and pull him closer. His hands go to my waist, which I sadly can't feel because of my big coat. I want his hands on *me*. "I don't feel like I've thanked you enough."

He nuzzles against me and kisses behind my ear. I suck in a breath, holding in my shivers.

"It's a good start," he says.

"What are we doing for our date tonight?"

He flashes me a look of pure mischief. "I have an idea, but it's a pretty bad one. You might not be in."

"Is it wrong I'm a little turned on?"

He fakes a pout. "Only a little?"

We lock up the warehouse and walk outside to Griffin's

truck. He opens the passenger door, revealing a pile of something stuffed in the back seat.

I stare at what he has back there. "Blankets?"

He bobs his eyebrows and nods at the truck bed. I peer in and spot two bundles of firewood.

"I thought we could have a little bonfire in the canyon."

I clap my hands like it's Christmas morning. "Holy cow, yes!"

He still looks skeptical. "It's awfully cold. We might not last long before we give it up as a one-way street to popsicle town."

"I'm completely one hundred percent in on giving it a try."

His grin gets my stomach swooping low. "Then let's do this."

Griffin drives the canyon roads like he can see in the dark and has every intersection memorized. I would have had the truck at a crawl, squinting at half-hidden signs in a desperate attempt not to get lost or plow us into a snowbank.

"How do you still remember where to go up here?"

"You underestimate how often I came out here."

He finds the gravel road he's looking for, barely more than a strip of white in the trees, but in another minute, he's parked in a turnout at a dead-end. He pulls off the elf hat and tugs a thick-knit beanie down low over his ears until he's nothing but a pair of hazel eyes and a chiseled jaw. Oh, the things I want to do to that jaw.

He opens the glovebox and hands a big flashlight to me, and we each grab a stack of blankets from the back. He pulls one of the firewood bundles from the truck bed, but he carries it all like it's nothing. We pick our way along the path by flashlight beam, the only sound the occasional hoot of an owl somewhere overhead.

"This is an excellent spot for an axe murdering," I whisper.

He pauses on the narrow path. "Do you want to go back to town? We can do something else."

I adore his earnestness. No guilting me, no hesitation, just if I want to leave, we can.

But to be clear, I don't want to leave. I lean into him, trying not to shine the flashlight in his face. "No, I want to stay. It's just so quiet out here. I can't see anything."

"You don't camp much, do you?"

"I've gone camping exactly zero times."

He nods forward and we continue on. "You live in a town surrounded by forest, and you've never gone camping? Not even as a kid?"

Everything the flashlight beam falls on casts strange shadows, like something could be waiting just beyond the light. It's weird and spooky out here, but no way will I admit that I'm on the verge of freaking out. I've waited over a decade to be at one of Griffin's famous bonfires. I'm not going to ruin it by telling him how big of a chicken I am.

"I don't think my mother knows how to rough it."

"What about you?"

"Let's find out."

We reach the stone fire pit he'd been heading for and start arranging blankets next to it. His bundle included a tarp, which he lays out first to protect us from the light dusting of snow, then the blankets in a cozy heap. Next, he sits me down in the middle like a pampered princess, pulling one blanket over my shoulders and another over my legs. Once he's satisfied I'm warm enough, he turns his attention to the firewood.

I shine my flashlight on the stone ring to give him some light to work with, but even this he seems to know how to do in the dark. After much newspaper twisting and precision log arranging, he pulls a long lighter out of a coat pocket.

"Here goes nothing." He ignites it and touches the flame to several spots until the fire crackles to life.

I open up my blanket throne so he can crawl in and share the heat. He burrows in behind me, snuggling me close in his arms and legs, then secures the blankets again. This isn't remotely what I imagined when he talked about roughing it, but I absolutely love it. I lean against his chest, not the least bit sorry we're here with snow on the ground instead of on a hot summer night. With him around, I'll never feel the cold.

The spooky stuff, I'm less certain about.

Griffin rests his chin on my shoulder. "You good?"

"Mm hmm. Is this what you used to do when you had bonfires out here in high school?"

He wraps his arms tighter around me. "I wish. Those were mostly guys from the baseball team telling stupid stories and throwing everything we could find onto the fire."

"It wasn't all guys. There *were* co-ed parties." I'd heard enough secondhand to know that much. Nothing very scandalous, but I'm not about to buy his "just me and the boys" version of events.

He kisses me right below my ear. "Yes," he says against my skin. "But not like this."

"Good."

We watch the fire dance higher into the night sky. Stars peek through the clouds at us in our own personal light show. I want to soak it all up. I lay my head back against Griffin's shoulder to get a better view.

"I need to paint this."

"I want to see it when it's done. Then you need to hang it in your store."

"Not this one. This one will be for you."

He hugs me closer. "You're amazing."

"And I'm going to put a tiny tractor in the corner."

His chuckle rumbles through me. "You know what I like."

The wind shifts, sending campfire smoke straight into our faces. I squeeze my eyes against the stinging smoke and try not to breathe it in.

"Does this always happen?" I say into the blankets.

"You really don't camp, do you? You're going to go home with your hair smelling like campfire and your eyes bloodshot from the smoke, and you're going to love it."

"I am, huh?"

"That's the plan, anyway."

"I've figured you out, you know," I say after a while.

He gives my arms a playful squeeze. "I'm in trouble now."

"Being in the woods is your Fortress of Solitude."

"I'm Superman in this scenario? Nice."

I twist to cut my eyes to him. "You're actually more like Iron Man. Isn't he the one who makes all the stuff? Am I thinking of Batman? Are they the same guy?"

"I can't believe you asked me that question. Go on about the Fortress of Solitude."

I settle back into his arms. "It's where you go when you just want to be you, without anyone else's expectations or pressures. It's your safe space. The river. The woods. That's your Fortress."

His breath is soft on my ear. "Maybe. Is painting your Fortress?"

"Maybe. Yeah. When I'm painting, nobody else is judging it. It's for me, even if I plan to give the painting away eventually. It's just me and the canvas, and I can do whatever I want."

"You can always do whatever you want. If people don't like your art or your festival or whatever else, screw them."

"Now you're giving me Hulk vibes."

His lips press against my temple. "I don't want you to worry about any of that, is all I'm saying. There are people out there who will give you a hard time, no matter what you do. You can't choose your happiness based on them. You need to make Hope happy."

"Is that how you live your life?" I'm treading on delicate ice here. I know he's not making himself happy, and he doesn't want to admit or accept it, either.

His legs nudge tighter against mine. "I should be so lucky to live my life making Hope happy."

My heart explodes like a little firework at that diversionary tactic. A romantic diversionary tactic, but still. "You know what I mean. Are you doing what makes you truly happy?"

He sighs softly. A whole minute creeps by, the only sound our crackling fire sending embers soaring into the night sky, and I think he's not going to answer me. Finally, he offers up a quiet, "I don't know."

I turn in his arms until I'm straddling him. I tug the blankets up around us, rebuilding our warm cocoon. Aside from the chill on my nose, I don't feel the cold. I can't, with Griffin holding me like this.

"Why won't you choose your own happiness?" My voice barely makes a sound.

He runs his hands under the edge of my coat to grip my hips. "Sweetheart, right now, that happiness is *you*. And I absolutely choose you."

My eyes have probably gone all hearty again, but I don't care. I kiss him softly, carefully, like I'm going for the Guinness record for world's slowest kiss. It's torture, really, when I'm one strong breeze away from completely letting loose with him. But out here, we can't get too wild. What are we going to do, risk frostbite on all our best bits?

Although I bet if I asked...

After a minute of my leisurely kiss-fest, Griffin takes control. One hand shifts from my hip, over my coat, up my back, until it cradles my head. He deepens our connection into something else entirely—all flame and passion and promise. My body is a wood stove, and he adds fuel until that fire burns so bright I get dizzy from it.

That's the other thing I'd go back and tell high school-me—Griffin is an excellent kisser, and if she'd ever stop their verbal sparring to experiment with a different kind of battle, she wouldn't be bothered at all to lose. Because every moment of this is a win.

The wind gusts smoke into our faces, and we cough as we break apart. Okay, maybe campfire make-outs aren't *all* wins.

He looks up at me, his face in shadow but oh so clear in my mind's eye. He releases my head and lowers his hand back down to my side.

"Hey. I need to ask you something."

I freeze, even though his hand keeps wandering over my coat along my back. He sounds so serious, I'm weirdly nervous. "Okay."

Both his hands move up to frame my neck, and he dangles my earrings with his thumbs. "What does the waffle mean?"

I throw my head back and laugh. I have to admire his willpower—he held out a long time. Personally, I would have asked the same day I got the mystery emoji.

I run my hands along the front of his jacket until they trail along his neck and jaw. "It's my favorite food."

"I see."

He shifts just a touch, almost nothing, but I can feel it. He's disappointed. He likes the joke, but he didn't want it to just be a random emoji sent to bug him. It isn't...so I offer up the rest of the truth.

I lean closer, my fingers splaying across his jawline. "I text it when I'm thinking about you."

He nods like he needs a second to ponder that. I don't know

why, but nerves wash through me. I've been making out with the man with abandon, but telling him I'm thinking about him feels like too much?

"You're not sending it nearly often enough, then. I want you to think about me a whole lot more than that."

And he pulls me back in for another kiss.

"I GAVE you the volunteer schedule for tomorrow, right? And your list of volunteers? It's got the map for where each Winter Wonderland piece goes on the back, and the phone number of the man who's lending us his patio warmers in case he forgets." Hope frowns. "He'd better not forget."

I flattered myself that I'd helped her relax a touch on our date last night, but she showed up today like a jittery chihuahua, boss mode fully activated. She shakes like she drank twelve coffees this morning in her store.

I wink and pat my chest over the folded itinerary in my pocket. "I haven't lost it yet."

She looks over her own agenda. "We might not see each other until tree lighting."

I'd noticed that, too. I'll be with my crew hauling Hope's Winter Wonderland pieces and setting them up in town square while she oversees the tree decorating and pretty much everything else. At least after this, she'll be able to relax.

Preferably, with me.

"I hope you gave yourself time for a lunch break."

"I'll pack something, I promise." She looks up Maple Street

toward town square as though she can see her little village set up there already. "I hope I can trust your crew not to damage any of the buildings."

I take her hands in mine and run my thumbs over her knuckles. Maybe she'll say it's too much out here in the open, but she needs a diversion. "Relax. I'll be in charge of the crew, and you can trust me. Everything's going to go just fine."

She pulls her lower lip between her teeth. "I'm going to hold you to that."

"I'm a fan of being held to things by you. All kinds of things." A flush tinges her cheeks, making my blood quicken. We have too much to do today for a moment alone, but I'm already thinking about our next date. And the next.

The truth is, I don't want to stop spending time with Hope. If I have my way, the end of the festival only means we'll see each other more. More days when she's not frazzled by a hundred responsibilities, and more nights...well, I just want more nights.

"Let's focus on getting these lights up, and let me worry about the Wonderland."

She nods, but I know I can't totally take her nerves away. She's dedicated to this thing—she's poured endless time and energy into it. Of course her heart's wrapped up in it. It's also probably the wrong time to tell her that my heart's wrapped up in *her*.

A dark green McBride's Landscaping cherry picker trundles up Maple Street to stop in front of us. Caleb agreed to help us get the lights on top of the lamp posts today and decorate the big tree tomorrow. Hope gently pulls her hands from mine before he can see.

I flex my fingers, working out the ache her absence leaves behind.

Caleb rounds the truck, a Cheshire Cat grin stretching across his face. "Good afternoon."

He's practically crooning. I don't think I've seen his "I know something you don't want anyone else to know" smirk since high school.

I shoot him a warning glare, silently reminding him of his promise to keep quiet. He just gives a tiny shake of his head like I shouldn't be worrying mine over it. I am very much worried. I don't believe for a second he'll betray the trust I asked him to keep...but he's still my brother. He'll make this awkward for me if he can.

"Thanks for bringing the truck to help us out, Caleb," Hope says. "We wouldn't have managed it without you."

He just grins at me. "I'm sure Griffin would have figured out a way."

We work together to string the lighted lengths across Maple Street, each with a festive garland-wrapped star in the center. Caleb mans the bucket while I feed him the wire, and Hope runs interference, stopping traffic whenever we need it. We hang tinsel-festooned candy canes, bells, and snowmen from the lamp posts, and make sure all the wiring is safe and secure from curious little fingers.

Daylight's fading, but we make good time. Caleb climbs into the bucket to secure the decorations to the final lamp post, and Hope passes him the last snowman.

"Did Griffin tell you how much he loves Christmas decorations?" he asks her. One of many leading questions of the afternoon.

She cuts her eyes to me. "He hasn't been super forthcoming about that, no."

"His favorite thing was our Mom's old wooden nutcracker. Why don't you tell her about that, Griffin?" Then, he slowly rises into the air, the whirring of the bucket motor serving as his laugh track.

She sidles closer to me, eyes wide and full of good humor. Of course she likes this reminder of my irrational fear.

"All right," I say. "Let it out. You can laugh."

"It's just cute."

"My childhood trauma's cute. That's nice."

She knocks her shoulder against mine. "You two are cute. And this thing you're doing with your face, trying to be all stoic and not embarrassed at the way he called you out? Super cute."

Hmm. I guess if she can think my continuing discomfort around nutcrackers of any size is an appealing thing, I'll let her. She doesn't need to know how badly I'd ground my teeth when I carried the two for her a couple of weeks ago.

"Cute's not the word you're looking for."

"I know." She leans closer. "It's sexy."

She drops her voice, dragging it out into a fake-sultry *sexay*. Laughter bursts out of me at how easily this woman can sneak right past my defenses and wrap herself around my heart. If she weren't so eager to play things cool, I'd pull her into my arms and kiss her right in front of my brother. Give him a taste of his own medicine, and really shove my love in his face.

Love.

My brain tests the weight of that word for a second. It's too much after only a few weeks with her, too heavy...but it fits her exactly right. She's taken up space in my life, and all I can think to do is make more room. She can have it all.

She can move in, redecorate, and stay as long as she likes.

Hope blinks up at me, her teasing gone. "What?"

I must be doing something—staring too hard, smiling dreamily, somehow giving these big feelings away. I've never told a woman I loved her before, but those words sit at the edge of my mouth. The sun sets over Maple Street, people wander all around us on their way to shops, and the smell of the cherry picker tinges the air.

I can think of a dozen prettier places to say these words. And more private, too.

The whirring of the bucket coming back down to ground level shakes me out of my daze. I don't want to tell the woman I love that I love her for the first time in full view of my gloating brother.

"I'll tell you later," I say just for her.

"It's looking good," Caleb says after he hops out of the bucket. "Like a vintage Christmas card."

Hope's eyes are full of something soft and sweet as she gazes at the view of Maple Street strung with garlands. "It's going to be so perfect when all the lights come on tomorrow night."

We tested each one after setting them up, but they won't come on permanently until tree lighting. Hopefully, the shock of it doesn't blow a fuse somewhere.

"Romantic, too." He smirks just enough for me to know he's still poking at this bear. "I'll have Rowan right by my side."

"As if she ever leaves it," I shoot back.

"What can I say? When you're madly in love, you want the whole world to know."

I narrow my eyes at him, but he's unbothered. "I'll see you tomorrow morning to help with the tree, Hope."

"Thanks again." She waves as he heads out.

As soon as she turns to me, Caleb points an accusatory—or possibly pushy—finger my way before he climbs into the truck. He pulls away, leaving Hope and me under the light of the lamp post freshly decked out in its holiday finest.

"You've done well, boss. You've got it looking like Bedford Falls around here."

Her eyes light up. "I knew it! I knew you secretly liked a Christmas movie that isn't about murder."

"What can I say? I like watching George Bailey lose it all right before he realizes just how good he has it."

She's grinning up at me with such a look of delight on her face, it's taking everything I've got not to toss her over my shoulder and hike the blocks to her house to watch the movie together. I would actually watch that one with her. Most of it.

Who am I kidding? If I throw her over my shoulder, my plans for her have nothing to do with a movie.

But then she looks past me, and her grin flattens out into one of her false ones. "Mom! What are you doing here?"

I turn to see Helena Parrish right behind me. She always looks like she just walked out of an important meeting and always smiles like she's closing a sale. I've got nothing against the woman, but her timing could be better.

"I was over at Crystalline talking with Thea about her plans, you know, when I saw you up here." She looks at the garlands strung overhead. A dozen stars hang over the street, covering three blocks of downtown. "It's looking so good, you two."

"Thank you," Hope breathes. "We're almost ready for tomorrow."

"I can't wait to see your finished Winter Wonderland." Helena shines her bright smile my way. "I'm sure you did a fantastic job for her."

"All the praise goes to Hope. Without her, they'd just be plain old buildings with no life to them." And I mean every word. Her painting gave those decorations a spark of magic I could never touch.

Hope beams at that, but not nearly as brightly as her mother does. "He's a charmer, Hope. You'd better keep him."

I'm puffing up a bit over that praise when Hope flails as if she's trying to dodge something.

"He's not *mine*, Mom." She doesn't look at me when she says this, like if she does, it will spoil the lie.

But...I don't know if it is a lie. My brother's teasing remark echoes through my head. *When you're in love, you want the whole world to know.* Hope wants to make sure nobody knows at all. Maybe she and I have different visions for what this is between us. I'm sitting here realizing I'm falling for her, and she's denying she has anything to do with me.

Suddenly, this wide-open street feels too close and confined. The walls I like to keep stacked up high around my heart haven't been doing their job.

"Oh." Helena glances between the two of us as though she heard the dismissal in Hope's tone as clearly as I did. "Well, you never know. The tree lighting can be a very romantic time."

Everybody wants to push us together tonight. Everybody except the one person that matters.

"Okay, Mom, we have to get these empty storage bins to the warehouse and close everything up, so..." She waves her mother along.

Helena doesn't take the hint. "But I invited Griffin to have dinner with the family as a thank you for your project. With Lila in town, I thought we'd do a big meal Sunday. What do you say?"

I'd say yes, except the woman I love looks almost horrified by the invitation.

"He'll keep that in mind, okay?" Hope's eyes are wide, expression drawn, desperate to end this conversation.

I know the feeling.

Helena laughs it off. "I hope you do. See you both tomorrow."

She finally walks away as if she didn't just breeze in here and set off a carefully placed charge. I think it was right over my stupid heart.

Once she's gone, Hope's showy fake smile disappears. I take a long, deep breath, letting the cold air sear my lungs.

"I'm sorry about that," she says. "She doesn't know when to stop."

"*Are* we going to the tree lighting together?" Of all the things tumbling around in my head, that's the one that falls out of my mouth first. I've imagined us there for these last couple of weeks, and I'm just now realizing she might not have seen that happening at all.

Her mouth drops open, and I'm practically leaning forward on my toes, dying to hear what she's about to say. But she hesitates.

I wait. And wait.

Public place, full of people, her big event. Countless watching eyes. Yeah, we're not going to the tree lighting together.

My heart feels like it's in a vise that's tightening beyond what it can handle. Something snaps in there with everything she says...and refuses to say.

"I hadn't really thought that far." Her voice is soft, an apology I don't want to hear.

Because, me? I've been thinking way too far ahead.

People walk around us on the sidewalk, and maybe even this is too private a conversation for her to have out here.

"I know you want to keep things between us under wraps, but I don't know if I can. If I'm with you, I want to be with you."

"I want to be with you, I just don't want anybody to..." She gestures vaguely as if that gives me anything.

"You don't want anybody to know," I finish for her. Why is that such a blow? We only reconnected a few weeks ago—I'd never ask to define what I was to any other woman so soon. But she's not any other woman.

"You don't understand."

I take a step closer to her. "I do. You want to play the part so nobody in town can possibly have anything bad to say about you. People are going to talk no matter what you do, Hope. You can't change that."

She shrinks back, but in the next moment, she shakes it off. "You think you're not playing a part, too?"

"How's that?"

"The part of the dutiful son who's working a job that doesn't make you happy to try to make amends for something you don't need to apologize for."

Hope's sharp words find their mark. I've got things I haven't owned up to, but these are very different scenarios. "Maybe I am playing a role, but that's for the benefit of my mom and brother, not because I'm trying to make everybody in town like me."

The indignant little sound she makes would be laughable if my stomach weren't twisting in on itself right now.

"No, because you don't care if anybody likes you."

"I care about one." And maybe that was foolish of me.

I'm not stupid enough to think she doesn't care for me, but I'm not blind enough to believe we can truly have anything that we have to hide. I don't know if I can get any further into this thing if it's going to go down in flames around me.

"Griffin."

She touches my fingertips, and even that's not enough—I want her hand wrapped in mine. I want her arms around me. I want her to be *mine*.

I want too much.

"I just...need some time to sort this out. Okay?"

I nod, because what else can I do? Throw her over my shoulder like I was thinking a few minutes ago? That'd destroy everything right quick. Tell her what's in my stupid, breaching heart? Not when it's this far away from what's in hers.

"I'll truck the empty bins back to the warehouse," I tell her. "Don't worry about locking up."

It's dark, but her Jeep's just down the block from here. She'll be fine.

And clearly, she's not mine to protect anyway.

THIRTY-FIVE
HOPE

I SLUMP INTO MY HOUSE, my mind on the bottle of wine in my fridge. My stomach twisted itself into knots the whole drive home, and now all I want is a glass of wine and a Christmas movie to distract me from the confusion of feelings whirling around inside me. *Feelings.* I told Wren I had feelings for Griffin, but I couldn't tell *him*. What is wrong with me?

Oh, just your standard crippling fear.

Lila crosses the room as soon as I'm through the door.

"Look at this." She holds her phone in my face. "Engagement is up something like three thousand percent on Instagram and Facebook!"

I slink past her to the fridge and open the bottle of wine. Ignoring the evidence Lila cleaned my refrigerator today, I pour a generous glass. "I really don't want to hear about your likes right now."

She probably started a whole new fashion trend or something but I. Do. Not. Care.

"Not my likes," she says, sounding a little put out. "The festival's."

She swipes the bottle and pours a glass for herself, still

holding her phone out to me. She takes a sip of the wine and scrunches her nose. "This isn't good. I'll give you some recommendations for a decent rosé."

"You got all that in a week?" Even a quick glance at the numbers proves she has a magic touch with social media. Although I guess her tens of thousands of eager followers already proved that.

"You don't have to sound so surprised. This is what I do."

"You're better at it than I am." I drop onto the couch. Add social media management to the list of ways Lila excels over me. I'd set up both pages over two months ago but haven't devoted much time to them in the rest of the preparations. Now, she's gained hundreds of actual fans for the fan pages in less than a week.

"Hey." She sits down beside me. "What's going on?"

I sigh but catch myself when it hitches and threatens to turn into a sob. "People have been telling me for months you would have done a better job at this, and now you really have. It's not your fault," I add before she feels she has to respond to that. "I'm glad you're so good at all this. I'm just feeling sorry for myself."

"You did stuff like this in Portland." It's almost a question. She's probably trying to figure out why I'm on the verge of a breakdown on my couch when she's given me such good news.

"Yeah, but I wasn't good at my job. I was miserable in Portland."

"You never told me that."

"I didn't want anyone to know." My laughter has a slight note of hysteria to it. "What's even worse, there's this guy, a really great guy, but I think I just screwed everything up with him. I'm so scared Mom's enthusiasm and all the gossip in this town is going to kill another relationship, I strangled the life out of it myself."

"Hope, don't worry about what people say about you."

I laugh again. So says the social media influencer with endless validation.

"That's easy for you to say. You've got a great job, a great fiancé—you're everything Mom ever wanted for us. You've got it all."

"Hope." Lila takes my hand and squeezes it tight. Tears shine in her eyes, but I go still when I realize that they're not for me. "I don't have any of that. I left Josh."

I'd almost think this is a misguided prank, but there's only honesty in her big blue eyes.

"What? When?"

"Almost a month ago."

I can't process that. Lila's not an especially private person—she has no secrets. She lives everything out in the open.

"What happened?"

"He cheated on me." She winces like just saying it hurts. "I think it was going on the whole time we were together. Of course, he fired me from his company when I gave his ring back. I moved my stuff into a storage unit, and I've been sleeping on a friend's couch, trying to find a new job."

I've thought my sister had it all together for so long, hearing that she doesn't has broken my brain. It's like I'm operating in a parallel reality and scrambling to make sense of it.

"Why didn't you tell us?"

She drops her voice to a stage whisper. "I was afraid of what people would say once they knew."

"Oh, Lila." I pull her in for a huge hug. She's soft and warm against me, and it hurts a little to think how long it's been since our last big hug. When we let go, I'm wired like the bell just rang in a boxing match. "I'm going to drop kick Joshua Brandt the Third."

She laughs and swipes her cheeks with the back of her hand. "I can't wait to see it."

"What do you need? How can I help you through this?" This is a massive upheaval of her life, and guilt crawls through my stomach thinking how I've been pushing her away when she needs me most.

"This is what I need. Being here with you and putting an end to my pity party. I'm not going to feel sorry anymore about breaking up with a cheater. Now, tell me about this really great guy of yours."

Oh, I want him to be mine. Even though I messed things up tonight, I want him.

"Griffin McBride."

She blinks. "That guy you hated in high school?"

"I didn't *hate* him, but yeah. He's been working with me on the festival stuff, and Mom's pushing us together. But after everything with Mark, I'm afraid to have anything be out in the open like that again."

"What's he like now?"

"He's amazing. There's nothing he wouldn't do for the people in his life. He's the best support, and encourages me, and believes in me when *I* don't believe in me."

Her wry grin is too knowing. "It sure doesn't sound like you hate him very much now."

"I think I love him." Think. Know. Is there a difference at this point? The hammering behind my ribs says it's all the same.

"Help me understand. You love him."

I nod. Now that I've named the feeling out loud, it's flooding through me, tinting every tiny part of me.

"And it sounds like he at least cares about you, too."

More nodding, because even though I screwed things up this evening, I know he does. We wouldn't have even had a problem tonight if he didn't.

If I'm with you, I want to be with you.

"And Mom wants you to get together with him."

"Yes, exactly."

She makes a face. "Then who are you keeping this a secret from?"

"Well...the—" I can't even form the right words. When she lays it out like that, I'm not sure of the answer anymore. "The town? When the gossips find out, they'll whisper about us, and he'll get scared off like Mark did, and..."

I hear it. I finally, truly hear it. I'm pushing Griffin away because I think the *town* might ruin my relationship with him? They're not the ones I needed to be worried about driving him away. "I'm an idiot, aren't I?"

"I was going to say misguided, but idiot works."

My heart goes into overdrive thinking about every foolish choice I've made these last few weeks, but I can still fix this. "I think I need to grovel."

I've always liked the big gestures in my romance novels, but I never really thought about them from the groveler's side. But I will find a way to prove to Griffin that I want to be with him, and I don't care who knows it.

THIRTY-SIX

GRIFFIN

I STARE at the only framed photo in my office. It's a picture of Dad, Caleb, and me from about five years ago. We'd been fishing all day, and our faces are pink from the sun, but we've never looked happier.

My heart twists and squeezes. I want that back. I know I'll never get it again—doesn't stop the wanting.

The front door to the building opens. It's after hours, but I'm not too worried about intruders. I saw the headlights when Caleb's truck pulled in. He comes straight to my office.

"I drove by and saw the lights are on. What are you doing here?"

I splay my hands over my desk. "Checking my inbox. I'll be back to work on Monday."

Not that there was anything waiting in my inbox.

"So? Doesn't explain what you're doing in here two hours after I closed up."

"I'm getting a jump on things."

He leans against the door frame. "Just tell me what you're really doing."

"What are *you* doing? Shouldn't you be home with your wife?" I'm kind of being a jerk right now, but he's unfazed by my attitude.

"Rowan's got a craving for salt and vinegar potato chips, and I'm the delivery boy."

"Then you'd better get on home and deliver."

"She'll be okay for a few more minutes." He winces like she somehow heard that and pulls out his phone. "I'll just let her know I'll be a little late."

He thumbs for a minute on his phone and then slips it away again. He walks in and sits in the chair across from my desk—a simple, uncomfortable-looking affair, because I don't usually visit with clients.

Don't really want to visit with Caleb right now, either.

"What's going on?" he says. "And spare me the work routine crap—I'm well aware of your work ethic, and that's not what's bugging you."

I run my hands through my hair, calculating the quickest route out of here. I could just walk right past him and leave it all unsaid. Leave it all bottled up where it belongs. But maybe I don't have enough fight in me tonight.

"Do you even need me here? Really?"

He blinks at my question, clearly not expecting it. "Honestly? We could do okay without you."

My laugh tastes bitter, but I appreciate the candor. "Good to know, I guess."

He leans forward in his chair. "But answer me this—do you even want to be here?"

I'm not inclined to be quite so honest. "Of course I do."

His smile is like the one he used to wear when he was a point up in pick-up basketball and about to destroy me. "Are you lying to me or yourself?"

"It's the truth," I lie.

He nods, clearly not buying what I'm selling. "You like this, do you? Running the office end of things for a landscaping company? Not using your skills or experience in any capacity? Good stuff for you, yeah?"

I grit my teeth but have to look away. "I'm happy here."

I've said it enough for Mom. Maybe Caleb will believe it, too. Only, the way he's talking tonight, I think I'm just digging my hole deeper.

"You sure don't sound like a guy who's happy to be here."

"What do you want me to do?"

"I want you to man up and tell me the truth."

I blow out a breath. "Fine. I'm not happy here. This isn't what I ever saw myself doing. I wanted to step in and help out, but I'm practically useless, and I hate it."

He leans against the chair back, his smile softer. "Finally."

He looks...weirdly happy about me admitting that I hate working for him. Not how most employers take that kind of declaration.

"It doesn't matter, though," I say before he can get comfortable with it. "I want to be here for you and Mom."

"Griffin." His voice is too soft. His "I love you, but I'm breaking some bad news" voice. "After Dad died, we were all lost. Mom and I needed you here, because we needed all of us to pull together. And I will never stop thanking you for stepping up and being here when I could barely keep myself going."

We'd had to remind each other to eat those first weeks, let alone figure out how to keep on top of our work responsibilities. Looking back on those days, I'm not sure how we didn't all collapse, and the business right along with us.

"But this doesn't have to be a permanent situation. Nobody wants you to hold onto a job that's not making you happy."

His words are so wrong, I want to crawl out of my skin. I hop out of my chair and go to the dark window, my hand in my hair again. "Dad wanted it. Before he..." I wave a hand. *Do not say the words.* "He asked me to come work with you guys permanently. But I turned him down."

That admission should lift a weight somewhere, but instead, it drops on the floor between us like a piece of discarded lumber.

"And you were right to do it."

I spin to face him.

"Of course Dad wanted you to work with us—this was his dream. But it was *his* dream. Griffin, if Dad hadn't died and you'd come to work with all of us, things wouldn't have been any different. You still would have wanted something else. And Dad would have encouraged you to go get it."

"You can't know that."

He lifts an eyebrow. "You would have had even less responsibility if Dad were here. How would you have liked that?"

"I wouldn't have." My shoulders slump, and I sink back into my chair. "Why do you sound so unsurprised by all of this?"

"Let me do you one better—why do you think Mom volunteered you for Hope's project?"

Because you guys don't need me here. But I don't say that.

"Because she wanted to give me a chance to do some carpentry again. She probably knew I missed it, and wanted me to enjoy myself..."

That eyebrow hitches higher, and he makes a *go on* motion with one hand. Filling in the blanks, my heart hammers hard.

"She wanted me to see I'm not happy here?"

He grins again. "We have a winner."

"She told you that?"

"Basically."

I'm not sure how I feel about all of this going on behind my back. "So you two schemed to get rid of me?"

"Correction. *She* schemed to help you remember what you really want. And if it got you closer to Hope Parrish, so much the better." He kicks a foot onto my desk. "Which reminds me, why aren't you with her right now?"

"She's...still figuring out how she feels, I guess." Although, I'm going to have to circle back to this revelation *Mom* was trying to get me with Hope from the beginning. But I'm not sure how much it matters now. "I'm trying to make a future with her, and she's trying to decide if holding hands in public is too much."

"If I can give you a word of brotherly advice?"

I repeat his *go on* gesture.

"Rowan's last relationship was...not good. When we started dating, she was afraid to get too invested because she thought I'd be like him and use her feelings against her."

I think about sweet, soft Rowan being trampled by someone, and my blood boils. "Kind of want to find that guy."

"You and me both, brother. But I knew I wanted to be with her. So I loved her as much as she'd let me. It took a while, but eventually, she knew she was safe with me."

That puts his showering Rowan with affection into perspective. I don't doubt he's doing it because he wants to, but he's also doing it because she needs the reassurance.

Hope needs reassurance too, I realize, just in a different way. Her impulse to keep us out of the spotlight comes from a place of wanting to protect us, not shame or unhappiness. The last guy she dated couldn't handle the small town gossip and ran off. Of course she's afraid to dive in too quickly.

When I walked away from her tonight, I didn't do much to reassure her I'm going to stick around. I want to kick my own butt.

"I don't know what's going on with Hope," Caleb says. "But can you be patient with her while she figures it out?"

Can I? Can I love Hope as much as she'll let me?

I've never been more sure of anything. Even if that means keeping *us* just between us for as long as she needs, I'll do it. I'll do whatever it takes if it means I can be with Hope. And if things don't work out, and it all goes down in flames?

At least I'll go down trying.

THIRTY-SEVEN
HOPE

THE BACON STARTED ARRIVING this morning. I texted Griffin first thing.

> Hope: I messed up last night. Will you meet me at the tree lighting? Because I want to be there with you

He hadn't made me wait long.

> Griffin: I'll be there

Then, he'd sent a bacon emoji. And he'd been sending one a couple of times an hour since. We worked separately all day; him getting the Winter Wonderland set up, me helping with, well, everything else. But those bacon emojis keep coming, letting me know he's thinking about me.

Letting me know I haven't ruined things between us. Because all I want is *us*.

I've got that cartoon bacon burned into my brain, I've smiled over those texts so often.

I straighten the canvas for the fourth time in as many minutes. My hands shake every time I touch it, and I'm tempted to tear it right back off the wall, but I can't help the little nudges. I hung up three of my smaller paintings this morning, complete with price tags.

The price tags seem like overkill when just having people look at my art feels this enormous.

The bells on The Painted Daisy's door ring, sending a blast of cold air through the store. I haven't been able to do more than peek out the front window at the growing crowds on the sidewalk since I returned from decorating the tree in town square. Going by the numbers in here, the turnout is even better than I'd expected, in large part thanks to Lila.

As planned, she shows up at The Daisy thirty minutes before tree lighting. She browses alongside other guests before winding her way to me at the counter.

"Have I said how much I love this store?"

That brief praise lights sparklers in my chest. "I love it, too."

Abby nudges her way through the shoppers to take her place behind the counter again.

"I hate that you have to miss tree lighting," I tell her.

She rolls her eyes at me. "Please. Like I'm going to let you miss the festival after you worked so hard on it. I'll see the tree lots of other nights. Now go. Enjoy."

I pull on my parka and knit hat and walk out the door with Lila. We stroll up Maple Street arm in arm like we did when we were little girls, eager to get to the tree.

Maple Street's parking is full up, and shoppers bustle in and out of stores on both sides. Night has settled over Sunshine, and the storefronts glow with fairy lights, sprigs of holly, and brightly colored ornaments.

Lila hugs my arm tighter. "I've missed this."

"You can have it again. But only if you want it. No pressure."

"I really think I do. I'm not sure how I'll make a living yet, but I want to try."

A small knot of people crowd around Henderson's window to watch the trains as they make their infinite loop around the tiny replica town. I added some real gems to the Christmas scene inside after Griffin and I set it up. A bright red wagon, an old wooden sled, several tin cars and trucks, plus felt dolls in all shapes and colors from The Painted Daisy round out the scene. Overhead, the string lights I rigged glitter like a canopy of stars.

Two little kids press their noses against the glass as they watch the trains go around, their faces aglow in the lights. Every murmur of appreciation just floats me higher on this cloud of pride and joy.

At town square, people press in around the twenty-foot tree, dark now as everyone waits for someone hidden off of Maple Street to throw the switch at the right moment.

My mother waves frantically, barreling toward us. I can't tell if Dad is parting the crowd for her or if she's using him as a battering ram, but they buzz our way.

"Look at everything you've done," Mom crows. "This is better than I ever expected—and I expected a lot."

"You've done well, Hope." Dad's praise is softer, but oh, I love that look of pride in his eyes.

"I saw Mayor Martinez earlier," Mom says, speaking loudly over the murmuring crowd. "He sounds ready to hire you on the spot for that tourism position if you think you could take it on."

"If he wants to talk about hiring someone, it should be Lila. I did a lot of work, but she knew how to bring in the crowds."

"Oh, you don't want a job down here." Mom's smile falters as she looks Lila over. "Do you?"

I give my sister's arm one last squeeze and let her go.

She steps closer to them, her arms out like she's ready to wrap them up in a hug. "Mom, Dad. We have some things to talk about."

I pat her on the shoulder. "I need to get to the Winter Wonderland, but you've got this."

Her happy little grin warms me right up. "Go get him."

Weaving through the crowd, I've got enough energy running through me I could light the huge Christmas tree myself. When I reach the Winter Wonderland, all the little lights in my chest spark and crackle like they're about to pop.

The small buildings stand all aglow, thanks to the string lights Griffin looped beneath the eaves. Children jostle each other for better views as they circle the buildings, cooing at the reindeer corralled between them. In the very center of the colorful village, Santa sits between two patio heaters, listening to earnest wishes. The line to sit in his lap stretches all the way back to the tree.

I could burst from joy.

In the distance, the soft tones of the church choir singing "O Christmas Tree" grow louder as they walk down Maple Street, and a hush falls over the crowd. A buzz fills the air as we wait for the magical moment the tree's lights will come on, ushering us fully into the season.

And then, my heart really does burst from joy.

Griffin steps out from behind the Wonderland bakery, his eyes locked on me. I want to fan myself, he's so handsome. That sharp jaw, those piercing hazel eyes that never miss a thing, that full, smirking mouth that gives as good as he gets—in *all* the ways.

Oh, I love this man. And I've been absolutely ridiculous to think I could or should ever hide that from anyone.

I had an apology speech running through my head all day, but in this moment, the words aren't as important.

With electricity glittering through my veins, I rush through the people around the Winter Wonderland and launch myself straight into his arms. He picks me up without hesitation, and I kiss him with everything I have, confirming enthusiastically that *I'm with him*.

Thankfully, he kisses me back just as eagerly. I melt against him, almost painfully happy in his firm embrace. Somewhere behind us, a round of applause goes up, and I remember all the little children scattered nearby. The kiss is fully PG-13, but that might have been too much for a few of the littler ones.

I pull back and cup Griffin's face in my hands. "I'm sorry I was afraid to tell you last night that I'm yours. I've been worried about the wrong things. I don't care what anyone else thinks—they can say whatever they want behind my back or straight to my face, but I won't let that stop me from loving you."

Okay, that went beyond what I thought I'd say tonight, but the words are out. Now, all I can do is see how he'll respond...

He hugs me closer, the triumphant light in those gorgeous hazel eyes making my legs go all mushy. I could sob from relief.

"This is why I'm crazy about you." We're surrounded by people, but his low voice is just for me. "I love your selflessness, and your enthusiasm. I love the way you create bright, happy art to share with the world. I love the way you don't back down when you're mad at me."

He sighs, settling me closer against him, like he's finally got everything he wants. "I love the way you make me *feel*. That shouldn't be a complete sentence, but for me it is. I'm not great with feelings, but I want to be, for you."

"What are you saying?"

His eyes sparkle in the Winter Wonderland lights. "You're going to make me spell it out?"

"Please do."

He moves closer until his mouth grazes mine. "I'm in love with you, Hope Par—"

I cut him off with my mouth, repeating my own "I love you" between kisses. His mouth smiling against mine is better than any tree lighting. My heart is so full, it could fill the whole town square. I'm with him, and he's with me.

Applause sounds around us again, and we break apart to a crowd of raised eyebrows and happy grins. My parents and Lila stand not too far away, clapping with the rest, my mom's smile biggest of all. A wolf whistle splits the air, and we turn to see Caleb, Rowan, and Kat, cheering us on just as madly.

"I don't think we're keeping this on the down-low anymore," Griffin says, still holding me close.

"I don't care." Now that I've flipped the dial on my PDA stance, I'm ready to go all in.

"I don't know, I might not want to be seen kissing my boss." His arms are wrapped tight around me like he has no plans to let me go. "Gossips might talk."

"Let them talk. Anyway, I'm not really your boss."

He smiles down at me until I think my knees will give out. "Yes, you are."

Town square quiets as the moment finally arrives. We turn to watch the lights on the tree switch on. Green, red, and white lights illuminate huge silver Christmas balls and golden bells in the huge pine. The choir sings "Silent Night," and swaying starts in the crowd like it'd been choreographed.

As though our singing called it down, fat snowflakes fall over us, and waves of laughter wash through the mass of people. A perfect ending for a perfect night.

I'm happy so many people are here to enjoy this moment, but I'm even happier that I've got my man.

Griffin turns me so his chest presses against my back, his arms wrapped around me as we gaze at the tree. He nuzzles his cheek against mine, making my stomach dip as I think about all the nights to come.

"Did you plan the snow, too?"

"Nope," I say, smiling against him. "This is better than anything I had planned."

THIRTY-EIGHT

GRIFFIN

I FEEL LUCKIER than George Bailey running up the snowy street in Bedford Falls wishing everyone a merry Christmas.

Hope pulls a batch of cookies out of the oven at her parents' house while she hums "Jingle Bells." The deep red sweater she's wearing just about makes me lose my mind, but I'm trying to focus. Her dad is telling me about his new driver, and I don't need it to be any more obvious that I'm nuts about his daughter.

They all know. I'm just trying not to be obnoxious about it.

"Do you golf, Griffin?" he asks.

"It's been a little while, but I play."

"We should play a round when the course thaws."

"I'd like that." Paul Parrish has welcomed me—I don't want to say into the *family*, exactly—but he treats me as if I'm one of their own. His gentle, fatherly affection means more than I can tell him. "But I'm pretty sure you'll beat me cold."

He pats me on the arm like we're old chums. "Don't worry, I'll go easy on you."

"Don't go easy on him." Hope slips up to me and slides an arm around my waist. "He likes a challenge."

I pull her close against my side, loving the feel of her against me. I can't love it quite as much as I might otherwise, with both of our families here, but it's still perfection.

Caleb moves into the kitchen as if he heard his cue. "Don't ever change, Hope."

"Shouldn't you get back to the hospital?" I say.

"I'm going. Came in here to say my goodbyes, actually."

Another wave of congratulations pours onto him from every side. Rowan gave birth to their son yesterday—little Colton James. Mom texted all day, giving progress reports on her labor that I would really have rather not known. All I cared about was the final score, I didn't need the play-by-play.

Hope's parents invited my mom and Caleb over to share in their Christmas celebrations, since ours have been upended by the baby's birth. I should probably be alarmed at how well our families mesh together, but I'm nothing but grateful.

"Tell her I'll stop by this evening," Mom says. She and Helena are in a corner together, probably swapping stories. I should probably be alarmed about *that*, too, but I'm enjoying myself too much to worry about it.

"I will. Thank you all again." Caleb ducks out, goodbyes following after him.

Lila waves a sequined arm in the air. "Are we going to watch the movie, or should I make another batch of caramel corn?"

All three parents turn to Hope and me.

"Give us a minute," I say.

Our moms glory in this like two little supernovas, but they usher Paul and Lila into the living room, giving Hope and me some privacy. I should have done all this a little less conspicuously, but between both Christmas traditions, there hasn't been time.

"Ready to exchange gifts?" I say. Honestly, Hope at my side smiling up at me is already a gift.

We grab our small, wrapped gifts from beneath her parents'

plush tree and duck back into the kitchen. She passes me the first of hers, a square papered in red and white snowflakes.

"I hope this isn't weird." She bites her lower lip. That little move makes my stomach tighten, but I focus on her nervousness.

"It's not going to be weird." I heft the small package, but then a terrible idea snags my thoughts. "It's not a nutcracker, is it?"

She laughs, but runs a hand over my arm, comforting me. "I'm not that cruel."

I slip the paper off the box, the excited tremor in my belly reminding me of childhood Christmases. Inside, I tug a red ribbon, and pull out a handmade ornament. It's a disc of wood painted with a perfect little hammer and saw on one side.

The ornament spins gently from between my fingers, and I see the back side is engraved. *McBride Woodworking.*

"It's sort of a pre-opening celebration," she says softly.

A well of emotion washes over me, lifting me up. I sweep her into my arms, the ornament held safely in one hand. In the spring, after Caleb returns from parental leave, I plan to open a custom carpentry business, with his and Mom's blessings.

Turns out that—and Hope right here in my arms—really were why she'd offered me up as a volunteer for the Christmas festival. Can't say I'm disappointed in the way things turned out.

I release Hope and look at the ornament again. "This is perfect. I love everything you paint."

Her smile flows like melted chocolate through my chest, warm and comforting. I love the thoughtful gift, but it's nothing compared to how much I love her.

"Now yours." I pass her the smaller of my gifts, not much bigger than the one she'd given me.

She frees the little faux-gold statuette, her soft "Oh, Griffin" letting me know she recognizes it. The Number One Debater Award hasn't lost its artificial shine. "Where did you find this?"

"In a box of high school mementos. I figured you should have it."

She positively glows. "Because you admit I really won our arguments back in high school?"

"Because it turns out I don't mind losing, as long as I lose to you."

That earns me a kiss, and I drag it out into a long, luxurious moment. When she pulls back, she's a little starry-eyed.

"Now for your second present." She passes over a thin package maybe two-by-two feet square, blushing in a way that makes my heart rate speed up. "I did promise you."

"Is this—?" I don't finish the rest, just carefully peel back the Christmas tree wrapping paper to reveal a work of art.

She painted that night we had a campfire in the canyon. The perspective shows our backs, bundled in abstract blankets on the snowy ground, looking up at the starry indigo sky. Everything from the glow of the campfire to the curl of smoke winding up through the trees brings out a visceral memory of that night.

"Sweetheart," I breathe. "You are magnificently talented."

I'm being completely sincere, but she breathes out a laugh. "So you like it?"

"I guess I appreciate art, after all."

"Aw." She leans in for a kiss. "Only mine, though, right?"

"Probably, yeah." I reach down and grab the big box holding her second gift. "We were thinking along the same lines."

She gives me a questioning look but tears into the wrapping paper. Inside the box, the gifts are nestled in thick butcher paper. She carefully unrolls the first one, and gasps when she finally sees it.

"Are these all—?" She sets the little house on the kitchen

island and makes quick work of unwrapping the other four. Her eyes shine with tears, but her smile tells me I did well. "I can't believe you made these for me."

In another minute, five little buildings stand before us, miniature versions of the Winter Wonderland Hope designed. They're about a tenth the size of the ones we'd made for the festival, perfect for a mantelpiece display.

"I thought you might like a version just for you."

She throws her arms around me and peppers kisses over my neck and jaw. "They're beautiful. I can't believe you did this."

"I painted the base colors, but there's room for you to paint the front details and make them magical."

She pulls back, her face just a breath from mine. "Is it cheesy if I tell you that *you're* magical?"

I tug her closer to me. "That's the best kind of cheese."

"I love you."

"I love you, too." I kiss her on the nose. "Merry Christmas, boss."

EPILOGUE

HOPE

SIX MONTHS *later*

Is it weird to find driving attractive? Because the way Griffin drives through the outskirts of town sends shivers up my spine. Maybe it's his confidence in knowing exactly where he's going. Maybe it's how safe I feel with him at the wheel. Maybe it's the way his T-shirt sleeves strain against his biceps.

It's a mystery.

"Lila asked me to send her photos from our hike. I told her she can't use me to farm content for her, but she didn't like that answer." She's taken on Sunshine's part-time position handling events, but she's angling for a full-time tourism job. "She's going to have to actually get dirty with the adventuring company if she wants to prove she can appeal to outdoors enthusiasts."

Lila and the outdoors don't mix, but she's determined. We'll just have to wait and see if she's determined enough to rough it on one of their five-day hikes, or if she'd rather keep stringing together part-time jobs.

"I bet she'll take them up on the offer. She's tenacious. It runs in the family."

He swings his eyes my way, and my whole body reacts. It's a perpetual side effect of being with Griffin—he does the smallest thing, and I light up. I don't make the rules, I just revel in them.

"Oh, I'm tenacious, all right." I bounce in my seat like I'm prepping for a boxing match. "I'm going to knock this mountain out."

Griffin laughs, my most favorite sound in the world. He's far more outdoorsy than I ever will be, but I'm learning to like some of the same things he does. Not fishing—he can keep the early mornings and lingering smells between him and his brother. But we take a lot of walks in the beautiful places he knows best. I swear, he's catalogued them all, and never fails to take me to a new gorgeous river, lake, or hillside view every time.

"Not very high up the mountain today," he says.

"I thought we were going deeper into the canyon."

I've been too busy admiring his arms to realize that instead of winding through the forest, we're skirting along the hills just on the edge of town. There are fewer houses out here, but they're pretty, custom homes like he typically works on.

McBride Woodworking is turning out to be a pretty successful endeavor. He contracts with a custom home builder and takes on private clients when he can schedule them. His carpentry will be all over this town one day, and I absolutely love that.

He turns his truck up a side street and parks. "Ready for a walk?"

"This is a neighborhood. We can't hike here." It isn't a very filled-in neighborhood yet, but I still don't like the idea of traipsing through someone's yard.

"Boss. Trust me."

Unfair that a name that implies I'm in charge manages to get me to do whatever he asks.

We get out of the truck, and he takes my hand, leading me to the end of the short driveway. Some of the land has been cleared, but pine trees mass together here and there to create privacy for the future house. He walks us to the center of the cleared area and nods over my shoulder.

I turn, and a little sigh escapes me. The hill slopes gently downward, and in the distance, the Olallie River is a ribbon of silver snaking through the green trees. I still feel a little guilty for trespassing, but the view is worth it. I burn it into my mind so I can paint it someday.

"It's beautiful," I breathe.

"You like it?"

"Whoever owns this lot is lucky to get those views."

"Yeah, we are."

I nod, still staring at the river, before I hear exactly what he's said. I look at him, and my breath stills as he smiles and drops to one knee.

My heart pounds like it's trying to beat out of my chest. He's holding a teeny tiny box, and he's looking at me with such trust in his eyes, I know he's really holding his heart in his hands. Griffin's perfect, precious heart he's so protective of—and he's offering it to me.

"Hope." His voice catches on that one word, he fills it with so much love and joy and promise. "I love you. I didn't know I could feel this much for someone, but I know I never want it to stop. I want us to go on loving each other and challenging each other for the rest of our lives. Will you marry me?"

I nod, crying just a bit now, and he leaps to his feet and wraps me in his arms. He's my best friend, my biggest support, and, once in a while, my biggest frustration. But I love this man, from his direct honesty to his fierce protectiveness to the way I know we'll never have a boring time together. I love his smirks and sarcastic eyebrow twitches. I especially love the way he always kisses me like he's going for a personal best.

He pulls back enough to slip the ring on my finger. It's a solitaire with diamonds along the band, and I might stare a little.

"You really bought this lot for us?"

"It's not official until Monday. If you want a different one, we have time to switch."

"No, this one's perfect." I want the one that drew my outdoorsman. "Do you have a house plan picked out?"

He spins me around so he's holding me from behind while we look out toward the river. "I have some ideas, but we can choose a design together."

"Will you do all the trim and woodwork?"

His laughter brushes my ear. "Do you think I'd let someone else do it?"

"Good point. Do I get to pick out the paint colors?"

"Do you think I'd let someone else do it?" he says again, nuzzling my neck.

I can almost see it, this house we'll design together, and build together, and live in and love in, and probably argue just a tiny bit in together. And I can't wait.

"We make a pretty good team," I tell him.

He nods, holding me close. "Best team ever."

THANK you so much for reading Mad About Yule! If you want a little bit more Griffin and Hope goodness, sign up for my newsletter to get a special bonus scene! Read on for a peek at Lila's upcoming book, Just Act Natural...

BONUS EPILOGUE

LILA

I THINK I MIGHT DIE.

Not in the overly dramatic way I usually toss that phrase around—"If I have to wait any longer for a table, I might die." "If MAC discontinues my favorite shade of red lipstick, I might die." "If I don't listen to the latest Taylor Swift album the night it drops, I might die."

No, this is in the literal "If I walk another mile today, my lungs will shrivel up and my heart will explode" way.

Everybody knows it, too. I think it's because I'm sucking in air like a malfunctioning Dyson.

Deena turns around on the trail about twenty feet in front of me and gives a tentative thumbs up. "All good?"

I flash her one back, but my thumb is full of lies. "Excellent!"

"We're about halfway to tonight's campsite."

Halfway. On day one of a five-day hike. I'm going to cry.

"Sounds good!"

More lies. No part of that sentence sounds good, especially not *campsite*. But if I want to get promoted from Sunshine, Oregon's part-time events consultant to their full-time tourism coordinator, I need to prove I'm interested and invested in everything the area has to offer, including all the outdoorsy stuff.

Even if I'd rather enjoy the wonders of air conditioning, unlimited WiFi, and running water than be out here in the great outdoors.

The rest of our group treks ahead of me, the steady *snick-snick* of hiking poles and boots playing a one-two beat in my head. Deena and her husband Mitchell run Horizon Hikes, and comped my place on the tour in exchange for some social media promo. They've enthusiastically told us more than I ever wanted to know about poisonous plants on the trail, the importance of filtering the water we'll collect in the streams along the way, and whether we need to look out for bears.

Hint: we do. It'd probably make great content if we came across one, but I'm only willing to do so much for good engagement.

Then there are the four guests on the hike—two married couples who decided a twenty-five mile hike would be the perfect way to celebrate all of them turning sixty this year.

That's right—my hiking companions are twice my age and already making me look like an absolute fool by not even being winded. They could at least fake a wheeze once in a while so I wouldn't be the only one.

And then there's me. Sweating through my clothes, chugging water faster than I probably should, and daydreaming about how nice it would be to sit down in the dirt for five minutes.

Maybe ten.

Normally, I don't want to do *anything* in the dirt, but my pride's as hard to find as my energy right now.

A giant bird swoops down between me and the others, and I suck in a breath, stumbling backwards. Strong hands grip my upper arms to steady me, and my back—well, my pack—runs up against something, keeping me from falling.

"It's just a hawk," a deep voice says from behind me. Once I'm sure of my feet again, he releases my arms, but I'm pretty sure I hear him chuckling.

So...that brings me to the last person on this trip.

Grant Irwin. Easily six-three, built like Superman and dressed like a Patagonia model, with dark wavy hair he sweeps back from his face so it doesn't fall into his eyes. I've been trying not to look at him, because that man is a problem.

Part of it is how his soft, Texas drawl makes it sound like he's caressing words as he speaks them. Part of it is the honest-to-goodness dimple in his chin. But mostly, it's the way he looked at me when we first met.

His eyes had skated over me, and his smile had turned from warm to chilly before we'd even finished introductions. Like he'd sized me up, taken stock, and written me off in five seconds flat.

It hadn't helped that I'd brought too many clothes with me and Deena had to set some aside for me to collect when we return, right in front of everyone. Or that she'd told them about my Instagram "fame" as though the rest of them should be honored to be on this trip with me.

And just maybe Grant heard the sound of dismay I made when Deena and Mitchell described the camp toilet they're bringing along, but I say that part's totally justified.

Doesn't matter. I don't need Grant Dimplechin to like me in order to get this promotion, I just need to complete this hike.

I'm honestly not sure which achievement sounds harder.

"Hawks are still carnivores, right?" I say with a breezy laugh

I don't quite feel. The bird is *big*, and now it's staring at us. Its beady eyes are unnerving.

Grant pulls up next to me. The trail is barely wide enough for two here, and our arms brush against each other as we maneuver our hiking poles. That unnerves me, too, but for very different reasons.

"I don't think it's going to carry you off."

"Speak for yourself. I'd make a portable snack." Unlike the big hunk of muscle at my side, I'm on the petite side.

Grant makes a sound of agreement but then clears his throat. "Just keep your distance."

Well, that's nice. I thought Texans were famous for their friendliness. I'm not in charge of how wide the trail is.

"*You're* the one who caught up with *me*. Keep your own distance."

A deep crease forms between his eyebrows. He stares so long, a weird, winding curl of unease sweeps through my stomach. I don't care a thing about his handsome face, but I care very much about how easily he dismissed me.

I got enough of that from my ex-fiancé to last a lifetime. No more.

"I meant keep your distance from the hawk," he finally says.

Oh. I focus on the trail again, sure my cheeks are flaming. If he didn't think I was a dummy before, he must now.

"But I wouldn't go broadcasting how tasty and portable you are if I were you," he says after a minute. "Bears like snacks, too."

Like I need the reminder.

"I think a bear would go for you and get the full meal." I'm going to blame this conversation on all the fluid loss from how much I'm sweating. I don't care what anyone says about how many changes of clothes I wanted to bring, I'm going to *need* them.

"A bear would take what they could catch first. That would be you."

No kidding. If a bear showed up right now, I wouldn't have the energy to run away. I'd just play dead and hope for a brief mauling.

"A gentleman would sacrifice himself to the bear so the lady could get away."

"Or the gentleman could use the bear spray clipped onto his belt, and they'd both escape."

I risk a glance at his midsection. Sure enough, he's got a small, bright orange canister in a holster there. But I don't look at the rest of him. Definitely don't catch sight of his big hand gripping his hiking pole handle like it's a toothpick. The only thing in my head is how he'd shut everything down when we first met.

He's probably married. No ring on that hand, but that doesn't mean anything. He could be like my ex, and think monogamy is too confining. Or maybe I'm just not his type.

Grr, no. Why am I even thinking about this guy? It's that stupid dimple in his chin, messing with my head.

"Nope," I tell him. "Too dangerous. A gentleman sacrifice is the only way."

His chuckle rolls over me like a liquid thing, spreading warmth through my belly.

"At least I know where I stand."

Four and a half more days out here in the brilliant green wilderness, but I don't think it's the hike that's going to do me in. It's Grant Irwin.

KEEP an eye out for Just Act Natural, coming in 2024!

A NOTE FROM GENNY

Thank you for reading my little Christmas festival rom-com! This story has been rewritten in several totally different versions, most of them way too serious for where I want to take my books now. Think grim medical diagnoses, family estrangements, and brotherly fistfights.

When I looked it over this summer, I decided I didn't want to give up on this story of reluctant co-volunteers, but it needed another rewrite. I only kept a few things: Griffin had to build Hope's Winter Wonderland. She had to accidentally hit him in the head while helping him. And they needed a sweet moment at the riverside.

That's it! Everything else is brand-new Christmas fun, and I absolutely love their story now. I hope you do, too!

To my earliest readers Kelly, Lindsay, Britt, Skyla, & Allison —you probably won't recognize this book anymore, but I'm still grateful that you read for me once upon a time!

To Claire, & Amanda, thank you for your feedback & support! I'm always grateful for your encouragement & reminders that I write pretty swoony books.

To my editor Cindy, thank you for your notes that helped me iron out the last of the wrinkles in the story's transition from serious romance to light rom-com! And my goodness, do I appreciate your eye for detail on my proofreads! I will never figure out where commas go, and for that I'm deeply sorry!

A huge thanks to Melody for creating Griffin and Hope so

perfectly in this cover! I'm always impressed by your talents and I adore this sassy Christmas scene!

Finally, to my sweet family. Thank you for your love and patience when I'm frazzled over a book—which is practically all the time now. I love you so much!

ALSO BY GENNY CARRICK

The Loch Effect

The Magnolia Ridge series

Say the Words

Have a Heart

Stay this Christmas

Make it Real

ABOUT THE AUTHOR

Genny Carrick is a sucker for an HEA, especially if there's a whole lot of laughter along the way. She writes romances and rom-coms about stubborn women and the men who fall for them.

When she's not lost in swoony reads, she's probably up to something crafty or trying to get her dog and two cats to love her.

Genny recently moved to Texas after a lifetime in the Pacific Northwest. She brought her brilliant husband and two hilarious kids with her.

Stay up to date with book news at gennycarrick.com

Made in the USA
Middletown, DE
12 December 2023

45410980R00187